Here Vultures Fly

RUDY RODRIGUES

First Edition

PAGE PUBLISHING, INC.
New York, NY

First originally published by Page Publishing, Inc. 2017

ISBN 978-1-68409-980-1 (Paperback)
ISBN 978-1-68409-981-8 (Digital)

Printed in the United States of America

To my entire family, whom I love. For my children, Philippa, Natali and Marc, who have endured prolonged and sustained periods of my absence, and who grew up without their father. To my grandchildren, Vivian, Johanna, Max and Zac who bring me tremendous joy and pleasure, and who restored my sense of family

Contents

Foreword

By Dr Reinhild Boehm

"Here Vultures Fly" is a remarkable autobiographical account which allows us a glimpse into the intense fighting in Afghanistan over a ten year period. The outsider typically only gets to know about this through articles written by journalists on short term assignments, or in recent years, through real-time social media accounts and observations. The war itself remains far away, and plays out in a country and culture few North Americans, other then the military, ever see from the inside.

Rudy Rodrigues served as an international professional staff member of the United Nations stationed in Afghanistan in the Central Asian Republics and the South Pacific from 1989 until 2008. Readers go on a journey of discovery with him, in which the ravages of war remain in the background, and the lives of children and their families affected by the conflict move into the foreground. The role of the various UN Agencies working in war zones is often mysterious to concerned citizens of allied countries, as is the war itself. How do these Agencies strive to alleviate suffering; bring urgently needed food,water, medical supplies, shelter and other services to the starving and displaces populations? How do they pave the way for an emerging democracy; help children go back to school and return to normalcy and peace? And, how is a person prepared, or even willing to do development work under such trying conditions?

Rudy Rodrigues has had a brilliant military career beginning with the Royal Military Academy Sandhurst (UK) and later the British Army Staff College. He saw active military service, which was probably the best preparation for the job. His military experiences, paired with years of solving strategic problems relating to droughts in Kenya's Northern Frontier District, and later in the famine ravaged

Sudan where the infrastructure had collapsed, making the logistics of moving food and other essential emergency supplies to the starving displaced population, almost impossible to surmount. No doubt a sense of compassion, paired with understanding of tribal societies, inspired Rudy to dedicate his working life to addressing these issues.

The path from army officer to a development worker may seem farfetched. Unfortunately, the toll on the personal life of family and children was great. However, extraordinary times demand extraordinary sacrifices, which in turn help healing and growth for so many more. The reader of "Here Vultures Fly" will appreciate the sacrifices, the gains and the courage development work costs the individuals involved, but also the joy and satisfaction that comes from serving "the greater good"

Stream of Cold Water - Masai place name

I would begin life among the lions in Nairobi, spend time among the sharks on Wall Street, and interact with terrorists in Afghanistan. I would work to save the starving, and I would marry an anthropologist from Freiburg and then a woman from Park Avenue, New York. My origins may have been simple, but my life was complex. From the moment I was born, I was a walking bundle of contradictions—born in one place, roots in another, parents from a third.

I was born in Nairobi, Kenya, of Goan parents. Goa was a Portuguese colony in South India, and my birth certificate listed my nationality as Portuguese. Already, there were conflicts. I was Portuguese, from India, living in Kenya. The name Nairobi is a Masai word meaning "stream of cold water," and in those days, Nairobi was just that—a pristine oasis, a place of hope, a lush playground for animals and expats. But it was also a British colony, and eventually, the injustices perpetrated by the British would become too much for the Kenyans to take.

My father worked for those British as a civil servant, and my mother, a socialite in India, was a housewife. I was the second of six children

We grew up in a segregated neighborhood called Park Road. This was an Asian quarter, and even though there was no official racial discrimination in Kenya at the time as there was in South Africa, society was starkly divided along racial lines. There was an unofficial pecking order with the English at the top, the Asians next, and finally, the indigenous population, the Africans. It was an isolating existence, being in this Asian ghetto of sorts, but it was not a painful one, and strangely, I never felt discriminated against. But in retrospect, mine was a silent generation. We were taught not to criticize but to work, endeavor, and never acquiesce. Sentiments were never to be flaunted in public but rather incarcerated within the individual. This served me well as a commander of troops in battle. It would be counterproductive to show sentiment in adversity. But in private life, this was repressive and eradicated one's capacity for self-expression.

I was an adventurous and a curious kid, pushing the envelope at every turn. And in Africa, that could be dangerous. One day, a friend and I ventured to the local racecourse, a vast expanse of savannah devoted exclusively for the wealthy white man. There, we began pretending to be racehorses, competing barefoot in the stubble of the freshly mown grass. Suddenly, our race was halted by the appearance of a huge lion, a "simba," emerging from the tall grass nearby. He swaggered casually up to us, stopped, and turned away. We were frozen in our tracks. It was only when we saw the vultures circling overhead waiting to feast on the leftover carcass—it was then that we realized our simba had just eaten, feasting nearby on some poor, unfortunate kill, and perhaps he was now too full to consume us. Eventually, he ambled off, and we ran home faster than any racing we had done at the course, or anywhere else for that matter. It was our last trip into the white man's fancy territory.

But Africa was like that—raw, wild, and full of the unexpected. The terrain was extreme, the weather was harsh, and the people were unpredictable. I learned early on that being prepared meant the difference between life and death, a lesson that remains with me to this day. Faced with such savage environs, my mother became obsessed with education, insisting that we get the best schooling possible and that we reach as high as we could. Education reinforced by aspiration. That was my mother—determined to see that her children, unlike her, were fulfilled in their lives.

Being the unconventional kid that I was, I turned to our family cook, Jugay, for much of my education. Jugay was a Kikuyu, from an educated and industrious tribe on the outskirts of Nairobi. He'd been with us for so long that we considered him family. I used to go to his dark little room, lit by a kerosene lamp, perch on a traditional hand-carved three-legged stool, and listen, riveted, as he wove tribal yarns all tied up in traditional mythology. But in among the fantasy was always the overriding message that this was an unjust world and that one should never let oneself be exploited, nor should one ever exploit another human being. I would notice his eyes dancing in the faint light, lit from within by his passion, and I would gaze at him in awe. More than anyone I knew at that time, I respected Jugay for his patience and wisdom. His lessons would resonate for the rest of my life.

My other hero was almost the exact opposite of Jugay: my Uncle Francis was a bon vivant, a renegade, the black sheep of the family. Francis lived with us for four years, and I worshipped him. It was from Francis that I received the warmth, humor, affection, and lack of judgment that I did not get from my father. He always dressed impeccably and smoked using a long ivory and silver cigarette holder. He took great care of himself, played social tennis and bridge, and partied frequently at the Goan Gymkhana Club, where he was a popular member.

He had just purchased a new 350 cc Norton motorbike that I could not take my eyes off of. It was black and chrome, and it called out to me in every way. Perhaps, I thought, one day I would be able to buy a bike of my own. For now, I had to be content with just polishing my uncle's machine for a shilling a week. As an added incentive, Francis would sometimes take me for a spin around the block. It was Francis who taught me to enjoy life, how to socialize, and that there were things out there worth aspiring for.

But beneath the placid surface of my life, there was a revolution fomenting in Kenya. It was a fight for Kenya's independence called the Mau Mau, an armed rebellion against the British colonial government. It was started by members of the Kikuyu tribe. And it was insidious because the Kikuyu worked in the homes of virtually every foreigner in Kenya.

I am often asked, why would a person who was trained to lead troops into battle spend most of his working life trying to avoid disagreement, advocate for better understanding among disparate factions, concentrate on promoting accord, and contribute to alleviating human suffering?

The answer is simple. I was disillusioned with our politicians and skeptical about what they said and what they actually did. It is evident that what we see what is not, in fact, we get. There are various factors and pressures that shape the political horizon, and this impacts on how decisions are made. In many instances, these resolutions do not best serve the public interest. When the going gets tough or rough, a typical ploy of our leaders has been to create a distraction to deflect public attention and defuse civic opinion. The armed forces have often been wrongly used for this propose. Having fought in a war, I am a firm believer that most armed encounters can be resolved through diplomacy, negotiations, and other peaceful means.

But before I continue, I wish to acknowledge my family and friends who spurred me on and offered every encouragement that they could, and I must also pay a tribute to our civilization—to commit to memory my lost colleagues who gave up their lives for what they believed in and to show gratitude and to acknowledge the complexity of our global culture, which in one way or another helped nurture, guide, support, and protect me. I am fortunate to have been able to spend so many years of my life living and working in a variety of cross-cultural and multiethnic environments in so many parts of the world. This experience has been exhilarating, educational, exciting, rewarding, and fulfilling.

I am uneasy about how we interact or fail to do so with our fellow human beings. Over the years, I have been troubled by seeing so many of my colleagues scramble for power, prestige, privilege, and money. My experiences have been humbling and have greatly influenced my philosophy on life and my being, character, spirit, mentality, and psyche. My life has spanned different periods in history. Some of them have been inspiring, even as others have been disheartening, moving, atrocious, inequitable, and discriminatory. But then, isn't this the veracity and quintessence of life?

I spent the last twenty years of my working life as an international professional with the United Nations, first with the United Nations International Children's Emergency Fund (UNICEF) and, separated from the organization, as their country representative in Papua New Guinea. I then joined the United Nations Development Program (UNDP) and served as a senior technical advisor to four different government ministers in Kabul from 2003 to mid-2007. Earlier, I was the executive director of the New York City Outward Bound Center in Manhattan, which was the first urban center in the nation that catered to the needs of inner-city juveniles. Preceding this, I worked as the country director for a Canadian nongovernmental organization in the Sudan during the mass famine in the early eighties and subsequently became the director of the World Food Program's Road Transport Operation in the Sudan, which delivered tons of food and emergency supplies to sustain over 2 million starving and displaced people in Darfur and South Sudan.

My experiences have been diverse, but the main focus of my endeavors has been managing programs providing aid in emergencies and support and protection in countries in conflict in many parts of the world. I spent over ten years in Afghanistan, spread over two tours of duty. During my first stint, I was the UN team leader in West Afghanistan based in Herat. This was during the Soviet occupation of the country. During the American invasion of Afghanistan that led to the fall of the Taliban, I was the head of the UNICEF country office in Uzbekistan and was instrumental in negations with the Uzbek government in the opening of the border to allow relief supplies to flow from Uzbekistan to Afghanistan.

A Single Rose Does Not Signify Spring - Afghan proverb

I wish to start by sharing with you some of my experiences in Afghanistan. I feel that they were impacted by local factors that prevailed long before I arrived. All the same, they are important in trying to understand the context of the current situation in that country. This is fundamentally a tribal society where religion and traditional values play a huge role in the daily lives of people. Most Afghans are deeply spiritual, and their Islamic faith forms the backbone of their society and shapes their values and thinking.

To me, democracy means different things to different people. Max Weber, the German lawyer, politician, and sociologist, believed that there were three ways of maintaining political legitimacy. These were to recognize and respect traditional authority based on the sacredness of a precedence. Second, provide charismatic authority and personal leadership like that provided by the late Ahmad Shah Mashood in northern Afghanistan. And the third was the rationale that requires obedience not to an individual but a structure—perhaps a religious one like Islam. It therefore follows that it is erroneous to assume that one form of democracy can be transposed from one country to another. The majority of people living in the rural areas of Afghanistan are illiterate. Forty years of continuous fighting interrupted, if not stopped, schooling for most, if not all, children. People know, understand, and respect their traditional values and customs. The majority believe that the new constitution is something that has been imposed on the country by the foreigners and therefore has little significance or usefulness.

The right to privilege and power, the craving for self-glorification, the paranoia, the disregard for traditional values, the racial profiling, the destruction by so many years of war have gnarled at the very basic fabric of society, and discrimination has further fueled Islamist extremism in Afghanistan. Even before the Soviet invasion, *Ma'alim fi al-Tariq* (*Milestones*), a book written by the Egyptian Islamist author Sayyid Qutb, became popular reading for the many frustrated academics and students at Kabul University.

They were perturbed by the inequality in society and their inability to get on in life. In this publication, Qutb outlines a plan and a call to rejuvenate the Muslim world on strictly Qur'anic grounds under Sharia law, or the laws of God. Less than a year after its publication, Qutb was arrested and tried in Egypt on charges of conspiracy and was sentenced to death by hanging in 1966. His death elevated his status to "shaheed," or martyr, to many Muslims around the world.

Qutb promoted the fact that Muslims must not only refrain from worshipping anything other than God, but they must also not obey anyone but God. This includes presidents, parliament, and any occupying powers. He saw Sharia as a complete and full way of life, based on one's submission to God alone. He condemned "the evil and fanatical racial discrimination" he experienced as a student in the United States of America.

Mullah Mohammed Omar, who helped form the Taliban, was a strong believer of the teachings and the philosophy of Qutb and was a staunch disciple using his thoughts, concepts on truth, and reality as the basis of propagating his brand of fundamentalism. All Taliban fighters share this philosophy and are prepared to sacrifice their lives to achieve their goals of installing a conservative Islamic Pashto government in Afghanistan that would preserve the status quo, traditional values, and customs and rid the country of all foreign troops.

It is common to hear people, especially foreigners, label the Taliban as "terrorists." However, the organization has never appeared on any "terrorist" list maintained in America, Europe, or elsewhere. There is no doubt, though, that the Taliban continue to use terrorism in their current rebellion against the Afghan government, who they view as traitors and stooges of the American government. They accuse the president of hawking national interest and traditional values to his foreign masters.

It is a fallacy to think that the Taliban were defeated during the American invasion. The fact is that they never really presented any concerted opposition to the invading forces. All they did was just take off their black turbans, hide their weapons, and melt into the woodwork of the Pashto areas of the country, ready to fight another day. There is a saying in Pashto that "revenge is a dish best served cold."

The only elements of the Taliban that were left to fend for themselves were, in essence, non-Afghan and non-Pashto fighters, many of whom had a vested interested in the drug trade. The few that were captured were incarcerated in an American detention prison at Bagram in Afghanistan or languished in Guantanamo.

The Taliban have now resurged with a vengeance. A recent Pentagon report gives little hope or expectation for success or improvement and states that the Taliban have now become a militant force that have "coalesced into a resilient insurgency." They capture and hold, for short periods, towns and villages in the east, north, and south of the country, where they impose Sharia law and punish those who listen to music or don't conform to their concept of the Islamic code of conduct.

The Taliban rely heavily on the active support that they have always received from the Inter-Services Intelligence of Pakistan, or the ISI, and operate out of bases inside Pakistan without let or hindrance. They do so because the government of Pakistan, in one way or the other, condone their actives and lend both active and passive support to the cause. Pakistan has always been viewed by the American government as a credible ally in the "War in Terror." NATO governments concur.

A fact that many people disregard or ignore is that the Pakistan military is the mainstay of the civilian government. In order to rule the country, the government must get the backing and support of the military. To a large extent, the Armed Forces are basically fundamentalist in outlook. They espouse a doctrine that stipulates that it is in Pakistan's national and strategic interest to maintain control over Afghanistan. Besides, the extremist political parties in Pakistan have a big following. However, their political clout appears to be diminishing.

But there is an even greater and more contentious issue that influences Pakistan's role in Afghanistan. It relates to the Durand Line that was arbitrarily drawn by the British Indian colonizers in 1893. This treaty artificially and subjectively divides the Pashto people between Afghanistan and Pakistan. This is a continuing source of tension between the two countries, and powerful traditional leaders on both sides of the border now advocate for an independent Pashtunistan. This hypothesis is supported by some very high-ranking Afghan officials, including government ministers.

The popular assumption in Afghanistan is that the Durand treaty was only valid and was to remain in force for one hundred years. This period ended in 1993. However, Pakistan is unwilling to give up any territory, and the acrimony continues.

One afternoon, the minister, who comes from a wealthy Pashto family from Kandahar, invited me to attend a festival to celebrate Pashto culture. Deputy Minister Ali, also a Pashto, would accompany me. Ali was not only a colleague but was also a true friend. I trusted him and valued his advice. He warned that this event was going to be highly political and, in a way, nationalistic. "Afghan nationalism?"

I inquired. "No, Pashto nationalism," he retorted angrily. He also cautioned me that I would probably be the only foreigner and non-Pashto invited to attend. No foreigners or non-Pashto are invited. Then he quickly consoled me by saying that I should not be worried, as I looked like a Pashto and nobody would realize I was not Afghan. But I had to keep my mouth shut.

For security reasons, I had reservations about attending and knew full well that I would have not got UN security clearance to participate. Encouraged by Mir Agha—my trusted friend, driver, and security overseer—I decided to attend. I would not tell anybody that I would wear a "Sharwal Kameez," the tribal costume. I felt confident that I would be safe and would pass as a local. Besides, this would be not only a fascinating experience but, more importantly, it would also offer me a unique insight into Afghan political thinking and ambitions.

The occasion started off being very festive. The gathering, as was expected, all male. The boys and men were dressed in their finest tribal ceremonial costumes. They held hands, sang, and danced in a very lighthearted and congenial atmosphere. Being of Asian descent, I blended in easily into the crowd.

When the more formal part of the function commenced, it became obvious that this event was designed to drum up Pashto nationalism and fervor to promote tribal superiority and encourage the dominance of the Pashto tribe that has ruled and would, it was hoped, continue to rule Afghanistan forever. The Pashto considers "Zna Zar Zameen" as central to their culture. It means that men are expected to protect women and treasure the land. Despite this, I found it odd that a senior government minister would be so actively involved and participate in such a controversial event, which focused on maintaining the power and privileged position of one tribe regardless of the provisions to the newly adopted constitution.

To me this went against all the norms of nation building. Pakistanis of Pashto origin also participated and some were clearly Inter-Service Intelligence officers. They eyed me keenly, and I did my best to ignore them.

The Pakistan army openly supports interventions designed to destabilize Indian-held Kashmir by covertly training, arming, and financing the insurgency there. Most of the fighters who are being sent to Kashmir are in fact trained at Taliban/Al-Qaeda camps in Afghanistan and have gained experience by fighting alongside the Taliban. Recently, after fierce fighting, ISAF troops captured a number of Taliban fighters. Some of them carried valid Pakistan military ID cards.

There can be no doubt that the Taliban is better organized today than they were before the US invasion. Recruitment into their ranks has received a tremendous boost by what is currently perceived as the Americans' crusade against Islam. The excessive force being used by Americans, NATO, and the "rent-a-guards" working for American security contractors further ferments the antiforeigner/anti-occupier feeling. It is common knowledge that using conventional tactics like aerial bombardment and shelling by field artillery in counterinsurgency operations in densely populated rural areas is nonsense, and such action will continue to indiscriminately claim innocent civilian lives.

In addition, the Taliban have been successful in winning the hearts and minds of much of the rural areas that they occupy. People are fed up of being milked of their meager resources by the flagrant and rampant corruption in government, in the police, in the judiciary, by parliamentarians, and by provincial administration officials.

All of this has contributed to the breakdown of law and order in many parts of the country. Unemployment in the rural areas is soaring, especially among the young, and therefore, many able-bodied men join the Taliban not out of choice but as a form of employment.

They are paid a regular wage, which is reported to be higher than the salary received by soldiers in the Afghan National Army.

Aided by the ISI, the Taliban have become experts at understanding the prevailing political conditions both domestically and in the home countries of the NATO troops serving in Afghanistan. They know that the hostile attitude to the war in both Iraq and Afghanistan is growing. With every foreign hostage they take and every soldier they kill, the opposition to the war is aggravated and accelerated. The taking of foreign hostages for ransom has also proved an important income-generating activity for the Taliban. They recently released a number of female Korean hostages for millions of dollars in cash and the release of some of their commanders who were in government custody.

People in both the urban and rural areas now feel betrayed. They initially believed in the promises made by the invaders and their local leaders, that democracy would bring peace, stability, and a better quality of life for all of them, which have not materialized. Several years after the invasion, they have witnessed a steady deterioration in their standard of living. The rich are getting richer, and the vast majority of Afghans are getting poorer. Security is worse than it ever was, and many of their innocent friends and relatives continue to be maimed or killed by the occupying forces. More women are being raped today, than ever before, and as a testament to this, the streets of Kabul are deserted as soon as darkness descends. The old custom of "melmastia," hospitality and asylum to all guest sseeking help, no longer applies.

One cannot ignore the resentment that is generally felt against expatriate Afghans. Those people fled the country soon after the Soviet invasion and made their homes in the United States, Canada, Australia, Europe, or the United Kingdom. They were educated and well to do, and this aided their mobility. Some of these men have now returned, but their families remain in the land they adopted.

Because of their education, their fluency in English, and work experience in the West, many now occupy positions of power and privilege in Afghanistan.

As we sat on our haunches on the front porch of his modest Kabul home, enjoying the fragrance and splendor of the roses that were now in full bloom, relaxing and sipping on sweet black tea, Fatha, a one-armed ex-mujahideen, started talking about some of the injustices that afflict Afghan society today. What aggrieves him and the others who took part in the "jihad" was the fact that they sacrificed their lives and limbs without let or fear. They waged war against the mighty Soviet Army, surmounting numerous difficulties and overcoming what the experts in the West assessed as insurmountable odds. "We succeeded in defeating the mighty invading Soviet Armed Forces, forcing them to flee from our beloved country."

"My brother, do you appreciate that this was a victory for not only Afghanistan, but also the greatest and most important one for the rest of the free world? We proved that the renowned Soviet military might was not invincible, and by doing so, we defeated Communism, dismantled the Soviet Union, ended the Cold War, and stopped the arms race. All of this brought peace and stability to the world. Nobody else in the history of mankind can claim such a victory!"

"Despite these successes and our contribution to our country and the world, just look at how we are rewarded. We are starving, have no jobs, have no homes, and cannot feed our families. We have served our purpose, were there when the nation needed us, but now our corrupt government has no further use for us because, among other things, they do not know how to deal with us. But more importantly, they are afraid of us. We are Allah's warriors and will prevail."

"I sacrificed my youth, my education, and my family to participate in the jihad. Despite this, I have now been discarded like a rotten apple. I cannot find work because I am illiterate, disabled, and labeled by the Americans as a 'war lord.' With no money, my family is starving. But I am a fighter and will fight again. We all will as that is the only thing we really know to do. In desperation, I am now heavily involved in the drug trade. As I am a *jihadi*, the authorities do not dare touch me. They turn a blind eye and leave me alone. Can you blame me for what I do? Is this how war veterans are treated in your country, Mr. Rudy?" he inquired.

For me, Fatha displayed a rage that I have seldom seen elsewhere. It is not common for an Afghan to vent feelings in the presence of a foreigner. I felt accepted, privileged, but it made me sad to witness the plight of these brave warriors. I had worked with them during the Soviet invasion, and being an ex-military officer, I admired their courage, determination, and ability to endure enormous hardship. But it also raised a red flag in my mind that it was an ominous sign of things to come.

"You see, Rudy, my brother, we believe and understand that this preferential treatment of these Afghan cowards is wrong and unjust. These people were members of the Communist Party. They therefore had the money and the influence to enable them to flee the country, with their tails behind their legs like scared dogs. We, the poor and really vulnerable, were left to the mercy of Allah and were expected to fend for ourselves. Our faith and the Almighty helped us to.

"But, Mr. Rudy, what is your opinion? We respect and trust you. Convert to Islam and I shall find you a young Afghan bride." Fatha waited for my response. I understood that he was seeking validation for his views and beliefs. This social encounter turned out to be more then I had envisaged or bargained for.

My timorous response was that it was not for me but history to judge who was right or wrong. Fatha's reply was not only sharp, angry but also insulting to me. "These people are selfish and self-centered. You are a man of moral integrity, and yet you choose not to join me in condemning them?"

I understood and shared Fatha's feelings. But then I was an International civil servant and, as such, had to be impartial. Besides being sympathetic, sharing some of his views and opinions, I was not at liberty to voice my personal opinion as this would be interpreted and understood incorrectly as the official UN position.

Exasperated, he concluded by saying, "These people are like leeches sucking the blood of their poor Afghan brothers and sisters." This outburst from Fatha made me uncertain and distressed about the future of this beautiful country that I have grown to love.

I have heard many Afghans say that they felt far safer and much more secure during the rule of the Taliban. The quality of their lives was generally better because there was no corruption, and they were better able to accesses the goods and services provided by government. The reality of their life today is that nothing is possible without paying a bribe.

In contradiction to this, however, was the experience of one of my staff, Majdi. He was traumatized and physically abused by the Taliban for no apparent reason and is, even today, extremely afraid, upset, anxious, and mentally scarred by this experience.

Because homes had no electric power or heat, most Afghan families generally go to bed on the floor early, to keep warm under communal blankets and conserve the oil used for lighting. The Majdi family was no exception. Suddenly one night, a pounding on their front door rudely awakened the whole family. On opening the door, Majdi was grabbed by two armed Taliban who whisked him away in an open pickup truck in full view and to the horror of his wife and children. Nothing was said and no reasons given.

Majdi was taken to a Taliban house on the outskirts of Kabul, where he was held captive in a hole in the ground that was sealed by a metal trapdoor. Slits in the door let in some light and air. Once a day, he was let out to stretch his legs and go to the lavatory, after which he received his only meal of the day, consisting of stale, dry bread and tea. On a few occasions, this bland and unhealthy diet was supplemented with leftover "kbuli pilau." This is a rice dish that has some meat in it.

One morning six months after he was taken hostage, he was startled by what sounded like calamitous commotion in the enclosed backyard of the house where he was being held prisoner. The Taliban were screaming at each other over the revving and roaring of the engines of their pickup trucks. He then heard tires screech, and his hole and home soon filled up with dust and grit as the Taliban sped away.

Soon the yard was all quiet again. He spoke about the mice and cockroaches that moved in an agitated but urgent manner across the filthy floor, feasting on scraps that constituted their dinner. It was now dark. He started to hallucinate. His head was full of strange and unfamiliar sounds and noises. He felt that he was on the threshold of going mad. The Taliban were certainly not house proud. They cared little about domestic affairs. Their focus and energy was on defeating the invaders and turning Afghanistan into a truly Islamic state.

When the dust had settled and it became obvious that the Taliban had fled, Majdi struggled for what seemed hours to open the trapdoor. He got cuts and bruises, and his hands were soon covered in blood. But he was determined to escape. At long last and totally exhausted, he was able to slowly push the trapdoor open and crawl out.

The yard and the house were deserted, except for a few live goats and two hens. The Taliban had all fled in extreme haste, leaving behind half-eaten meals of rice and meat, clothing, and a small transistor radio. Being famished, Majdi started to greedily consume the leftovers. He soon began vomiting, became disoriented, and passed out.

When he came to, it was dark, and the house was eerily quiet. He was cold, afraid, and unsure what to do next. He heard sporadic small arm gunfire in the immediate neighborhood. He started thinking about his family and trembled in horror and fear. A dusk-to-dawn curfew had been imposed on the city of Kabul before his capture, and he assumed that this was still in place.

Majdi was not allowed to wash or bathe over the whole period of his captivity, so when he found a bucket of freezing water, he soon indulged. He noticed that his body was reduced to skin and bone, his clothes were in rags, and he had sores all over his body. The good thing was the Taliban had left behind some clothing, so he was able to change. At dawn he left the compound and was startled by the people he passed in the street. After all, he had not seen or spoken to anyone for six months.

He walked for miles to reach the shack where he had left his family and felt the tension was driving him insane. His worst fears then materialized. His family was not there. The landlord had ordered them onto the street, the day after his capture. Nobody knew or would say where they had gone.

The struggle and emotional torment that followed was far too painful for Majdi to narrate. He just could not think or talk about this frightening, distressing, and shocking experience. I could well understand.

After wandering the streets of Kabul for weeks, he met Abdul who had gone to university with him. They hugged but said nothing. Once they had gathered their wits, they held hands and walked in silence to a bombed-out building near Kabul airport. Majdi was overjoyed that soon he would be reunited with his family. But what would he find? He was afraid and wanted to run and hide in the hole that was his forced home for so many months. Abdul sensed this panic and clutched Majdi's sweaty hand firmly. In a tiny room that had no doors or windows, Majdi was reunited with his family. The room was blackened with smoke, there were shell scars all over the walls, and the air smelled of poverty and deprivation. His wife was alive but ill, and all the six children were dressed in tatters and on the brink of starvation. But they thanked Allah that they were alive and together again. He could not explain or find a valid reason why he was taken hostage but surmised that it was because he is Tajik and a Shia by faith. This was the new Afghanistan.

Learn to wait, there is always time for everything -
Indian saying

He told me this story when I interviewed him for a junior support position on my team. The fact that Majdi shared with me his extremely distressing experience created an emotional bond between us. I could clearly see in his eyes, face, and expression the pain and suffering he had endured, and reliving this experience caused him further grief. It almost was as if he could no longer reconcile his body, mind, and soul. I took comfort in the belief that by talking, he was able to come to terms with what he had been through. Majdi did not have the skills or experience that I was looking for. But then, this was an imperfect world. Here was a man with six starving children with no income, shelter, food, or clothing. I could not reject him, not after all that he had been through. He deserved a respite. I decided to hire him on compassionate grounds. Difficult to justify, but I was prepared to pay the price. Majdi understood this and always made a concerted effort to give his very best. With the resurgence of the Taliban in Afghanistan, Majdi wrote me an e-mail recently, requesting my support to help him and his family to immigrate to Canada.

I was returning to Kabul not so long ago when the immigration officer at the Kabul international airport tried to computer read my passport. He was illiterate, and it soon became obvious that he did not know how to use the scanner. "This passport is forged," he charged. "No, but I think that your computer has a problem," I replied. "However, if you allow me, I may be able to fix it." I explained in sign language how he should scan the passport. Following my instructions, he was amazed that it worked.

He then struggled to find a valid visa. Understandable, as my passport was full of visas and entry/exit stamps. I requested that my passport be handed back to me, and I then opened the appropriate page for his scrutiny. After studying the page in great detail and squinting to read the writing, he ceremonially told me that my Afghan visa expired. On checking, I noticed that the visa was valid for another six months. The officer responded that the Dari version of the visa had expired despite the fact that the stamp was in both English and Dari. However, he was willing to compromise, to spare me any inconvenience, especially since I was a UN official and an adviser to a government minister.

The officer now adopted a playful mood and was in no hurry to get things done quickly. I was tired after my long flight back to Kabul from New York. All I wanted to do was to get to my guesthouse, shower, and sleep. "What country do you come from, my brother?" was his next question. His eyes conveyed shrewdness and slyness, and he his demeanor was as sly and cunning as a fox. It was difficult for me to maintain my cool, but I understood that it was important that I should.

"From Florida," I responded politely. "But you look like a Pashto, like one of us. Or perhaps you are from India? We in Afghanistan love the Indians. They are the same as us but for their religion. They help us a lot. You know that all the Airbus aircraft that Aryana, the national airline, uses were a gift from the people of India. And so are the Tata Milee buses. More than one thousand operate in Kabul alone, and the fares are very low. Besides, Pakistan is their enemy, and we Afghans hate all Pakistanis." The people standing in line behind me were starting to get impatient, and the official yelled in Pashto that they should move to another immigration booth.

I was now all alone, and I could sense that this fox was ready to make the kill. "I think you are doing a lot to help my people, so I want to help you too. I do not want to make things difficult for you, my brother. But please understand that I have problems too. I have a family of fifteen people, relatives and their children living with me. They have no jobs, no money, no house, so I have to support all of them. Buy them food, clothing, medicines, and pay bribes to corrupt officials so that they are not arrested. In Kabul you can be arrested without cause.

"That is why when you people in the UN talk about human rights, it's just hollow words and means nothing. So if you give me only $150, I will stamp your passport and you can go." I did not intend to give him a dime, but $150 as a bribe appeared steep, as his monthly wage could not be more than $30 per month. Apparently, he could read my thoughts and quickly added, "I must give $130 to my commander, and the rest is mine." This was certainly a well-oiled machine. I fully understood his position, and the plight of all public servants are the same. With inadequate resources, they have no alternatives but to seek out other ways to generate income like demanding bribes. This is the standard pattern of behavior and is considered normal in today's Afghan society. Not so during the reign of the Taliban.

After a while, I responded that I fully understood his plight and I wished that I could help. But because I was traveling from New York, I had no cash on me. The streets of New York are unsafe, and one is in constant danger of being mugged if you carry cash. "Oh! So your New York police are same as the Kabul police. They are robbers in police uniform," he asked.

"Not so," I said. "There are of course good cops and bad cops, but most of them are good cops. So all I have on me are credit cards, and these are of no use in Afghanistan." I showed him my Visa card as he had never seen one before, and it was impossible to get him to understand how the card worked. For some strange reason, this was a turning point in our relationship, especially in regard to how he behaved toward me. His attitude changed, and he now treated me like a long-lost member of his tribe.

He then said that he would drive me in his cab to my guest-house for a modest fare of only $25. "But you cannot leave your post," I interjected.

"Don't worry," he countered cheerfully. "Nobody really cares."

"But our security regulations do not permit UN staff to travel in non-UN vehicles. Besides, I was certain that my driver was waiting for me outside." The issue of the Visa had evaporated, so I shook the officer's hand and invited him to a kebob lunch the following day. It always helps to have a contact at the airport.

This incident reminded me of an event that may have resulted in a crisis. I was returning to Afghanistan from Tashkent by road after an R & R break. I used the "friendship" bridge to cross the mighty, fast-flowing Amu Daria River. I arrived at the impressive new Afghan immigration and customs complex built by the UN. It looked even more imposing because it was surrounded by structures that were damaged or destroyed in the war. The facility was impressive, and the first impression that travelers got was of an efficient, well-run state. The Afghan immigration officer declared that I did not have a valid visa to enter the country. I asked for my passport, and to my dismay, my visa had in fact expired over a month ago.

I therefore could not enter the country and would have to drive back to Tashkent and apply for an Afghan visa. But I only had a single-entry Uzbek visa and therefore could not reenter Uzbekistan. Was I doomed to spend the rest of my days camping on the "Friendship" bridge in no-man's land? I had long learned to keep my wits and asked to see the commanding officer of this border facility. I was ushered into the general's plush office.

To my great joy and pleasure, I knew the general, who also immediately recognized me. Hajji Nadir and I first met during the war against the Soviets. He was then a mujahideen commander in Western Afghanistan. After embracing and going through the lengthy traditional Afghan greeting, we sat down on the floor to drink green tea and eat almonds and raisins. We reminisced about the war and the many victories that Hajji Nadir and his holy warriors had scored over the Communist forces. He recalled how UNICEF had provided essential drugs and food to his village and said that without this support, many women and children would have died.

About two hours later, the general asked for my passport. He then unbuttoned the front of his smart general's tunic and pulled out a rubber stamp and an ink pad and inserted a visa into my passport. Problem solved. So I jumped into my white Toyota Land Cruiser and headed for Mazar-i-Sharif.

An Afghan colleague wanted to renew his passport. He went to the passport office in Kabul, and after standing in a line for four hours, he was told that there were no more blank passports books left in the country. New ones were being printed, but these would not be available for at least another six months. However, if he gave the officer $350, he would issue him with a new passport immediately.

In order to obtain a driver's license, an individual does not necessarily have to know how to drive. All that is required is payment of a bribe of $100 to be issued with a valid driver's license immediately. As a result, Afghan roads are death traps, with the number of accident fatalities increasing by the day.

A person that I had tremendous respect for was the commander of the Kabul international airport. He was from the old school of Soviet-trained officers, always immaculately turned out in his uniform. General Rahim was courteous and gave the impression of being reliable and a person one could trust. There were rumors that he was corrupt, but these were never substantiated. Counternarcotics officers search the possessions of all travelers flying out of Kabul airport. On a Saturday afternoon, a well-dressed Afghan woman traveling to Dubai was arrested when police found four kilos of heroin on her possession.

She was escorted to the main terminal building, yelling and screaming that the police had no right to arrest her. She would get them all fired if she was not allowed to board her flight immediately with all her belongings. General Rahim ordered the arrest and detention of the woman, and she was taken away in a police vehicle. This appeared to be very normal. The next day, the local press reported that General Rahim had been relieved of his command and was facing corruption charges. The woman who had been arrested and charged with trafficking was released and no explanation given. Actions like these perpetuate corruption. It clearly demonstrates that segments of the population are above the law and can get away with murder.

History shows that individuals or parties wishing to gain political power are not averse to making promises to gain popular support. The Taliban are no exception. When they ruled Afghanistan from 1996 to 2001, they were able to stamp out corruption, security in both the urban and rural areas was very good, and most importantly, they were able to eradicate the cultivation of the opium poppy.

They continue to use these accomplishments to show that the present Afghan government is ineffective as its activities are confined to Kabul only. They contend, and many Afghans agree, that the government is dysfunctional and unconcerned with the plight of the ordinary person.

Despite the billions of foreign aid dollars that were poured into the country for poverty alleviation, very little, if anything has changed, and the ordinary families desperately struggle to make ends meet. The majority of people continue to live in abject poverty, malnutrition in young children is extremely high, and health care services are almost nonexistent in rural communities, where the roads are so bad that farmers have great difficulty in getting their produce to market while the bazaars are well stocked with produce imported from Iran and Pakistan. Electric power and running water continue to be in short supply in many urban areas and are not available to most of the people living in villages.

The Taliban repeatedly pledge that when they regain power, they would use all foreign funds to bring about a sustainable and positive change in the lives of the masses, unlike the current government officials who only look after their best interest and are busy lining their individual pockets.

A recent UN survey shows that opium cultivation in Afghanistan has reached an all-time high in 2006, rising by almost 60 percent over the previous year, producing 6,100 tons of opium and yielding about $755 million in revenues. Of this, it is estimated that about 92 percent goes to the warlords and corrupt government officials and about $20 million into the coffers of the Taliban.

It should be noted that government revenues over this period were around $350 million. There is now ample evidence that the Taliban are using this narco money to fund their current insurgency operations. NATO commanders in Afghanistan have accused Iran of arming, aiding, and abetting the Taliban. Why would a fundamentalist Shia government side with a fundamentalist Sunni cause?

The drug trade in Afghanistan flourishes because the drug and warlords are well connected. Many noncorrupt officials have been punished or dismissed when they attempted to bring traffickers to task. They have now learned to turn a blind eye. During the fall of the Taliban, many of the warlords who acted as surrogates for the Americans, in their hunt for Al-Qaeda, filled a vacuum and took control of the drug trade.

There is almost no difference between the attitudes of these warlords and of the Taliban. Most are dictators who do not tolerate dissent, their outlook is regressive, many are guilty of war crimes, lots of them participated in the destruction on Afghanistan between 1992 and 1996, and all are extremely wealthy and well connected. As they were seen as key allies in the war on terror, their active participation in the drug trade was largely ignored and at times even condoned.

Their enormous wealth has now put them into a position of power and privilege, local officials are at their beck and call. De facto, they have more authority and power than government and are the respected, if not feared, rulers of the region that they control. It is widely acknowledged that the CIA initially sponsored the drug trade as a weapon to defeat the invading Soviet Army. Lessons had been learned in Vietnam, and these were now being applied to Afghanistan. The logic was to sacrifice the drug war to win the cold war.

The irony is that senior government officials are also involved in the drug trade in a very important and fundamental way, and this undermines the very principles and the structure of the British-funded counternarcotics program.

When I was the adviser to the Minister of an article appeared in the *New York Times* naming the minister as one of the major players in the drug trade in Afghanistan. I had heard this allegation on many occasions and also that the ex-president's brother and the minister worked together and were major players in the drug trade.

On most days, the deputy minister and I joined the minister in his private dining room for lunch. One day during lunch, the minister turned directly to me. Staring at me unswervingly, he stated that the *New York Times*, in a lead article, had named him as a major drug lord in Afghanistan. "Rudy . . . what is your opinion and advice?"

I had of course read the article, which in my view demolished any concept that the minister possessed any principles or adhered to high moral standards required of a serving government minister. We took big bites of our grilled baby lamb chops, chewing steadily and noisily, and thoroughly enjoying the Afghan gourmet cuisine. At the end of the meal, the minister turned to me as he said, "Rudy you have not responded to my question about the *NY Times* article." The reason I had not was because I was uncertain how to ask the tough question. But diplomacy aside, I had to take the bull by the horns and ask the difficult question. Looking the minister straight in the eye, I asked, "Your Excellency, are you involved in the drug trade?" He was taken aback by my boldness and the directness of my question.

I glanced at the deputy who was discreetly looking out of the window, obviously uncomfortable with this confrontation. People in power in Afghanistan are not accustomed to being challenged. They expect their subordinates to be, "yes", men endorsing everything they say. So the minister was taken aback by what I am certain he felt was insolence on my part. The deputy minister's jaws dropped as he looked at me in absolute amazement that I stood my ground.

But the minister was not a person to get angry and consumed by emotions in such circumstances. It took him a few seconds to regain composure. When he had, he burst out laughing, and in a cool, calm, and collected way, he said that he has never had anything to do with drugs.

In that case, my advice was that he should get himself a good New York lawyer and file a suit against the *New York Times* for slander. I said that I would be glad to identify a suitable litigation lawyer and give him some idea of cost, process, and possible outcomes. The minister nodded and said that he would think about it. A few days later, I broached the subject again, and the minister responded that he did not care about what was written about him in America. If someone made the same allegations in Afghanistan, that would be a different matter.

A week later, I was invited to the minister's guesthouse for lunch. I was told that all the movers and shakers in Afghan would be there. On my arrival, the parking lot was crammed full with high-priced SUVs, all black with their windows tainted. Well-armed bodyguards in smart Afghan-army-type uniforms stood around or sat in their Toyota pickup trucks. Mir Agha said that these people were all Kahandaris and Pashto.

A banquet had been laid on, and I felt slightly out of place in this gathering, so I took a seat in the back and watched. Looking around, I had no doubts that the guests, who were all male, were extremely wealthy. They wore gold Rolex watches, had diamond rings, and were dressed in flashy Italian suits or the traditional sharwal zameez.

Suddenly, there was a flurry of activity, and in walked the ex-president's younger brother with his huge entourage. It was evident that he and the minister were bosom buddies. These people were the Pashto elite. After lunch, the minister invited some of his guests to join him in another room. They were obviously going to discuss topics that they did not want the rest of us to be privy to. This gave me the opportunity to leave.

Over the past four years, I have served as senior technical adviser of five different government ministers in Kabul. I have been able to observe things from the inside and therefore have an entirely different perspective that most foreigners get. To be accepted into the inner circles of Afghan hierarchy, I had to win the trust and confidence of the government ministers I worked with. This I was able to do, and therefore, I became privy to much of the infighting and lack of purpose within government.

My background and experience helped me in achieving this. The fact that I was an American with no political or tribal axe to grind facilitated this. True, the country has a constitution that was agreed upon by warlords and fundamentalist mujahideen commanders. However, the majority of the population who are, by and large, illiterate know nothing about it. The drafting of the document or the debate that followed was not inclusive or transparent, and it is common knowledge that the outcome was arranged through intimidation and bribery.

One of the main pillars of the constitution is to guarantee the rights and freedom of the population. However, the very government ministries that are supposed to deliver the goods and services to the population are dysfunctional and not able to do so because of corruption, nepotism, greed, and a total lack of human capacity. To be effective, the approach of these ministries should be holistic and integrated. In actuality, they are individual fiefdoms whose turf is jealously guarded by the minister and a few trusted henchmen.

I was exposed to the inner wheels of government when I was an adviser to the minister of Frontier and Tribal Affairs. In the past, this ministry played a key role in the administration of Afghanistan. Its authority and influence covered all aspects of life, and every Afghan would, at one stage or the other, have had some form of official contact with this ministry. I really enjoyed working at the ministry, but my driver, friend, and bodyguard often advised me not to take my duties seriously.

I once asked him to explain. His response was sharp. There was a tone of anger in his voice, but I sensed that he tried to hide his fury. "Rudy, this is not a government of the people for the people. It is a government for individuals. The people in power want to grab everything for themselves, for their families or relatives. The rest of the population does not matter." His comments made me sad, but then, this was the reality.

Now that the constitution was a reality, I asked the minister if the Kuchi (nomads) who number about five million had heard of the constitution. Kuchi affairs were part of the ministry's mandate. Distracted and disinterested, the minister said that he was certain that like the majority of Afghans, they would not have a clue what parliament, the constitution, or democracy was all about.

These were "foreigner" values that were of little interest to the locals. I advised that perhaps the ministry should develop a strategy of bringing the constitution to the people. The conversation ended with me being requested to do whatever was necessary, but this was certainly not something that the minister or senior management would be involved with or pay much attention to because they considered it irrelevant.

I had developed a profound respect for the Kuchi. These proud nomads were able to carve out a living in areas that were marginal. They were born conservationists who respected the environment, understood Mother Nature, and were in perfect harmony with the environment that they lived in. They are proud and fiercely independent. Even during the Taliban regime, their women refused to wear the burka, and out of deference, the Taliban did not insist in conformity as they did for the rest of the population.

I decided to meet with the National Kuchi Shari (group of elders), which I helped constitute to plot a way forward. The Kuchi have always contended and complained, and rightly so, that they have been sidelined, their rights are not being recognized or respected, and their special needs were not catered to by any of the National Development Programs, and therefore, they received no benefit from these.

The elders, many of whom were literate and wise, were surprised that I should presume upon their time to discuss something that did not affect them. The constitution was something abstract that had consequences for the people who lived in Kabul but had nothing to do with the Kuchi. They had never heard of parliament, the constitution, or democracy and felt that their tribal "shuras" and traditional customs and laws adequately served their needs.

I set the record right and stressed that unless they participate in the parliamentary processes, they would continue to be marginalized and would remain second-class citizens. This hit the right cord. I was assured that all the men would register and vote.

This was not good enough, I insisted. Women represented 50 percent of their demographic profile, and they too must register to vote. The fact that the women would have to be photographed for voter registration was a major deterrent. After a great deal of debate, a compromise was worked out. Their women would be allowed to register if females carried out the process. Polaroid cameras would be used by women photographers, and the resulting photograph would be pasted on the voting card that would be handed to their woman directly.

I was exhilarated by the fact that perhaps this would be a start to mainstreaming and inclusion of the Kuchi into Afghan society. But my satisfaction was short-lived. Voter-registration stations were located in population centers miles away from the Kuchi winter quarters, where transportation was scarce and costly. Besides, a mother with young children is unable to leave her young children alone in a tent while she spent the whole day traveling on foot or donkey to get registered as a voter.

One of the main complaints of the Kuchi was that they no longer received the veterinary or health care services before they started their summer migration. They lost a lot of their animals to disease, and their children were dying due to the lack of healthcare. I raised these issues with senior management at the ministry and the fact that the Kuchi were denied their traditional right of way during migration.

To my dismay, there was no political will to try and address these issues, let alone resolve them. Frustrated and angry, I met with officials from the Ministries of Health and Agriculture. The Ministry of Health gave me a copy of their glossy five-year health strategy, which was based on fixed health care centers. I inquired about the Kuchi and was told that they were free to access these. "Not so," I retorted. "They are turned away because they do not live in the area, and besides, there were no provision made for drugs to treat nomads."

I was beginning to lose my cool and inquired what a mother living high on a mountain pasture with a critically ill child should do. The smug answer was that she should take it to a health center, at best five days' walk away. What disturbed me was the fact that these officials lacked the compassion or interest to come up with viable solutions to the problems. Mobile clinics were used in the past, and these could be reinstated, I suggested. Not in my lifetime, I understood.

My meetings at the Ministry of Agriculture were equally pointless. I was able to meet with the minister who politely told me that besides being predominately an agriculture-based economy, his ministry was understaffed and lacked the resources to provide even the most basic agricultural services. They received no funds from foreign aid, and the international donor community did not see support to the Ministry of Agriculture as a priority. No wonder the peasant farmers are driven into the clutches of the drug lords.

On returning to the ministry, I went to brief the minister on my unproductive morning. He was not surprised or interested and abruptly ended the conversation by requesting me to do what I felt was necessary. He then invited me to lunch in his private dining room at the ministry. By now, the cooks knew that I was on a low-carbohydrate diet and served me with mountains of lamb and beef.

The rest of the guests were business partners of the minister. After lunch, I met with the chair of the Kuchi National Shura. I was embarrassed to inform him that I was unable to get the powers that be to focus on or come up with solutions to the problems that his people faced. I assured him, however, that I had not given up and would remain in touch. I got the impression that he had heard these reassurances before.

Later in the week, I was invited to attend a meeting with the US military that was chaired by Deputy Minister Ali. The American army had realized that they were losing the battle for the hearts and minds to the Taliban. They had therefore created a civil affairs team commanded by a senior officer to work closely with government, religious, and tribal leaders.

At such meetings with foreigners, I was expected to be the administration's unofficial spokesman. I explained that in the past, the Kuchi had always played an important role, and besides being the main producers of meat, wool, hides, and skins, they also acted as the eyes and ears of government in the remote parts of the country. Because of their nomadic lifestyle, they were to be found in the most isolated and inaccessible areas. This made them valuable assets for firsthand, on-the-ground intelligence gathering. I was certain that this information would ensure that I received the undivided attention of our guest.

The military team was made of reservists who had been in Afghanistan for only a few weeks. They therefore knew little about the country, the people, their religion, or their culture. Even their young Afghan translators, who were "kabulis," had little information about the Kuchi. As livestock was the lifeblood of the Kuchi, veterinary services for their animals were as important as health care for their children. The senior military officer present said that they had vets in the staff who were part of the army's K9 unit. He would speak with the commander and get back to me.

The Kuchi had started their spring migration, and I had noticed that a few were encamped on the Shomali Plain just outside Kabul. When the colonel commander of the vet unit called on the ministry a few days later, I suggested to visit the Kuchi camped on the Shamali Plains. I led the long convoy of military and government vehicles to the tent of chief of this group of Kuchi. They were warned of our visit and welcomed us with fresh yogurt and warm home-baked flat brown bread. I viewed this as a real treat, but the Kuchi were disappointed when the American service men and women did not partake in this simple but delicious customary traditional fare.

Many of our military guests had not been out of their camps, and for some, it was their first opportunity to get out into the countryside and meet Afghans. It is therefore easy to understand that what they saw fascinated them. The elements in the environment provided excellent photo opportunities for all. The Kuchi chief told me that one of his wives was giving birth in a tent next door and asked if the colonel, who was a woman, and a vet would assist. The colonel was apprehensive but went accompanied by two female subordinates.

Apparently, the woman who was delivering was alone and lay on the dirt floor in the company of a few newborn lambs. There was no water. I have been a soldier and have seen blood, sweat, and tears. But nothing prepared me for this. The mother had just delivered with nobody to assist her. Now she struggled to cut the umbilical cord by biting on it. This was too much for me to take. I felt helpless and ignorant about the realities that these wonderful people face in their life. I beat a hasty retreat. There was commotion. "We need water, help . . ." The colonel had fainted watching this scene. I took comfort in the fact that I was not the only one who could not stomach this real-life drama. She was quickly carried out and came to a few seconds later. The expression on her weather-beaten but beautiful face was one of absolute shock.

The chief had effectively demonstrated the dire need of his people and asked in a very polite but assertive way what was being done with the billions of dollars in foreign aid that was being poured into Afghanistan. His people applauded and were very outspoken in condemning the corrupt government and blaming the Americans for destroying their ancient way of life. This outburst by the Kuchi had a lasting impression on the American service women and men. In a subsequent conversation that I had with their commander, he said that he was alarmed, disappointed, and filled with apprehension at the opinion and general feeling these illiterate people had about their American liberators.

He had learned a valuable lesson and appreciated the fact that strategically, the US Army had to win over the hearts and minds of these people. He was going to discuss the matter with the overall commander of US forces in Afghanistan and would inform me if outcomes were positive. My objective had been achieved. I knew that I could not gain accesses to the top American military commanders, and therefore, it would be impossible to explain to them the plight of over five million of these proud nomads.

Besides, working at the ministry, I became aware of the fact that the Kuchi were an excellent tool for intelligence gathering. They moved across borders freely, they had relatives in Pakistan and Iran, but more importantly, they traveled over vast distances on foot into areas that were remote. They were the government's eyes and ears on the ground. The foreign military had yet to appreciate what a valuable asset this was to help with the planning and execution of timely military interventions against the Taliban.

The following year, the American military sent out a veterinary team to the winter quarters of the Kuchi just outside Jalalabad, where they were able to treat and vaccinate about seventeen animals. But the problem was not only with livestock. More importantly, it affected Kuchi children. I got a report in Kabul one day that a Kuchi elder would not allow the children in his clan to be immunized against basic childhood diseases. I could not understand this, so I decided to visit. I found the clan camped in their winter quarters just outside Jalalabad in southern Afghanistan.

The encampment was located in a dry riverbed where a few hand-dug wells provided brackish brown water that was used for human and animal consumption. There were just a few goats around, and the chief's tent was apart from the rest. Chief Abdullah was a dignified man. He sat on a threadbare carpet in his tent, and I was surprised to see that there were very few personal possessions around.

Abdullah invited me to join him on the carpet, and he offered me green tea. He looked tired and troubled. His eyes were bloodshot, and I got the impression that this man was tired of carrying the problems of his tribe on his shoulders. The Kuchi are proud people who, despite all the hardships and problems that they face, never give up. Abdullah was a broken man who was giving up on life.

The members of his clan were now beggars. After two years of drought, they lost most of their livestock to famine or disease. Their animals are their only means of survival. They provide milk, meat, hides, and wool. Most of the men are too weak to work, and in any case, there is no casual work in this area. He had lived for many years—through droughts, wars, and disease—but he had never seen things so bad. There was only despair and no hope. Feeding his people was now impossible, and they were starving to death before his eyes.

So there was no point of immunizing the children. "I would much rather the children died of disease . . . preferably to starvation. Death from disease is common among my people. But death from starvation carries a great stigma for me, their chief. My successors would be blamed for generations." I understood the logic of his argument and was saddened by their plight.

I used my radio to call a colleague in the World Food Program and inquired if these people could be included in any emergency feeding program. Jake was familiar with the plight of the Kuchi in Southern Afghanistan and said that he would arrange for these people to receive emergency food rations immediately. The ration would include rice, dried beans, cooking oil, wheat flour, sugar, and tea.

The news immediately changed the demure Abdullah. A glimmer returned to his eyes; he was reenergized and happy that his clan would soon be back on their feet again. He requested that I arrange for a vaccination team to visit his camp immediately and immunize the children.

If the Kuchi were to meaningfully participate in the democratic process, they had to remain informed about the local news during their long summer migration. The problem was that most could not afford the batteries for transistor radios, and those who could had nowhere to buy replacement batteries when they were on the move. I explained this dilemma to the civic affairs officer of the US Army. He quickly saw the importance and advantages of getting this segment of the population politically engaged and involved. He said that he would arrange for the free distribution of Grundig windup radios to the Kuchi.

At noon each day, his unit would broadcast a special one-hour program to the Kuchi. It would cover topics on health, politics, education, and traditional music. This was an excellent initiative of the US military. They were able to win over the hearts and minds of the Kuchi, and the tribe was able to remain in touch with what was going on in the urban areas and in the country.

Being a UN staff member, I had no voice. However, more than often, I felt obliged to speak out. The Ministry of Frontier and Tribal Affairs was responsible for the "tribal militia." Thirty men from each village that surrounded the borders of Afghanistan were selected to serve in this Militia. It was an honor and privilege for young men to be selected for this service, and they all were prepared to give their lives for their country.

The tribal militia needed no logistic support, uniforms, transportation, food, or accommodation. They lived in their villages and carried on with their daily lives. However, in a time of need, they were called upon to serve. Each was armed with an AK-47, and the unit was under the command of the village council of tribal elders. They served as the eyes, ears, and the nose of the government for over one hundred years. They were an excellent source of intelligence and greatly assisted the central government to maintain administrative control of these remote and inaccessible areas.

With my military background, I felt that this was a tremendous asset to the government. The minister was under intense pressure from the president, who was acting on instructions of the US ambassador and military commanders, in particular, to disband the tribal militia, as they viewed them as a private army controlled by tribal warlords. The minister asked my opinion, and I strongly advised against the disbanding of this militia. Prior to this, I held protracted consultations with militia commanders who were all regular officers in the Afghan National Army. The minister lacked the political will or the proclivity to act in the best national interest. His main focus was on his extensive businesses enterprises.

As a result, major policy decisions that were advocated by foreign advisers were adopted by national politicians without due care and consideration as to what would best serve the national interest. The minister would laugh and chide me for taking my duties too seriously. In response to my bewilderment, the minister would then quickly add that I had the authority to speak out on his behalf at meetings with foreigners. I understood that he did not want the responsibility for incurring the wrath of the foreign advisers and was happy for me to be the fall guy.

Not withstanding this, I felt obliged to speak out and made a credible case for the militia to remain in its present shape and form. As a result, some ISAF commanders viewed me as an obstructionist. The tribal militia was eventually disbanded and the borders with Pakistan immediately became porous, and the government lost its ability to police or control these remote regions. Fighters, drugs, and weapons were transported across the borders without let or hindrance, which is a prime cause for the escalation of violence in Afghanistan today.

Foreign field commanders soon realized that disbanding the tribal militia was a costly mistake, and they were paying dearly in terms of the escalated fighting and the loss of an increasing number of their soldiers. A decision was hastily taken to reform the tribal militia. The easiest but a contradictory approach was adopted.

The powerful warlords and drug barons who provided surrogate fighters in support of ISAF against the Taliban indicated their willingness to immediately fill in this vacuum. They saw this as an opportunity to legitimize their private armies and, to crown it all, have the government pay for it. As a result, their private gunslingers are now better armed and equipped, but best of all, they are on the public payroll. What a windfall.

Girls' education is one of the big successes touted by the United States and NATO. Hundreds of schools have been built, and over two million girls have gone back to school. All of this is true. However, we automatically assume that now that they are back in school, these two million girls are now receiving a quality education that would one day enable them to eventually play a major role in the development of Afghanistan. Unfortunately, this is an erroneous belief.

According to the Minister of Education, over 85 percent of all teachers in the Afghan school system are illiterate. This void is therefore being filled by "religious scholars" in rural areas who, in effect, turn the schools into religious "madrasahs" where the girls are taught only the Qur'an in parrot fashion. The Taliban targets schools where a regular curriculum is being taught, and a number of schools have been burned or otherwise destroyed. In addition, many of the schools that were built are currently not open because of major problems with accessibility or the lack of funds to furnish, equip, and operate them. Therefore, I do not believe that we can credibly claim that girls' accessibility to meaningful education is a major achievement of ours.

The Koshal Khan School sits on the outskirts of Kabul. It is surrounded by orchards, and at one time, this school had the reputation of providing an excellent education for Pashto boys and boasted achieving the highest grade scores in the nation. It was founded and funded by the late king, and besides academic subjects, Pashto values, customs, and tradition were also instilled into students. Many Kuchi boys attended this school as it catered to their nomadic lifestyle. At the start of the spring migration, some Kuchi parents dropped off their boys at this boarding school before moving to their summer pastures in the mountains of Northern Afghanistan.

However, after the withdrawal of the Soviets, there was heavy fighting among the various mujahideen groups to gain control of Kabul. The Hazara faction that loathed the Pashto was determined to settle old scores. It was now payback time, and they started to obliterate anything Pashto in their sights. Using artillery and mortars, they constantly shelled the school. It came under constant tank and machine gun fire that reduced the establishment to rubble. A few of the school buildings that remained standing had major structural damage and were no longer fit for human habitation. However, a few of the old academic and administrative staff still living in the area dreamed of reviving their beloved institution. Thanks to their vision, will, and determination and with little help from the Ministry of Education, they reopened the school. The facilities were primitive, but classes had started, and they had enrolled one hundred boys as fee-paying boarders.

At the request of the minister, I visited the school. I really did not know why I had been asked to go there and what to expect. As it was located just out of the city of Kabul, there were security implications as well. I loved going out into the countryside and felt like a caged animal being confined to certain security zones in Kabul City.

On arrival, we were greeted at the gate by the principal, staff, and students. Obviously, this visit had been prearranged even though I was told that we were just going to "drop in."

The boys sang us a Pashto song of welcome, and the principal then invited the deputy minister and me to his office for tea and cakes. I politely declined, as I knew that these refreshments were being paid for by the headmaster himself out of his paltry monthly salary of $30. We were then shown around the school, and I was appalled at the living and sanitary conditions. Students subsisted in shell-pocked rooms with no doors or windows. There were no heat, lighting, water, or toilet facilities. The dormitories and classrooms no longer had the structural integrity to be deemed safe, there was little or no furniture, and minimal school supplies were available.

At lunch the following day, I briefed the minister about what I had seen. He was well aware of the situation, and he had intended for me to be shocked by what I saw. He was certain that this would motivate me to get personally involved. The old fox was right—yes, cunning, as only the Pashto can be. But I must admit that I was also impressed by the fact that despite all the constraints, the staff and students made best of the little they had and were determined to prevail. So far, all the minor improvements at the school were done by students, teachers, and some parents on a self-help basis. My feeling was that the minister and his staff had an ethical obligation to support the school.

The minister was delighted with this opinion. He said, "Rudy Jan . . . as my trusted advisor, you must act on my behalf. Yes, something must be done to provide immediate assistance to the school. You know that I have so many problems of the state on my shoulders. I therefore have to remain focused and have no time to do this project on my own. But I know that you have the skill, knowledge, experience, and respect of donors to do this in my name. I need to show my Pashto brethren that I have their best interest at heart. It's all political, you understand?" As I had anticipated, the buck had stopped on my desk. But then this task did not fall within my mandate. It was highly charged and had serious political ramifications. I could and would be accused of working toward perpetuating Pashto dominance in Afghanistan.

But then, I was touched by the will and determination of the people I had met. They deserved better, and all of them understood full well that the only support that they could possibly count on would come from the international community. I just could not let them down. This was regardless of the consequences.

Despite all my other duties, I just had to raise funds to rebuild this school. This became an obsession, and I spent all my free time thinking about and strategizing on how I could achieve this goal in an environment that was very competitive for donor funds.

I met and spoke with numerous donors and wrote endless proposals. But the competition for donor support was fierce, and all the powers that be battled each other for their share of the "pork." Money was allocated without rhyme or reason but entirely on personal relationships and trust—that the person receiving the funds would deliver an acceptable product at the end of the day. Little attention was given to feasibility, sustainability, and the bringing about real, sustainable change.

After attending countless meetings with the military brass, the American military at last understood why supporting this school would create good will among the Pashto and this was in our best strategic interest. After what seemed like an eternity, the commanding general of US forces allocated $800,000 for the renovations of the Koshal Khan School. I was overjoyed when I received this news. I rushed in to brief the minister. With the money, we could build new classrooms, dorms, a kitchen with gas-burning stove, a dining room, solar energy would heat water for showers, and a generator would provide lighting and accesses to the Internet. We would also construct toilets and create recreation facilities. This was a generous grant that would enable us to once again turn the place around and restore it for history. What an opportunity.

However, I was soon to realize that all of this was wishful thinking on my part. The minister informed me that his deputy had a construction company and that the contract for the renovations should be awarded to them. Corruption was raising its ugly head yet once again. I quickly understood that the bulk of the funds would be siphoned off into the pockets of the already rich and famous. The good news was that the deputy manager appointed a British subject from the Lebanon to be the site manager. I first met Nassim when he acted a business adviser to the minister. We became friends, he was an expert at what he did, he was hardworking, and I trusted him. I took comfort in that fact that all was not lost.

When work started, it was obvious that Nassim had no control over the project. Decisions were made behind his back, his attempts to enforce quality control were futile, and he concluded that he was there just to give the project a hint of credibility. Nassim complained that the work being done was just cosmetic; the buildings remained unsound as none of the structural problems were being dealt with. He felt that being involved was an insult to his intelligence, but he made no move to dissociate from what was going on. In Nassim's estimation, only $120,000 of the $800,000 was actually spent on the project. It's anyone's guess where the rest of the money went. The contractor "certified" that the contract was completed in accordance and compliance with specifications. In the eyes of inexperienced service members, it appeared as though it was.

I have now been transferred as the senior technical to the minister, Ministry Labor, Social Affairs, Martyrs, and Disabled when three separate ministries were merged into one. Many of the disabled were mujahideen who fought the Soviets and also battled one and other. As "holy warriors," they hold a special place in society. However, there is grave dissatisfaction in their ranks as they feel that they have been shut out of the reconstruction and development processes.

An unloaded gun makes two people afraid - Afghan saying

Today the city was abuzz with rumors and speculation as to why a member of parliament from the north had been assassinated in Kabul the previous day. On our way home from work, all the traffic was stopped at the Masood Square roundabout for the funeral cortege that was taking the body of the murdered MP to the airport. It was a cold winter's day. There was slush all over, and water flooded the roadway as none of the newly constructed drainage system worked. About a dozen women in their tattered burkas sat on the curb begging for alms. These women were obviously homeless and were forced to beg to feed their children. These broken human beings were forced to live like animals. The only difference is that as women, they could not fight back as the wild dogs that infest this city did.

We were forced to wait patiently as all the roads were blocked off, and there was no telling how long we would be stuck here. But the consoling fact was that we were warm and comfortable in the vehicle, unlike the poor women who were cold, wet, and shivering on the curb. Half an hour later, the evening silence was shattered by the wail of police sirens. With lights flashing and driving at breakneck speed, about ten police cruisers sped past us.

They were followed by at least fifty high-priced black SUVs with tainted windows and bodyguards hanging out of the sides pointing their weapons at the people who were forced to line the streets. The speeding vehicles splashed mud and slush on the poor women. Despite this torture, they squatted patiently, opening their palms in a begging gesture. The contrast between the haves and have-nots was on full display in plain, unambiguous, and harsh terms. Mir Agha turned to me in disgust and said, "This is our democracy. I hope you observed how we, as good Muslims, treat our poor."

Today was another day in Afghanistan. No two days are ever identical, and I have arduously stated that I should always expect the unexpected. When watching the news this evening, I received a frantic call from an Afghan colleague and friend who was my national counterpart at the ministry. He wanted to meet immediately, and over the phone, he sounded as if his world was coming to an end. But today is Friday, the only day in the week that I try to take off and imprudently call my own to do what I want when I want. For security reasons, we were by and large confined to our guesthouses.

Because of the tone and urgency in his voice showed apparent graveness of the prevailing situation, I invited Amiri to come over to what was commonly known as the "UNDP guesthouse." Inviting Afghans, even if they were expatriate, was not encouraged by our local regulations as alcohol was available and the female residents dressed as they wanted on their day off. So this rule was designed not to compromise residents. This was a valid argument, but I felt that it was somewhat irrelevant, as many expatriate Afghans drank and dressed as they pleased.

As a child, Amiri was critically injured when a bomb demolished their family home in Kabul during intense fighting between the invading Soviet forces and the mujahideen. His parents and two siblings were buried under the rubble. He fled with relatives to Moscow and later settled in England as refugee. Although a British national, Amiri decided to return to his country of origin and help with the rebuilding of his devastated motherland.

We now work at a government ministry where I am the senior technical advisor to the minister. As a team, we act together in an open, honest, and collective way. The milieu in which we operate is corrupt, with the majority of people jostling to get rich quick.

Amiri has displayed incredible, unselfish veracity, functioning for more than a year as a volunteer, during which he lived off savings that he had accumulated in England, where he had worked for fifteen years. I respect him for protecting his reputation and for his knack of remaining cool, calm, and collected even in the most trying circumstances.

It was already 8:30 p.m., and because of increasing insecurity, the streets of Kabul are deserted by 9:00 p.m., when most residents are seeking the comfort and the protection of their homes. Also, after this time, the streets are choked by police roadblocks, which provide officers with ample opportunity to solicit and take bribes.

Hence, we must be facing some sort of emergency that even the United Nations Security Unit is oblivious of. When Amiri arrived at my bastion of a guesthouse, he was unshaven, dirty, and dazed. He held a bouquet of artificial lilies in his right hand. I had never seen him look so disoriented and disgruntled. I suggested coffee in the living room. His preference was to seek the solace of my room instead. This we did, and once the door was locked, he buckled under the strain and began crying hysterically. I poured him a drink of scotch to soothe his nerves.

When he regained equanimity, he spoke in a sobbing, sad, and stuttering voice. He started by saying that I had gained the esteem of the Afghan people because I empathized with their anguish. He too cherished his country and was ready to die for it. I was the sole person whom he trusted in Kabul. The feeling of isolation was intimidating to him. His anguish was caused by a number of death threats he had received today.

A fellow Afghan expat in the secret services confirmed that that they had credible information that he would be killed. I was unable to garner the reasons for this coercion. Was it related to personal or professional issues? In Afghanistan, scores are still settled with the sword and not the word. Exerting pressure on corrupt officials can have serious implications. His fear was for his yea-old daughter, whom he loved dearly. He shows blatant contempt for crooks, and this has perhaps triggered their hate and kindled a desire to harm him.

These lilies were for me. They were a token of friendship that would remind me of him, his values, integrity, and devotion to his people. He appreciated my disdain for artificial flowers, but then, these blooms were all that were available. Besides, they would not wither and die, as he definitely would. Amiri was in shock and in a state of severe depression.

He confessed to being disheartened by the corruption, the egocentricity of elected leaders and those in public office. He was scandalized by the fact that only a negligible part of the billions of dollars of aid was actually getting to the people that needed support most. I interjected by saying that in Afghanistan, corruption was not considered an encumbrance because with time, it had really become part of the routine. But this was not the time for dialogue.

He was critical about the lack of political will to address the foremost challenges facing his country and at the escalating anti-American sentiment, instigated by their egotistical behavior and the use of unwarranted excessive force. This continues to cause death and injury to destitute and innocent people, destroying their homes and livelihood. As a consequence, he understood the resurgence of the Taliban in presence and power. They now had the ability to easily attract volunteer suicide bombers that inflict casualties and death on foreign soldiers and innocent civilians.

He was astounded by the inability of NATO to restore peace, stability, and security to the country so many years after the invasion. The fighting continues to escalate, innocent civilians are killed or maimed on a daily basis, and he could only see the situation deteriorate even further. He was saddened and distressed by the resurrection of the centuries-old animosity between minority tribes and the

Pashto majority. This was carving up along Sunni and Shia Muslim lines. He had dreamed of Afghanistan becoming a utopia but now recognizes that dreams can be boundless and are a distraction from the ruthless realities of life.

I asked Amari if he had sought guidance from the British embassy. He had and was told to leave the country immediately. But this was not a viable option. He is married to an Afghan woman in England, and they have a child. However, she ran away with another man and refuses to get a divorce. This distressed Amari, and to escape the humiliation among fellow Afghans in Britain, he decided to return to Kabul. Here he married a young village girl, and they have a beautiful daughter. He wanted to return to Britain with his young bride but could not, as he is still legally married. This prevents him from making a quick exit.

"What is the way out for me, my brother?" he inquired. It was clear that he had to leave the country as soon as possible. What then came to mind was the fate of a Scottish colleague of ours who was also an adviser to a Government minister. He was ambushed and shot dead in broad daylight in Kabul just outside his residence, which is located along the well-guarded Embassy Row.

He was due to leave Afghanistan for good the following morning. The motive for his murder and the identity of his killers remain unknown. After so many years of carnage, bloodshed, and death, life and limb no longer have value, and it takes little to get on somebody's hit list.

I suggested that he take his family to Europe, and there, in an atmosphere of peace and tranquility, he could figure his next move. "But, Rudy, my wife and daughter will never get a visa to visit Europe." The following morning, we were scheduled to meet with the French ambassador on some other business. I suggested that he broach the subject of the visa then.

This requiem was tragic, poignant, and upsetting. It left me tongue-tied and emotionally deficient. I utterly agreed with Amiri's sentiment. These were the veracity's of the day and the reasons for my frustration, disappointment, and anguish at not being able to initiate meaningful change. But as an adviser, I have no executive powers and can only counsel the minister, who has decisive authority even if he lacks the proclivity to do what is right.

To me, Afghanistan is on the brink of anarchy. With the disruption and distraction posed by Iraq, we lost focus on Afghanistan. The Taliban reemerged with a vengeance, and our knee-jerk, overkill reaction has served to fuel anti-American sentiment. The infrastructure remains in shambles, power supplies in Kabul are still intermittent, opium production is at an all-time high, and the Taliban control parts of the north, south, and east of the country.

Because of the hazards posed by this volatility, aid and reconstruction efforts to these provinces have now come to a grinding halt. The battle being waged by the Taliban is far more robust and relentless then many in the UK or USA dare admit. The labors of a corrupt, insolvent, fragile, and feeble government cannot equate to the power, dominance, influence, and financial clout of the warlords who rule the rural areas.

The pathetic institutional capacity of the administration and its agencies are immense impediments to the reconstruction and the development of this beautiful country. The Pashto now refer to themselves Afghans. This means the people of Afghanistan. They call the minority communities Afghanis, people who live in Afghanistan.

To me this is an ominous sign. There is a sort of paralysis that has gripped the country, and with this coupled with the mounting disenchantment, people will continue turning away from the government and, by default, support the Taliban or try to illegally migrate to Europe. What is obvious but ignored by most is that both the

Afghans and Afghanis cannot build and have a future without first reconciling with their past.

The president may be an honest and a well-meaning individual. But the feedback I get from some of his ministers is that he is weak, afraid of offending his opponents, and steers clear of altercation, and all of these factors make him vacillate. Afghans are used to and have come to expect their leader to be resolute and strong-minded. Consequently, the warlords who are members of government have free reign to do what they please when they please.

Amari and I met with the French ambassador the following day, and after business was done, Amari had a private meeting with the ambassador. On the way back to the office, he gleefully told me that his wife and daughter would get a tourist visa to France. I was relieved but realized that he did not have the cash to make this travel possible.

He sought my counsel, but little did he know that I already had a possible solution. If only he would get paid for the eighteen months he had worked for the ministry as a volunteer, his troubles would be over. So overnight I wrote a project proposal for five million dollars for national capacity building in a budding democracy and good governance in postconflict countries and solicited funding from the Ministry of Finance through the World Bank. The project was approved, and the ministry received the money. Subsequently, the minister paid Amari $26,000 in back wages. He was delighted and wanted to celebrate. I felt that this was premature as he was not out of the woods yet.

The following day, his wife and daughter boarded a flight for Paris. I asked Amari where they would stay as his wife did not speak English or French. His curt reply was that they would be flying on to Stockholm. This took me by surprise as I was not privy to this part of his plan. In a way, I felt betrayed as I had invested so much time, effort, and emotion in this venture but was not kept fully in the loop.

About two weeks later, Amari said that his wife was uncomfortable in Sweden and wanted him to join her immediately. Where was she? I inquired. He then told me the story. His plan was to get his wife and daughter to some place in Europe. They would then travel to Sweden and claim asylum as soon as they arrived there. This is what they did, and his family was now in a camp with other would-be immigrants. Her complaint was that the majority of inmates were Somali males, and as one of the few women around, she felt threatened.

After all that we had been through, I felt that I had been used by Amiri. But then, this is what Afghanistan is all about. What you get is not what you see. One morning I was woken up at 5:00 a.m. by one of our security guards. A government official wanted to see me. With great reluctance, I dressed and accompanied the guard to the gate. It was Amiri, and he had come to bid me a teary farewell. He said nothing but just locked me in a tight embrace and departed. This was the last I ever saw or heard from him.

Nobody at the ministry had any idea of his plans. The minister was perplexed and looked to me for answers. Unfortunately, I was not in a position to provide any. The police searched Amari's rented apartment and concluded that he had departed in a hurry.

I got to the ministry early this morning because of an important deadline. Much to my frustration and flurry, there was no electricity, and therefore, I could not start functioning. I have a small generator but discovered that the fuel had been stolen overnight. Nobody but our night watchmen could have been responsible. Not the best way to begin any day. By about 9:30 a.m., the key ministry staff started to roll in, and slowly but steadily, this arm of government came to life. I was happy to get started, but no sooner had I done so, the senior national adviser to the minister entered my office and said that for security reasons, I must leave the building immediately. This was bizarre as the city was calm and quiet on my way to work. He is a devout Muslim, or else I would have assumed that he was inebriated.

He persisted, and I understood that he was genuinely concerned about my safety. All UN staff members are obliged to carry VHF walkie-talkies at all times. Mine was in my car, and my driver, Mir Aga, politely walked into my office to inform me that "White City" had just been declared by the UN Security Chief. This code indicated to all UN staff members that the security risk level had risen to "extreme," that there should be no movement and that staff and vehicles should freeze until further notice.

The local radio stations were now broadcasting live reports of riots that had broken out on the streets of Kabul. The cause was a traffic accident involving the American army and a civilian vehicle. The president, who was chairing a cabinet meeting at the time, was whisked away by US troops to a safe haven. The situation deteriorated very rapidly after that.

Extensive looting and destruction of foreign-owned property was taking place all over the city. The size of the mobs was being swelled by all and sundry joining in. Many of the Chinese brothels frequented by American security guards were looted and set ablaze, and people chanted anti-American/government slogans. At the ministry, we sat in the deputy minister's office, discussing the causes and consequences of the ongoing day's events, when word came through that two police stations had been ransacked and all the weapons stolen and distributed to the rioters. While some of the police fled, others removed their uniforms and joined the rioting mobs.

Gunfire soon erupted broke in the vicinity of the American Embassy, which is not about five blocks from our offices. A Black Hawk helicopter gunship hovered in the skies, tanks rumbled by, and the sirens racing police cars filled the noon air. All the mobile phone networks were congested with the high volume of traffic, making it impossible to call or receive calls. My Afghan colleagues felt really isolated and were worried for the safety of their families.

A commercial radio station announced that troops, weapons, and other assets of the Afghan National Army were being hastily deployed around the city to contain the situation. It takes a lot to frighten the average Afghan, but today they were visibly scared. "The country is going up in flames," said Hajji Nadir, who normally served us tea. He had been through numerous wars and was a wise old man. He told Mir Agha in Pashto that he should take me home immediately as the mobs would attack government offices next. Mir Agha was very concerned as he was also responsible for my security. But his hands were tied. We could not move from where we were.

The Afghan people have seen, suffered, strained, and endured a great deal of pain and torment in the past, which in a way has left them numb to pain suffering and even death. They have become fatalists and believe that whatever will be will be. Nothing appears to excite them. However, this situation was different. They too were getting gravely concerned, distraught, and agitated. I watched with sympathy as they evacuated the ministry in dribs and drabs, not to draw attention that they worked for government and eager to get home to their loved ones as quickly as possible.

The live radio coverage of the security abruptly ceased. The deputy minister felt that this was on the orders of the government as the broadcasts were enticing people to intense anger and action. Instead, the sound waves were now filled with soothing Indian music. As the shooting intensified, the UN security services instigated a roll call of all international staff. This was done by call sign, which masked the identity of the user. We were required to report our exact location, how many other UN staff was in that location, and our safety status.

As dusk approached, the gunfire subsided and a semblance of law and order restored. We were ordered to muster at the bomb bunker in the UNDP country office compound. Heavily armed escorts from the UN Protection Force provided security cover for the move. I decided that it was too dangerous to use my UN-marked car, so dressed as a national, I got an Afghan colleague to drop me of at the collection point. The streets were eerily calm with no cars or people around, only troops, tanks, army trucks, and military roadblocks.

Evidently, members of the newly trained police force joined the rioters and were now being replaced by the Afghan National Army. Some UN property had been damaged, and two foreign female colleagues were fortunate to escape with their lives when they were attacked by frenzied mobs hurling bricks, sticks, and stones. One received head injuries and was traumatized. I helped to arrange for her evacuation home to Australia for specialist therapy. Numerous deaths and injuries were reported, however; the exact numbers vary according to the source.

The ferocity of public reaction astounded me, but my Afghan colleagues were not surprised. To them, the causes were clear. Government had failed to meet the expectations of the masses by not delivering on any promises. The buzzword now was *regime change*. Is there a connection concerning the result and its cause?

To me, the Afghan police are a joke. The majority are illiterate, and this make policing very difficult. They have little or no understanding of the law. Yes, they wear a uniform, are armed, and drive fancy patrol cars, which are a gift of the German government and are paid about $40 per month. There is little doubt that the majority are corrupt and use their uniforms as a means of generating extra income for their bosses and themselves. This why they were not able and perhaps lacked the will to restore law and order during the rioting.

No foreign power has ever won a war in Afghanistan. The British twice tried but were unsuccessful. Despite deploying a massive invasion force, the Soviets lost after ten years of occupation and war at a cost of many lives—not only because the Afghans are excellent fighters, but also because they know the country, understand the people, speak the languages, are able to endure adversity, and fight with no or logistic support.

To me, the basis of the prevailing situation is clear. The majority of local Afghans, excluding expatriates, resent foreigners meddling in their affairs with total condescension to their culture, customs, and religion. This makes them passionate, involved, and dedicated to brusquely resist the occupying forces and all that they represent.

Sad news met me when I returned to the guesthouse this evening. I normally popped into the kitchen to chat with the staff and find out what was cooking. It was sort of a community ritual that we all enjoyed. It also facilitated my keeping a finger on the pulse. As I entered, I noticed Hassan, the assistant cook who was twenty-one years old, sit on a stool with his head held in his palms bowed over a sink. He was crying, but as soon as he saw me, he jumped up and started brushing away the tears. Hassan was like a son. He was always cheerful, totally trustworthy, hardworking, and not afraid of long hours. He and his extended family lived in two rooms rented by him, and he was the only wage earner in the family. He grew up during the war and witnessed the death of his father and three siblings. Life has dealt him a brutal hand, but he never complained and, as a brave young man, survives as best as he can.

He hugged me and said, "Rudy Jan, today there was fighting in the streets of Kabul. My brother-in-law, who is a policeman on traffic duty, was shot in the chest and died on the street. Rudy, he has a wife and seven children, and now they will all move in with me. I am responsible for their food, shelter, and clothing, and you know I only earn $400 per month. I have no money saved, and I hear that this guesthouse will soon close for security reasons and I will be without a job." In fact, we had no option but close the house but had decided that members would give the reserve fund of $50,000 to the staff as compensation and they would also inherit all the furniture, linen, equipment, which was valued at $50,000.

"Melmastia," I responded. I will extend hospitality in terms of money to all relatives seeking help. The burden on this young man was enormous. He cares for his ailing mother. She has high blood pressure and suffered from arthritis, but unfortunately, he cannot afford to take her to see a doctor or buy her medication. We often sat in the garden in spring and admired the perfusion of roses and the budding grape wines. We conversed about his lost childhood, his powerlessness in trying to obtain an education and his evaporating dreams of being married and having children. This was a young man with so much potential, astuteness, commitment, and a burning desire to progress. But providence eluded him as there were no prospects in Afghanistan for honest people like him. I hope that he, like so many young Afghans, does not give up hope and, in desperation, turn to drugs to blunt their pain and despair.

I suffer from high blood pressure myself, so I gave Hassan one tablet of my medication and diuretic to try out on his mother. Most of the drugs that are available in the bazaar were counterfeit and have expired. The next day he came to my room, bursting with joy. The pills worked, and his mother was feeling much better. I was due to travel out of the country soon, so I gave him most of my medication with the strict instructions that his mother should only take two pills a day. When I returned to Kabul, Hassan greeted me on arrival with the news that his mother was now "normal." I am glad that I had bought her six months' supply of the drugs in Dubai.

Five British troops were killed here during the last three weeks, and six American and one Romanian soldier died in combat in the past four weeks. Last night, five more American soldiers, two Canadians, and three civil contractors were injured in a Taliban rocket attack. These heavy losses over a brief period have rattled senior military field commanders. They had expected exacting opposition but nothing like the determined, well-planned, and devious hostility they were now forced to deal with. But who is the enemy?

How does one identify them? They certainly do not wear uniforms or badges that can be used to identify them. The enemy are in fact ordinary Afghans who have become disenchanted with their quality of life; they have no trust in their leaders or government and loath the corruption that plagues their daily lives.

I have worked with the deputy minister at the Ministry of Labor, Social Affairs, Martyrs, and Disabled for over a year. We have an informal, friendly, and relaxed relationship based on trust, and he finds it refreshing that I have no political ax to grind. He is an intellectual whose integrity, commitment, fairness, and unassuming nature continues to impress me. He is one of the few bureaucrats whom I have so far met who will not use his position and power to enrich himself. He is a devout Muslim, and during the war, he was a close ally and adviser to Ahmad Shah Massoud, the famous mujahideen commander and national hero who was assassinated by two Arab terrorists posing as international journalists.

Even on a mountain there is still a road - Afghan proverb

I accompanied His Excellency to New York when he led the Afghan government delegation to the sixth UN Ad Hoc Committee drafting the new international treaty on disability. At this forum, he displayed mature political acumen and was able to dialogue with international donors on their terms as an accomplished equal, thus attaining their respect.

Each member country of the United Nations maintains a permanent diplomatic mission in New York. Member countries appoint an ambassador to head their mission, and their responsibility is to ensure that the best interest of the member country is reflected in all proceedings at the general assembly and the Security Council. This was the first time that Afghanistan was represented at the Ad

Committee despite the fact that the country was emerging from a conflict situation and disability was one of the major challenges facing the Afghan government.

After the accreditation processes and in accordance with protocol, we paid a courtesy call on the Afghan ambassador. The reception was cordial, and we lunched with the embassy staff. Out of the blue, the ambassador announced that he would like the deputy to introduce an amendment to the draft resolution on disability that had been discussed and crafted by members over a two-year period. The deputy minister asked me to respond to the ambassador. I started off by saying that in my opinion, it was a bit late in the day to try and introduce changes. What was the nature of the proposed amendments, and could I see the language? Had the embassy staff canvassed the delegations of other member states to see if there would be any support for the Afghan proposal? I also asked the ambassador if he had spoken with the New Zealand ambassador who had been elected chair of the Ad Hoc Committee.

I could guess what the answers would be, but for the record, these questions had to be asked. The embassy staff had not participated in any of the deliberations of Ad Hoc Committee, there was no draft of the proposed amendment, and in the ensuing discussions, I tried to flush out the substance of the change that the country wished to table. It was obvious that nobody had read the draft resolution that was in the processes of being finalized by the Ad Hoc Committee. What the embassy was now proposing was already covered in articles of the draft resolution.

I was concerned that the deputy minister would make a fool of himself and lose credibility among other delegates if he made an intervention in the assembly hall and proposed changes in the framework document at this late stage. It was obvious that diplomats at the Afghan mission were not at all familiar with how the UN functions. They were unfamiliar with politics, the behind-the-scenes lobbying and canvassing by member states and other interest groups including nonmembers like the nongovernmental organizations, etc. On our way back to the hotel, I asked the deputy what was his impression of the caliber of the embassy staff. He put his hand on my shoulder and said, "Rudy, some of these people came to New York to work as drivers and security guards. They are relatives of ministers and were sent here to do private business and not to serve the country. It's the same with all our overseas missions."

I suggested that that the deputy minister should have side meetings with heads of delegation from donor countries. These delegations came from their capitals, and they would have to report back to their governments on their return. These meetings would give the deputy minister an opportunity to meet on a personal basis his counterparts, it would help network, and it would expose them to the professional qualities of Afghan government leadership. I advised that during these meetings, the minister should stress the fact that in Afghanistan, disability is not only a human rights issue, but it also has serious security and political implications. He could brief them on the prevailing situation in the country, the progress that has been in rehabilitation and development, and end by outlining the unmet needs of his ministry.

These meetings took place in the members dining room at the UN headquarters in New York. Located on the top floor, the dining room had a commanding view of the Hudson River, the food was excellent, and service was superb.

The deputy performed brilliantly at these one to one sessions. His remarks were clear and concise; he answered questions with ease and took time to listen. It is a real pleasure collaborating and working with a person of his caliber. I must quickly add that this is more the exception rather than the rule. We have worked closely on a number of issues, including formulating institutional capacity-building initiatives for staff, drafting of policy relating to disability, and coordinating the activities of all nongovernmental organizations providing services for people with disabilities in Afghanistan.

Because of his leadership and management qualities, personnel are slowly accepting responsibility, showing diligence, and becoming accountable for their actions. I felt buoyed that some progress was at last being made and momentum was growing and that ministry staff were beginning to become conscious of the fact that they were there to provide service to the people.

Today was atypical. When I arrived at the ministry, I felt that all was not well. There was no shouting in the corridors, and staff hassled to get out of the way. On the executive floor of the ministry, I found the team subdued, with deadpan expressions on their faces. The scene reminded me of the many Afghan funerals that I have attended. But who or what had died on this day? Gone were the effervescing greetings I usually received on arrival. A messenger came into my office and said that the deputy minister wanted to meet with me immediately. When I entered his office, he cordially requested his other visitors to leave. He was tense, preoccupied, and despondent.

There were winkles on his young brow; the rings around his eyes were dark, his eyes were bloodshot, and his eyelashes twitched nervously. His demeanor was sedate, somber, and sad. I was perplexed. What was the cause of the crisis that was intrinsic to this anomalous behavior? The deputy is well connected to the Northern Alliance, and the alliance wielded great power and controlled key ministries like the Ministries of Interior, Defense, and the Intelligence Services. They are powerful and their people are well protected. So what did he see that I could not?

In typical Afghan fashion, the conversation started off with endless greetings, forced smiles, handshakes, and small talk. When this was done, the barrage began. He had decided to resign immediately. He was disenchanted, disturbed, distraught, and outraged. His reasons were legitimate and based on fact, clear rational thought, and a levelheaded analysis of the prevailing situation.

He was a senior official at the ministry but had no authority. The minister did not trust or confide in him. He was a puppet, and his title was pseudo. This came as no surprise to me as the minister was always free and frank with me. So I thought. Senior members of government lacked vision and commitment. They were cynical, tired, ineffective, erratic, and preoccupied with making as much money they quickly could. Devoid of sensible supervision and coupled with lethargic management, the country was like a wreck being tossed around the ocean in a gale force wind.

The minister lacked expertise, experience, intelligence, and interest to exert his authority in the best interest of the most vulnerable that his ministry is mandated to care for. The deputy said, "Rudy, I have enough of this sham." Another national advisor who was also present was of the same opinion, and the analogous appraisal of the prevailing situation was salient and upsetting.

The blatant abuse of public power for personal gain is definitely detrimental to the best interests of the country. It siphons off into private pockets, millions of dollars intended for reconstruction and development. The real victims of this delinquency are the poor and helpless and people with the greatest needs.

Fraudulent practices sap the energy of this nation, depriving it of direction and determination, decreasing growth, and discouraging foreign investment. But most importantly, it totally emasculates the authority of the newly created but still fragile political institutions and puts into question the constancy and legitimacy of government.

Unfortunately, none of the Afghan government officials that I worked with had been appointed on the basis of merit. The government of "unity" was just a way of appeasing the different warring factions and had little to do with the sustainable development of the country. Each minister viewed his or her ministry as a private fiefdom. Senior staff members at the ministry are, without exception, all relatives of the minister, and the majority of them lack even the most basic understanding of the functions of government. There was no interaction between government ministers or their staff. In fact, the opposite was true.

I knew that there was no real unity in cabinet. This is because ministers are appointed for various reasons and come from disparate backgrounds. Besides, it was an ongoing battle for power, turf, and resources. One minister in the Afghan cabinet was a shining star. He was educated in Britain, has a very strong background in development, speaks excellent English, and surrounds himself with a loyal core of foreign advisors. Because his ministry was able to deliver a quality product, donors showered him with resources. This made him unpopular with other members of the cabinet. In this context, another minister said to me, "Rudy, in Pashto we have a saying, 'If you see one rose, it does not mean that spring has come.'" On another occasion, I was told that he was a communist who lost his leg fighting against the mujahideen. This is when he fled and was able to get an education in Britain.

I was unofficially asked by a minister to mediate and try and pour oil on these troubled waters. However, I certainly did not believe that this was my role and strongly feel that as senior members of the cabinet and professionals, these two Ministers should sit down and iron out their differences in the best interest of the nation. But this would of course never happen. I was concerned about being sucked into Afghan politics. It's like the black hole of Calcutta, and the end game was never clear.

The cultivation of opium poppy is now rife in Afghanistan, making it the largest producer of heroin in the world. Currently, the drug trade generates about $2.7 billion annually, which amounts to more than half of the country's legitimate economy. In addition, it is estimated that there are now over one million Afghan drug addicts.

Many political analysts have categorized this nation as a narco state. I don't share this inference but acknowledge that because of ineffective—and the complete absence of—good governance, it is fast becoming one.

Donors have invested vast amounts of money in counternarcotic programs, but most have been ineffective. Traffickers continue to thrive, and drugs keep on engendering enormous pecuniary revenues for the most significant accomplices in the trade. They use this money further their spheres of influence, energetically and ingeniously expand their empires, to buy influence, corrupt officials, finance terror, instigate aggression, force people into repression, circumvent government structures, and consolidate their personal positions of supremacy and notoriety.

Narcotics-funded terrorism is now thriving globally and is especially successful in influencing and radicalizing young and disenfranchised Muslims in Europe and North America. Another factor is the abuse of human rights as displayed at Guantanamo Bay, Abu Ghraib, and Bagram air base in Afghanistan. These fuel the feeling that "the war on terror" is in fact a crusade against Islam and is promoted as such by radicals.

Many Afghan drug barons are now full-fledged members of global, organized crime syndicates. Their local trade operates on a sort of "futures" system. Peasant farmers borrow money using their land as collateral. This money is spent on tractor hire, fuel, fertilizer, and insecticide. When the poppy crop is harvested, the farmers are obliged to pay back their loans in full by giving the lender an agreed amount of poppy resin.

If the grower is unable to make the quota to pay back the loan, his land is seized and the family forced off the property. Therefore, eradication programs that aim at destroying the poppy crop only increase and intensify poverty. In 2005, the United States pledged $780 million on eradicating poppy cultivation. I feel that this money would be better spent creating alternative livelihoods to enable farmers engage in legal agricultural activities like poultry production, fish farming, and growing horticulture products for export.

Flush with cash, the drug lords are able to exert more authority than the democratically elected government. They can react rapidly to the urgent needs of their people and therefore command the respect and loyalty of their communities. Volatility and anarchy is necessary for the narcotic trade to flourish, and therefore, these close-knit and influential groups operate together in many ways to further discord.

The drug trade only provides a very basic livelihood to the rural masses, but it enriches a few. A national financial system dependent on drugs cannot promote genuine development. These wealthy people pay no taxes, own senior officials, maintain standing armies, and have the unquestionable right to privilege. Their power is ingrained and omnipresent.

Much of their money is stashed away or invested abroad, making little contribution or impact to the growth and development of this country. The war and drug lords gained legitimacy by joining forces with the American military and CIA to fight the Taliban. This set a disparaging example and spread misgivings about America's resolve to eradicate the drug trade in Afghanistan. Many of these commanders have now become police chiefs but deem it more lucrative to contravene the rules rather than implement them.

I have heard and read emphatic statements and claims about how the Taliban was crushed by the US-led invasion. This was not the case. They just melted into the woodwork so that they would live to fight another day. That day is today. At present, claims of victories against the Taliban and Al-Qaeda are based on the number of enemy fighters killed.

These figures are inflated by including many innocent civilians killed in the crossfire and then branded as enemy combatants. Apart from this, it is obvious that there are many Taliban volunteers waiting in the wings to replace the dead. I do not believe that the Taliban can be crushed or eradicated in battle. The counterbalance to this bloody carnage is real sustainable rural development that truly and quickly improves the quality of life of ordinary people.

The issues relating to endemic poverty must be addressed and the basic infrastructure swiftly improved. Rampant corruption and poor human capacity have so far stalled meaningful progress. The bulk of the development funds are either drained off by corrupt officials or used to pay high-priced foreign experts and consultants. In addition, the United States made no effort to appease the population that was angry, agitated, and displaying aggressive behavior.

The sanguinity that came with the promises of liberation and affluence has now given way to all-encompassing dissatisfaction and disappointment even as the administration continues to squander its limited legitimacy. People are agitated by the presence of foreign troops that sometimes show contempt for the local culture and beliefs. The feathers of the coalition partners were further ruffled when it became obvious that the government was attempting to bully and intimidate the local press by issuing a seventeen-point dos and don'ts.

Among these were instructions that the press should not broadcast or print material that "weakens public morale or damages the national interest" or that the press should use "freedom fighter" as opposed to "warlord" when describing former anti-Soviet militia leaders. The revival of the religious "vice and virtue police" has also caused alarm in the donor community, and the Afghan Human Rights Commission expressed concern as a similar force was a tool used by the Taliban to violate human rights. Then it was as if people had no eyes, no ears, and no tongues because they were deprived of their right to use these senses.

Democracy denotes different things to different people. In Afghanistan, it stands for peace, prosperity, proper housing, health care, education, and access to pure water, electricity, and employment. So far it has delivered naught and therefore no longer has significance.

As a result, the Taliban bacterium continues to spread. A senior US military commander is quoted as saying, "It's all right in the city, but if you go outside the city, they are everywhere, and the people have to support them. They have no choice." The majority of the people now feel that the Taliban should be tolerated, and this signifies that they are winning the hearts and minds of populace. The Taliban now openly operates roadblocks a few miles from coalition bases and flout their authority by putting on trial and sentencing people using "Shariah" law. They also continue to burn off girls' schools with impunity, and about two hundred have so far been destroyed.

The US administration now faces the possibility of additional adversity in Afghanistan. More worrying, however, is that we have little idea of how to resolve this impasse? For what it's worth, I feel that we should rely more on the traditional, religious leaders, and take heed of customary law as it forms the backbone of society.

Afghanistan is a land of abundant proportions. Because of its location, it has always been strategically significant. It is a country having common ethnicities and sectarian groups with adjoining states, its borders are exceptionally porous, and it is landlocked. The people rejoice in, and are proud of, their dissimilar and time-honored ideals and customs.

They respect traditional values that govern their modus operandi and behavior in society, even if the gun is sometimes used to upholds these. They expect strangers to maintain a code of integrity that is congruent with the local culture and religious beliefs. All of this is recognized by many foreigners but still remains an enigma to most.

Over the years, invaders have tried to transpose their own narrow prearranged structures of viewpoints, values, and dreams on Afghanistan. All intended to influence the pedestal of social, economic, and political philosophy and priorities of the people. None have so far succeeded.

Afghanistan has an astounding but manipulative effect on the outsider, with countless characteristics that are so similar to the highly addictive heroin this state is notorious for. Once physiologically and mentally addicted to the challenges and the real opportunities for sustainable development that this muddled environment offers, it is difficult to withdraw. I first came to this country after the Soviet invasion. I had previously lived in Manhattan and led a safe and comfortable life.

One faces numerous restrictions working here. The corruption, physical hardships, restricted movement, day-to-day moral dilemmas, security threats, frequent power outages, interrupted IT connectivity—all hinder one's capacity to act in ways that are credible, constructive, and intended to bring about real change to lives of the majority of people who now live in a state of immense hardship, deprivation, hopelessness, and misery.

It's difficult to justify my current conduct and actions that are considered by my family to be irrational and unacceptable. Using plain words, I have consistently tried to elucidate from a logical and balanced perspective, my reasons for being here. However, I have failed again and again. There is no intermediate position. You either love or hate working in Afghanistan.

Revenge Is A Dish Best Served Cold - Afghan proverb

But my involvement with Afghanistan started unexpectedly. It all began when a friend offered me a consultancy with the United

Nations, based in Peshawar but requiring extensive travel into Afghanistan, a country that was being laid to waste by the war against the Soviet Union and communism. I apathetically accepted. Stefan gave me little indication as to the nature of the assignment. What he did infer was that it was clandestine and that I would be briefed on arrival in Peshawar, Pakistan.

Preparing for this mission was complex. I knew about the raging war but little else. In December 1979, the Soviet Union invaded Afghanistan to prop up a puppet Communist government against the mujahideen. The mujahideen, or holy warriors, brought together incongruent Islamic factions who did battle by the guiding principles and philosophy of Islam. The mujahideen received massive military and financial assistance from the United States. The CIA used the Pakistan's Inter-Services Intelligence (ISI) agency to Afghanistan as a conduit for delivering these weapons and supplies.

A common belief by the USA, and rightly so, was that Islamic fundamentalists would provide the best resistance to the occupying Soviet forces. Therefore, from 1980 to 1990, the CIA made enormous sums of cash available for the recruitment, training, and disbursing the operational cost of the thousands of volunteer fighters, recruited from many Muslim countries, including Saudi Arabia, Yemen, Sudan, Somalia, and Pakistan. Among them was Osama bin Laden. It is well known that many of these fighters later became disenchanted with American policy and joined Bin Laden to form Al-Qaeda and fight against America's interest worldwide.

The mujahideen's stunning successes achieved over an immeasurably superior Soviet Army under exceptionally difficult battlefield conditions encouraged the Regan administration to sharply escalate covert support to them, amounting to about three billion dollars in the 1980s. It is estimated that the United States was also sending vast quantities of arms and ammunition to the Islamic warriors annually.

I was thrilled to be met at the Peshawar airport by Stephan and his team of foreigners but was surprised and perturbed by the size and makeup of the welcoming party. During the drive to the house, Stephan said that he was pleased that I had accepted this challenge, as he knew I would. There were many candidates, so he personally made the choice. Nice to hear, but I was more interested in the beef than the bun. On arrival, we immediately went into the operations room, where consultations began.

The donor community had received complaints and read public statements about dissatisfaction among the mujahideen. While they did battle and tussled with the invading Soviet forces, their villages and families lingered behind, waiting for outside donor support, which had not yet materialized. Their relatives were now facing serious problems relating to health, water, nutrition, hygiene, and sanitation. This was impeding motivation, so the United States pressured the United Nations to immediately initiate humanitarian assistance programs into mujahideen-controlled areas.

I was relieved to hear this, as to me, there was nothing covert about this operation. However, I could see the real need for absolute secrecy to ensure our own safety. As far as the Soviets were concerned, the rural areas controlled by the mujahideen were "no-go areas" and designated as battle zones. All intruders would be targeted and destroyed. This was no idle threat as the skies were subjugated by Soviet airpower.

Their lethal MiG-23 and MiG-27 swing-wing fighter/strike aircraft flew so fast and low that it was only possible to hear them long after they had passed over the target. SOO helicopter gunships that traveled through the air, hugging the mountainside, backed these fighter jets and unleashed rocket and cannon fire with deadly accuracy. All air strikes were instantly pursued by helicopter-launched ground assault by crack Soviet commandoes.

Our task was to select a site north of Kandahar and build a forward operating logistic base for the provision of humanitarian assistance to the villages in the region. We were also to meet with the local commanders and gain their support and protection. My mission was to provide technical advice, plan the operation, lead its execution, and act as military/security advisor to Stephan during our stay in Afghanistan.

This region was the hub, from where the bulk of covert aid from Pakistan was sent into Afghanistan. Soviet intelligence maintained vigilant surveillance of the region using spy planes and paid informers. My military background and experience would certainly be put to the ultimate test here. This was a high-risk operation that, unless well executed, could easily result in the massive loss of life and limb. I took time out to contemplate, calculate, pray, plot, and plan.

The core of my strategy was simplicity. We would only travel at night, off the main roads to avoid land mines, and use mountain tracks well known but seldom used by the mujahideen, and our convoy would be spread out to avoid presenting a worthwhile target for the Soviet Air Force. I consulted with the various Afghan factions in Peshawar to get firsthand knowledge about the terrain and prevailing circumstances.

I was careful, in control, and in no hurry. I knew that these informers also provided the CIA with "inside" information in return for large sums of cash. They therefore tended to be deceitful and inclined to concoct much of the information that was fed to their clients. I also met with some commanders who operated out of Pakistan.

The route I chose was circuitous, tortuous, and went through remote mountain terrain. We would link up with our mujahideen escort just inside Afghanistan. Our convoy consisted of three new long-range Toyota Land Cruisers, painted in UN livery, and fitted with high frequency and very high frequency radios, global positioning systems, and mobile satellite telephones.

Departure was at 6:00 p.m. from Peshawar. Our weighty vehicles were loaded to capacity with fuel, food, water, medicines, and spares. Both Stephan and I decided that it would be safer to drive ourselves. We were met by an Afghan guide on the Pakistan side of the border and quickly crossed over into Afghanistan. The Pakistani government had endorsed this mission.

Our escort on the Afghanistan side of the border surprised me. They were a scruffy group of thirty heavily armed, black-bearded mujahideen all dressed in traditional black pajamas and wearing black turbans. They were festooned with an array of Soviet weaponry and ammunition, appearing menacing, undisciplined, disorderly, and vindictive. They traveled in the back of five Toyota ½-ton pickup trucks, and after scrutinizing us with stares that conveyed no emotion, they clambered aboard and were ready to depart.

Having been first commissioned the British Army and then the Kenya Army, it was odd for me to be allied with this band of dispirited guerillas. The convoy now spread out, and we drove at breakneck speed on surfaces that were rough and strewn with rocks and boulders, passing through a number of mujahideen checkpoints to gain local security information about Soviet troop activity in the area.

Our path took us well away from Kandahar, a major Soviet garrison town and strategic air base, but despite this, we triggered the launching of illuminating flares to the west that lit up the night sky for miles. The lead vehicles did not stop, so I assumed that the Communists did not catch sight of our passage. During the journey, Stephan and I maintained strict radio silence, and all vehicles drove only with sidelights, subjecting the vehicles to an atrocious pounding on the very rough surfaces we drove on.

By daybreak, we approached our destination. Part of the land was now cultivated, but the destroyed, burned-out buildings and charred Soviet fighting vehicles bore testament to the ongoing battles and ravages of the war. Reaching a village, our protection force leaped out of their trucks as if springing into action. Stephan and I were asked to sit tight.

Soon we were greeted by a dumpy weather-beaten guy with a long black beard, dressed in black, and crowned with a black and silver turban tied very differently from the rest of the men we had travelled with. In Afghanistan, this is significant as this indicated that he was the chief. His gaze was more like an intense stare. He was Mullah Naquibullah, the local commander. The only people around were men, and I guilelessly wondered where all the starving women and children had gone. We followed Naquibullah into the house, where we were served hot sweet tea, freshly baked flatbread with yogurt all spread out on a carpet on the floor. It was only now that I realized how hungry and thirsty I really was. I guess that the adrenaline just kept pumping me up, and I forgot about eating or drinking.

Stephan talked, and Hadhi, a student from Peshawar, translated. I immediately took a dislike to the mullah. He had a dubious look in his eyes and gave the impression of a manipulator who got what he wanted for naught. The two new deluxe Toyota Land Cruisers parked outside attested to this. He traveled frequently to Peshawar to update the CIA about his may combat conquests and collect his payoff.

My instincts told me not to trust this man. He made many demands, saying that by collaborating with the UN, he placed his people in harm's way. My counter to this claim was that with all his battle successes, he was already a prime a target and therefore endangered us. He then demanded 1,000 MT of wheat flour, 200 MT of cooking oil, 50 MT of sugar to feed his men, in addition to six new Toyota pickups to replace the ones that they were now using.

We then inspected the site for a base. It was isolated and on the side of a rocky hill. This virgin land would require a great deal of work before becoming inhabitable. We would require a large labor force to build the perimeter wall, clear rocks, cut down the thorny shrub, and dig shelter trenches for ourselves. Our offer to pay the mullah with food for the work was rebuffed point-blank. He only wanted cash—in US dollars!

My hunch about this character was correct. He certainly was not a preeminent partner whom we could rely upon and trust. Our first supply convoy had now arrived, and we quickly erected a pre-fab warehouse to store the food, medicine, and other humanitarian supplies. Two days later, four trucks in the second convoy carrying wheat, oil, sugar, and high-protein biscuits were hijacked and looted. Mullah Naquibullah asserted his virtue and was ignorant of this incident.

Sandbags surrounded my tent, and I soon discovered that besides the Communists, we were also vulnerable to the vast verities of snakes, scorpions, hornets, and reptiles that called this patch of earth home. One evening at sunset, I was sitting in my tent, reading, when through the corner of my eye, I noticed a glitter. It took a few moments to spot the source. When I did, I was dumbfounded. Less than a foot away, a sand-colored carpet viper was poised ready to strike. Its pale-pink-colored mouth was wide open, and its twin-dagger-like fangs were exceptionally menacing. It was so well camouflaged that it was almost impossible to trace its complete form.

I froze in fright and was vigilant about provoking an attack. Then, in desperation, I looked around for something to shield myself with. I realized that my life dangled on my every move. On hand were a powerful flashlight and an empty one-liter plastic water bottle. Keeping my eyes glued to the noxious viper, I inch by inch reached out for the flashlight. I was now sweating profusely, my eyes were watering, and my throat was parched. I wanted to urinate, and I desperately needed to sneeze.

After what seemed to be time immemorial, I managed to get my fingers wrapped around the flashlight. Anxiously and at a snail's pace, I directed the powerful beam into the snake's eyes. In a flash, it vanished. I lunged out of the tent and yelled for help. Immediately, mujahideen encircled the tent, their AK-47 rifles cocked and ready for action.

It did not take me long to explain. Dropping their weapons and arming themselves with picks and shovels, they instantly tore down the tent. There was a great deal of communal chanting that reinforced their feeling of shared support and backing. I was too dazed to see how, but the snake was eventually killed. The venom of carpet viper is lethal. It causes the blood to immediately cloth, and the casualty also starts bleeding profusely.

Death ensues if antivenom is not administered right away. Despite our meticulous planning, we had not taken any antivenom. In any case, it has to be stored under refrigerated conditions, and we did not have the facilities to do this. I spent the rest of the mission sleeping in my vehicle with my boots left outside the vehicle. In keeping with an old habit, I always tipped my boots before putting them on. Just as well, as one morning, I dumped out a large eight-legged poisonous scorpion, its tail upturned, ready to sting. The effect of a scorpion bite is acute pain, swelling, frothing at the mouth, and convulsions.

The base was now up and running, the warehouse was full, and our replacements had arrived. Mission accomplished, we started to prepare for our return to Peshawar. The day before our departure, our camp was abruptly buzzed by a pair of high-speed, low-flying MiG-27s. They did two supersonic sweeps over the site but did not fire. We watched from our foxholes as the pilots maneuvered to get an accurate fix of our encampment.

Soon after, we received a radio call from the UN in Kabul, informing Stephan that the supreme Soviet commander in Afghanistan wanted to know why the UN had erected a large "aircraft hangar" in the south. Their demand was accompanied by a threat to destroy the facility if they did not receive immediately and adequate reply. There was no further Soviet military activity that day. This had been an exciting, complex, and dangerous assignment. I was thankful that we had left nothing to chance. Detailed preparation and Stephan's ability to guide, direct, and influence people had ensured successes.

I am confident that Mullah Naquibullah and his band of cantankerous men were the rudiments of the Taliban. In Pashto the word means "student." They were indoctrinated into a fundamentalist interpretation of Islam in "madrassas" in Pakistan. They had also received military training from the ISI with financial support from the CIA. It was obvious that over the years, many, if not all, of these commanders, with the help of the Americans, had become rich, powerful, and a law unto themselves. Several were despots who flagrantly abused human rights and eliminated any opposition to their power, privilege, and absolute rule.

Pakistan has played a major role in Afghanistan. Besides being host to over four million Afghan refugees for over twenty-five years, it has supported the mujahideen and later spawned and continues to nurture the Taliban. The ISI is Pakistan's intermediary for covert support to the Taliban and in sustaining the opium trade. The people of the self-governing North-West Frontier Province of Pakistan known as Wazirstan share a common history, religion, and culture with the Pashtuns living in southern and eastern Afghanistan.

Many Pakistanis went to the same madrassas and therefore share the Taliban's elucidation of Islam. In fact, most present-day Afghan Taliban were born and raised in refugee camps in Pakistan. There are more Pakistani than Afghans, and they prefer to speak Urdu as opposed to Pashto or Dari.

Iran also finds itself in a perilous position. Two of its largest neighbors have been invaded by the United States, and one is experiencing increasing sectarian violence even as the other faces the threat of it. Both run the risk of all out civil war. Iran remains anxious even though American foreign policy has inadvertently enhanced the fundamentalist agenda in many ways. For instance, it eliminated the menace poised by the Taliban from Iran's eastern borders and defused the problem, threat, and danger posed by Saddam Hussein on its western flank.

The instability in the Middle East, promulgated by the United States meddling in the region, has also helped at one time by driving global oil prices to an all-time record high, giving the radical Islamic government in Iran the financial clout and confidence to do what it desires despite world opinion. Many people in Iran were envious when America invaded Afghanistan.

They felt that with US presence and support, Afghanistan would be catapulted into the modern world. This growing groundswell of support from the moderates was worrying to the fundamentalist. But when things started to sour in Afghanistan and Iraq, they swooped down and capitalized on the idiocy of these incursions. Because of its proximity, Iran has always exerted influence of the affairs of western Afghanistan and continues to host a large number of Shiite refugees within the country. It would like to become more immersed in Afghan affairs, but its main focus has now shifted to Iraq.

However, Tehran still sustains single-minded determination to mold its relationship with this region to be consistent with its own vested interest. The western provinces of Afghanistan have a long border with Iran and are mainly populated by Shiite Muslims. The Iranians foster intelligence and trade links with the West and maintain a wary eye on Pakistan and the American forces that are now constructing permanent bases and airfields close to the border purportedly for use by the Afghan military.

My consultancy had come to an end, and during the long flight back to New York from Islamabad, I was able to contemplate on the time I spent in Afghanistan. I was distraught by the ferocity of the war and the ensuing pain and suffering that it inflicted on the poor. My idealistic perception of the mujahideen had diminished. True, there are many commanders who were genuinely committed to the cause, but the motives of many others were only for personal gain. I became cynical about the involvement of the foreign powers and their roles as proxies to this conflict.

I was taken aback by how glib but gullible some of the CIA operatives whom I met were. I am convinced that the Soviets would be forced out of Afghanistan, but the real losers in this struggle will be the long-suffering common folk living in the rural areas.

I realized that despite the complexities, I was able to make a constructive contribution to the success of the mission. Stephan was ecstatic about our achievements and insisted that we team up again when the next opportunity presented itself. I was touched by the warmth and spontaneity of the Afghan people and subconsciously felt that I would someday return. I returned to New York on completion of this consultancy.

The wound of a gun will heal but not that of the tongue - Afghan saying

A few months later, I once again met with the late Peter a celebrity of the nation and of the American Broadcasting Cooperation and my wife's colleague, who was also an exponent and a longtime family friend. We knew each other, and Peter graciously offered to introduce me to James, the executive director of the United Nations Children's Emergency Fund (UNICEF). I had a vague notion that the agency was the United Nations arm for children. The next day, I got a call from Mr. James, chief of staff. A meeting had been arranged for the following day that would last for no more than fifteen minutes. I should therefore be explicit about what I wanted to discuss. I was to be at the executive offices twenty minutes ahead of schedule.

I had no expectations and was consistently inspired but goaded by James. He was charismatic and committed and presented an inimitable missionary vision of the world. His aspirations for its children were imaginative and farsighted. He looked intently at me with piercing eyes during the whole meeting. He spoke with zeal and authority but also had the patience to listen to what I had to say.

We discussed various topics, but he was most interested in my work with inner city kids from the Bronx and Harlem. Our meeting lasted two and a half hours, much to the exasperation of his support staff. It was my privilege and pleasure to be in his company and was enthused by his dedication. Just before departing, I noticed that James had scribbled the word "hire" on a pad next to him.

A week later, I received a call from Ekrem, the UNICEF country representative for Afghanistan, inviting me to a meeting. Ekrem looked like a Turkish eagle ready to swoop down on its unwary prey. He monitored my every move and waited for me to open the tête-à-tête. His hidden smoke eater did nothing to conceal the fact that he was chain-smoking in what was hypothetically a "smoke-free environment."

On his desk was the latest issue of *Time* magazine that contained a feature story that related to my life in New York. He, scrutinizing me, my dress, and I, sensed that he had made up his mind about who I was. I understood and accepted that he had placed me in an unfavorable box.

Ekrem later said that he had written me off as a good-for-nothing Manhattan socialite. Little did he know the veracity. UNICEF offered me the position as head of their office in Western Afghanistan. I caused consternation by instantly accepting.

My duty station was the ancient city of Herat that, according to legend, descended from the ancient town of Artacoana, which was established before 500 BC. Alexander the Great spent time in the city in the fourth century and Genghis Khan destroyed Herat in 1220, and a story that has been passed down by generations has it that the only people who survived this massacre were those who hid in the Blue Mosque. In the north of the city stand four tall minarets, which were the corners of a madrassa built by Queen Gaward Shah in 1457

Its grapes are reputed to be the best in the world, and the theory is that the Aryans first started growing grapes in the region around 2000 BC. The famous Mashid-Jame, or the Blue Mosque, overlooks the Old City from a prominent position that dominates the neighborhood. During the communist regime, the city was extensively used by the Soviets and even before the invasion they had a substantial presence in and around the city. In 1979, the army under the command of Ismail Khan mutinied, killing more than 350 Soviet citizens in one day. The Communists quickly retaliated in an unrestrained, violent, and vicious way, with sustained air and artillery bombardment. Before the recapture of the city, they caused massive destruction and were responsible for killing about 20,000 people. Intense fighting continues in the region, and the Communist government maintains a large military garrison and air force in the city. But despite the obvious risks, I was enthusiastic about this assignment.

I arrived in the fall. The leaves had started to turn, but no sooner had we landed than we came face-to-face with the harsh, ruthless, realities of this brutal war. The sound of battle was deafening and was rapidly approaching the airfield from the east. Black plumes of smoke were clearly visible, the reverberations of explosions penetrating and filling the air with the pungent odor of explosives.

The captain of the UN plane gunned his throttles for a hasty takeoff as the aircraft made a mad dash down the runway. To avoid being hit by antiaircraft or missile fire, he went into an almost vertical climb and then circled the airstrip to gain precious height. We were aware that the CIA had recently armed the mujahideen with the deadly "Stinger" ground-to-air missiles. Communist armor and artillery scrambled to take up battle positions, helicopter gunships with rotors revolving were geared up to provide air support, soldiers were sprinting in confusion as if their hair was on fire, and the Soviet major commanding the garrison was irritated because we had observed the bedlam.

Katabi, my national program assistant, was at the airport to greet me. He had lived in this war zone for many years and was impervious to the furor that surrounded us. Despite this, he was now agitated and yelled that we should leave immediately. We boarded our mine-plated land cruiser and made a dash for the safety of the city.

Even with the devastation and carnage, Heart still had a vague semblance of a once-elegant city. Massive old pines line the streets, and the people remain proud of their rich intellectual traditions, tombs, viewpoints, and custom for religious and racial tolerance. In the early sixties, the city was home to a flourishing Jewish community, and even today people of different ethnicities live here.

The city could certainly have been from a period in ancient European history, between antiquity and the Renaissance, with its narrow streets bristling with action and commotion. Blacksmiths, cobblers, tailors, barbers, carpenters, silk weavers, chemists, and carpet sellers, all working with diligence at their trade or occupation.

The calm, clean serenity of Manhattan was a far cry from the unforgiving realities of Herat. The damage and destruction around me was startling. Most of the shops and houses bore the ugly blemishes of battle, the streets were strewn with the remnants of destroyed and burned-out fighting vehicles, artillery pieces, and civilian cars that were inopportunely trapped in the cross fire. These relics bore obnoxious testament to the savage fighting taking place in this forgotten, forlorn part of the world.

The once-solid concrete road from the airport was pitted and potholed, caused by the high volume of tanks churning up and down. Our movement from the airport was closely monitored by UN security, and Katabi told me that I was only the second UN international staff member to be permanently based in Herat—a consoling thought.

My home was my place of work, and soon we approached one of the few stone buildings that were not completely gutted by fire or fighting. On the roof was a tall mast from which proudly fluttered the flag of the United Nations. The roof was cluttered with radio antennae, masts, and other communication paraphernalia.

A high stonewall topped by razor wire encircled the house, giving it a fortlike appearance. Iron gates that were kept under stringent control by well-armed guards barred the entrance. All authorized visitors were body searched before being allowed to enter. The homes of our neighbors were little more than rubble and skinny; barefoot children with snotty noses and dressed in rags played in the street.

I had never worked or lived in such a dilapidated building before, and the prospects were exceptionally depressing. But there was a positive side to it as well. Only segments of our roof had caved in because of the shelling, and not all the external walls had cavernous shell holes in them. A well in the yard provided water, but the quality was highly suspect. Rumor has it that bodies were dumped into it by the KHAD or the secret services.

A small generator powered the communication equipment during the day while oil lamps provided gloomy, flickering light for a short time at night. There was no running water or heat, and some of the windowpanes were smashed and functioned as wind tunnels for the freezing winter gusts. I was fortunate, however. Although my room was blackened by smoke, damp, and cold, it was otherwise virtually intact and would provide adequate shelter from the sun, rain, and snow.

I had a bed with boards substituting for a mattress, there were drapes that covered the gaping holes in broken windowpanes, and there was a communal squat toilet with no running water. The accommodation was basic, but under the circumstances, it was adequate. But I must admit that I dearly missed one luxury—my down pillow. I just cannot find true sleep without it. Was it the texture or perhaps the comforting aroma or the fact that I had spent so many years sleeping on it? I don't know.

Johan, a Swede, was with United Nations Refugee Agency and was the other foreigner based in Herat. He had arrived earlier and had survived the past two months, making him a veteran who was now accustomed to this Spartan lifestyle. To celebrate my arrival, we drank a hundred grams of vodka to fortify our nerves and spirits.

Dinner was served by the faint glimmer of light from an oil lamp, which offered little illumination but belched clouds of kerosene fumes in recompense. The food was insipid, cold, and greasy. But it was sustenance. As soon as it got dark, the fighting started in our neighborhood, and we were entertained by a melody of tank, rocket, and small arms fire, sprinkled by the sporadic detonation of a rocket-propelled grenade or a land mine.

The war had destroyed most of the infrastructure of the city. Many parts had no running water or electricity; the garbage was piled high all over and scavenged by a mélange of street children and packs of wild dogs. The Herat Hospital was a sanatorium only in name. Once a contemporary facility, it now was dirty and devoid of drugs, furniture, and equipment. The few dedicated medical staff made Herculean efforts under daunting conditions to provide the most rudimentary health care services to their patients.

The lack of water and poor hygiene and sanitation created conditions that contributed to a gargantuan infection rate, causing additional but avoidable death. The incinerator had broken down, and medical waste was heaped all over. A large number of wild cannibal cats congregated around the operating theater, gorging themselves on body parts tossed out of the window during surgery.

One of my first challenges was to restore power to the hospital. I hired an Indian engineer to refurbish the two titanic generators, and electricity was returned in a fortnight. UNICEF then made available all the essential drugs, detergent, and medical supplies that were urgently needed to improve the quality of medical care and cleanliness. We started a supplementary feeding program to carry out therapeutic treatment for the hundreds of severely malnourished and dying children who were brought to the hospital each day.

There was no blood bank, so I instituted a system of walk-in donors. We pretested and categorized potential donors, and when a particular blood group was required, an appeal was broadcasted by the local city radio station and donors encouraged to walk in and donate blood for direct transfusions. This simple, timely, and effective measure saved many lives. The water supply was finally fixed and tons of garbage disposed of. I now looked for a hospital manager to ensure that these interventions were sustainable.

With the return of electricity, many parts of the hospital, including vaccine cold storage, was revitalized. Once restocked, the immunization of children in the entire region was resumed. I was shocked and saddened to see so many mine victims, mainly children with shattered limbs, broken bones, and battered bodies, transported by wheelbarrow, donkey cart, and bicycle or on horseback to the emergency room for treatment. Because of the lack of rudimentary medical facilities, an average of five child victims of mine-related injuries bleed to death each day. This state of affairs was truly barbaric.

Despite severe censure from my supervisor, I approved funding for the renovation of a small section of the operating theater, and with expert technical help from an international NGO, the unfortunate victims of this absurd carnage received immediate and appropriate medical attention that conserved the lives of many innocent victims.

Many people derived consolation and reassurance from our presence in Herat. Being in their midst and witnessing their pain, torment, and suffering gave them encouragement and hope. It was a lifeline that provided hope and sanguinity. We were powerless to react to many of their critical humanitarian needs, but they were nevertheless buoyed because they were not abandoned.

For these reasons, we were given unhindered accesses across lines and into areas controlled by the Communists, the militia, and the mujahideen. Before venturing into these regions, however, I first consulted with the appropriate authorities who then felt obligated to protect us. Consequently, we had entrée to secret military information on operational plans and activities of adversaries. This made me uncomfortable because I realized, recognized, and had to admit that many of the people I worked or collaborated with, and who shielded me would themselves get killed in these imminent battles.

With time, I became more in tune with the milieu. The need for superficial features of comfort no longer concerned me. I was focused, methodical, and in command. My biggest trepidation was for landmines. There were minefields all over. Some were marked, but many were laid haphazardly and not identified. The mujahideen certainly maintained no records where they planted theirs and had no institutional memory either. Roads attracted the main interest of all warring parties, so I never used them. I only drove cross-country using a compass and placing my life in the hands of the Lord. Landmines in Afghanistan have killed many of my colleagues.

In a fierce battle, the mujahideen commander Hajji Ahmed lost jurisdiction of a large town to the north, to an atrocious militia commander Dhost. Horrendous reprisals followed, creating a catastrophic humanitarian emergency. An assessment mission was ordered by Kabul that would be lead by Kizoto, a Japanese colleague from the World Food Program. I was to accompany him. Our mission had three Land Cruisers and a Russian GAZ four-by-four truck. This vehicle has excellent cross-country traction, and the sound of its engine is similar to that of a Soviet tank.

Knowing the area and having traveled through there a number of times, I volunteered to lead this mission.

This is not devoid of risk. As a rule, any land mine in its path usually blows up the front vehicle. Entering the town was eerier. Shops, houses, and fields were still ablaze, coal-black spirals of smoke rose from burning fuel dumps, and the sign and smell of death and destruction was everywhere. Dhost, who seemed sedated, his narrow eyes bloodshot, and his guise menacing, received us. His fighters were well armed, unrestrained, vicious, and vehement, with the look of bloodthirsty scavengers. Without a doubt, they were high on drugs.

I had previously worked with and trusted Hajji Ahmed, so we decided to spend a night with him at his fallback position in a village across a dry riverbed only two kilometers away. It was getting dark, and I did not want to be forced to spend the night with these hooligans. Being inexperienced, Kizoto took his time, and we eventually departed soon after dusk. I took the lead and was quickly able to navigate my way across the stones and soft sand of the riverbed.

My colleague, however, got bogged down, and I could hear him gun his engine, trying to break free from the wet sand, but instead, he was digging himself in deeper. It was dark as I spun around, with the GAZ pursuing and dashed to the rescue. Kizoto, who had never driven under such conditions before, had managed to bury his rear axle in the sand. We hitched his car to the GAZ and, with the engine roaring under the strain, towed out the bogged vehicle. It was a pitch-black, still night, and we had created an awful commotion getting through this obstacle, which I was certain was covered by mujahideen small arms and rocket fire. No sooner had I crossed over to the other side of the luggar than I came under intense machine gun and small arms fire aimed directly to my front, and tracers with illumination flares lit up the cloudy black skies. I instinctively slammed on the brakes, left the engine running with the headlights on, and turned on all the lights in the cab before ordering all my passengers to abandon ship and take cover.

Fortunately, I had stopped by a huge irrigation ditch that led up to a thick mud wall. My crew used the cover of the canal to crawl toward the wall, their heads bobbing in the water like floating corks. The water in the ditch was cold, stagnant, and inundated with bugs, the stench overpowering. The unpleasant smell immediately gave me an allergic attack.

Looking back, I saw Kizoto's vehicle stationary out of harm's way. The firing continued for what seemed like eternity, and we heard bullets penetrate or ricochet off or the vehicle. As quickly as the shooting started, it stopped. People began scampering down the hill toward us, screaming in excited voices. Soon they walked into the headlights of my vehicle, and I recognized Hajji Ahmed.

Dashing up to him, we embraced, but he instantly chided me for risking our lives by traveling in the dark. They were certain Dhost and his men were attacking this position with tanks. They recognized that we were friends because I had stopped immediately and left all lights on. They almost engaged us with antitank rockets. We were fortunate to be alive, and I thanked the Lord that it ended well. But it was not over yet. Soon we were being engaged by another ambush position located on a hill directly to our front.

Once again, we dived for cover in the putrid waters of the ditch while Hajji flashed light signals to the ambush position that we were friends and not foe. I reeked like a polecat and felt pooped and hungry. I spoke to Kozoto on the radio and informed him that it was safe for him to join us and notified Kabul about our encounter with faith.

Winter was fast approaching, and most of my colleagues were preparing to go home for Christmas. As the UN team leader for

Western Afghanistan, I had to remain in the country and hold the fort. Our living quarters had been improved and were now comfortable. I had also shifted my office to another building as my program had expanded and we needed more space. It was a joy not having to live and work in the same house. Besides, it was essential for the people I assist to have easy accesses to me with some degree of confidentiality.

But it certainly did not feel like Christmas. There was nothing to cheer about or with. I was alone, the weather was glacial, and there were skirmishes around the city, with ongoing battles in the countryside. I was depressed and dejected. On Christmas Eve, I was in bed at 8:00 p.m. but quickly got lost in happy thoughts that perceived physical, practical, and the emotional joys of previous Christmas celebrations. I imagined and understood how fortunate I was at having so many possibilities in life and being able to grow up healthy and live in peace, harmony, and prosperity. These were gifts from God that I glibly took for granted.

My personal life was a mess, but I was alive, strong, fit, and flexible. I realize that life can be better understood by scrutinizing the past, but it can only be improved by concentrating on the future. On the morning of December 25, I rummaged through the kitchen, searching for something to eat. Unfortunately, the cupboard was bare. With nothing to do and nobody to talk with, I decided to drive to the office.

In your childhood you are playful, in your youth you are lustful, in old age you are feeble - Afghan saying

The gale force wind was blowing plumes of snowflakes that spread a white blanket over the trash and filth that littered the streets.

At the gates to my office, I saw two young kids wearing rags, sitting huddled on a snowdrift. They clearly were very cold. The guard told me that they wanted to meet me, but with no reason, he would not let them in. I requested him to show them in and call for my translator.

The kids had anxious, scared looks in their tender, watery eyes. They were unresponsive and impassive. The girl hobbled on a prop on one leg and was about ten, and her brother was perhaps seven. They were dirty, frostbitten, their skin lacerated with abscesses, and both were badly malnourished. I asked my translator, Malhia, to give them a hot shower. My driver was sent to the bazaar to buy warm clothes, shoes, and food.

Mahila ushered the children into my office after they had devoured their meal. Both chose to sit on the floor. They were traumatized and miserable, and the disfigurements of a deprived and difficult childhood were clear for all to see. This was truly a poignant scene. Malhia used all her vigor, vivacity, and ability with the children to get them to talk.

In a slow, heartbreaking, faltering, and toneless voice, the girl started to tell all. She did not know how old they were. One day, running to keep warm on her way from school to home, she stepped on a mine that smashed her right foot and killed her friend. She remembers the intense pain and the blood that made her faint.

No medical help was available, and her parents had no money to pay for transport to Herat. The barber was the only person with cutting skills, and he hacked off her crushed limb. Her parents begged for pills, but nothing took away the extreme, excruciating pain. She remembers her parents yelling that it would be better if she were dead. But she was petrified of death and wanted very much to live.

When she got better, her father cruelly told her that without a leg, she was worthless. No one would marry her as she was unable to work. Consequently, he would not feed her, and therefore, she had too go and fend for herself. At first, she did not understand what he was saying.

When he threw her only pair of shoes onto the street, she understood. Her young brother was taken aback and decided to accompany her. They hitched a ride to Herat on a donkey cart and have stayed alive on the streets by contending with wild dogs for the few scraps of food on rubbish dumps. They were petrified of these ferocious animals and often waited till they had their fill before savaging for the rest.

I was not only scandalized but also humiliated by the torment of these poor, innocent souls. The International Committee of the Red Cross ran an orthopedic facility in Herat that made and fitted prosthetics. I called them on the radio and got an immediate appointment with a foreign technical expert. He examined the stump and said that the amputation was so crude and clumsy that reamputation was necessary. Our surgical unit at the Herat hospital would perform the operation immediately, but the prospects terrified the child. She was still distraught by her previous experience.

Mahila spoke to the patient in a warm, loving, and calming way, explaining that foreign experts would do the surgery in a new facility. I was concerned about parental consent and called the governor to obtain clarification. The outcome of the surgery was good, and with the proper care and attention, the recovery and healing processes were quicker than expected.

During this whole period, both children remained detached and bemused. They sat in silence, holding hands, and it was obvious that their anguish had created a solid bond between them. They showed no feelings, did not react or communicate, but just endured.

The time had come to measure and mold the prosthesis to the stump. Other amputees who had been trained painstakingly undertook the procedure. Because of their personal experiences, they were compassionate and committed. After numerous fittings and adjustments, the artificial leg was ready to be put on. Patients are then thauht to walk and undergo weeks of gate training.

With her false leg strapped on, the little girl stumbled and then fell. But her brother was quick to help. Once standing again, she balanced herself on her brother's shoulder and took her first step. She walked slowly but unsteadily toward the door. Just before they exited, both kids spontaneously turned towards us, waved, and gave us endearing smiles, their faces brimming with euphoria. Their childhood had been restored. With tears of joy, we rejoiced at receiving such a wonderful Christmas present.

I often wonder what became of that child, her life parentally scarred by this war. But then we could not be bogged down trying to find answers or reasons for the many dilemmas that confront people in their daily lives.

The plight of so many homeless children caused me grave concern. They lived off their wits on the street and were victims of both sexual and physical abuse. I often spent time talking with some who were manual workers under dangerous conditions. What I learned from them was that they were survivors. In order to live on the street, you need cunning, the mental acumen, intelligence, and the will to survive. Because they have been exploited, they trust nobody but themselves.

Without exception, they felt that by learning to speak English, they would be able to find better work and get off the streets. I identified a donor who gave us 100 Sony Walkmans. We installed Dari/English tapes in them, and rechargeable batteries powered all. These were distributed free to the kids. Besides being a status symbol, it gave them the opportunity to learn English as they worked.

But more important for me was the fact that they were obliged to come to our offices when the batteries in the Walkman needed recharging. Herat did not have electricity, so generators powered our offices. The visit by these kids to our offices gave my staff the opportunity to assess their health and mental and physical state. We were able to identify kids that were being abused and provided them protection.

I often spent time in the bazaar, sitting crossed-legged on the carpeted floor, drinking sweet green tea, and chatting to the locals. It was relaxing and felt like balm to the hurt mind. It gave me a unique opportunity to connect and understand the real difficulties that the poor and oppressed faced in their daily lives. The UN can only effectively plan useful program interventions if they are constantly aware of the ever-changing environmental circumstances that impact the lives of the most vulnerable.

At that time, the majority of people that I met worried about and spent all their time and energy in ensuring the safety and survival of themselves and their families. It was an hour-to-hour existence, and nobody could predict what would come next. This caused tremendous stress among the adult population.

Overmedication or narcotics was the only coping crutch that sustained and supported people to muddle through their daily lives. Pills of dubious origins were available at a price. Nobody knew what they were or what ailment they were intended to treat or, for that matter, cure. They were labeled in the language of their country of origin. The self-styled "doctors," many of whom were semiliterate, dished these out at random depending on the patient's ability to pay.

The implications of this irresponsible and criminal behavior are obvious. My driver was called Kamal. He was almost seven feet tall and a lion of a man who was unafraid of anything. He claimed to be a descendant of Genghis Khan, and his blue eyes and fair complexion could well be a testament of this. Indira Ghul, his eight-year-old daughter, had an effervescing character with oodles of energy for living and a spirit for appreciating the little things in life. Watching her giggle, skip, dance, and play all day among the roses was a tremendous source for joy to me.

One Thursday afternoon, she was bundled up and perched on a donkey for a three-mile trek to visit her grandparents in the village. Two days later, Kamal returned home a broken man minus Indira and wife. I was astounded to see the "shir" (lion) behave like a lamb. Kamal understood that I loved Indira as my very own. Despite being a Muslim, he poured me a drink and then broke down and told me the story.

In the village, Indira drank some water from a stream and soon became ill. She started vomiting and ran a temperature. Kamal took her to the village clinic, where the doctor prescribed six different types of pills and charged Kamal the equivalent of $20. Indira reacted adversely to this medication and soon lost consciousness. By morning she was dead.

I was dumbfounded and asked Kamal if he had any of the medication. He gave me a dirty brown envelope that contained most of the pills. My international colleague who was a physician with the World Health Organization advised that I send the pills to a laboratory in New Delhi for analysis.

The results indicated that some were antibiotics with contradictions that could not be taken together. The other pills were for diabetes, high blood pressure, and nervous disorders, certainly not to be taken by children. The bottom line was that Indira was poisoned. I was incensed and asked for an audience with the governor. We met, and he understood how upset I was. In a very cool, calm, and collected way, he explained that Afghanistan was not the USA or Canada, and therefore, I should not hold local officials accountable to Western standards or practices. I could not believe my ears as to me this was a fundamental human rights issue.

As human beings, is it too much for us to expect to receive basic but safe health care? Indira was a delicate blossom, a symbol of hope, vibrancy, and vitality—a symbol of hope with a basic expectation for a better future. Unfortunately, she was born and raised in perhaps the bleakest years in Afghan history.

Thanks to her parents, none of this adversity adversely affected her because she was raised with love, sacrifice, and the promise of a better tomorrow. Like everything else in Afghanistan, things that could bring about the slightest expectation for change are stifled before they can germinate, take root, and become a strong agent for transformation.

But despite all these constraints, the majority of people adopted a very positive outlook on life based on the belief that God willing, this war would soon be over, all the refugees would return from Iran, people would start rebuilding their homes and lives, children would go to school, basic health care services would be restored, there would be pipe water in every household, electricity would lift the constant veil of darkness, and the people of Herat would once again prosper. I did not share this optimism or the luxury of this belief, nor did I expect or hope that someday things would turn for the better and that all the peoples of this beautiful land would live in peace, harmony, and prosperity.

But this was not to be. One evening, I was told about the serious escalation in fighting between the mujahideen and the militia in two villages not far from Herat. The reports were grim. A school and a clinic that we had built had been set alight after being ransacked. This infuriated me as the school was the only form of normalcy in the completely disordered and out-of-control lives of children of the villages. The clinic provided essential, basic, but easy-to-access health care services for people living in the area.

I sent a message to a mujahideen commander from the area with whom I had worked on previous occasions, informing him that I intended to visit the area to assess the damage. We set out early next morning in three white vehicles with UNICEF clearly marked on the roof and two sides of each vehicle. In addition, we flew a large UN flag at the tail of each SUV. This made in easy for both sides of the conflict to easily recognize that we were neutral and were not part of their conflict. We were there to assess the situation and possibly provide whatever humanitarian assistance that was necessary.

Sporadic fighting was still going on and one of the villages had been partly destroyed, the inhabitants had fled the area, and the mujahideen forces that had previously ruled had been pushed back by the militia to defensive positions about two miles away. The air was still filled with the smell of explosives, and the stench of the dead and bloated bodies lay where they had fallen. My instincts told me that we were in a hornet's nest and that our lives were in jeopardy. My national team agreed and suggested I find a way to extract us from this village as quickly as possible.

Soon militiamen surrounded us. Their bloodshot eyes could indicate that they had had a sleepless night. Through my translator, I asked one of them to take me to their commander. It was clear that the person I spoke with was either drunk or high on drugs. He haphazardly pointed to a white brick structure, and I drove to the front entrance.

There were rocket launchers and machine guns stacked at the entrance, and two Soviet-made tanks with their engines idling guarded the building. We agreed that this was a well-funded group. The commander, in his late twenties, spoke with a slur and gave me a bear hug to welcome me. An empty bottle of whisky lay on the carpet where he had been sitting.

The UN is well respected by all parties in this conflict, and this afforded us a certain amount of protection. Hajji Mohammed, my translator, was disgusted. He warned me to cut this meeting short. The commander, whose name was Hussein, was in the mood to party. He ordered his men to slaughter one of the sheep they had taken as booty.

I knew that it was imperative that we made a graceful exit without loss of face. I told Hussein that I had been having severe diarrhea and that I could not stop vomiting. I suspected that I had cholera, and I certainly did not want to infect him and his men.

Despite his state, the message got through, and he ordered his men to give us safe passage through the village. Now I understood why they were able to cause such unjustified and malicious destruction to the people and their homes and village. On our way out of the village, we met medics from the ICRC that provide first-line medical services to combatants in a war zone. They were amazed that we had entered these two villages when we did. Perhaps I was somewhat naive or even stupid doing so.

A trader whom I got to know well was a man called Hajji Sultan Amide. Hajji, as all fondly knew him, ran a gift shop in the old part of the city. His family had been involved in this trade for years, and his ancestors blew the famous Herat blue glass for decades. Over a cup of green tea, Hajji told me how his family had prospered. In the early sixties, Herat was a magnet for the hippie generation.

They came from all corners of the world because they enjoyed the culture, the historical significance, and the tolerance of the people of Herat, who always made them feel welcome. Besides, high-quality hashish was readily available. At the end of the summer, the hippies loaded up with silk carpets and blue glass and headed home. They would sell these in their home countries, and the proceeds would pay for their trip to Herat the following spring.

Hajji showed me photographs and letters from these flower people who only wanted peace and detested war. What would they say of Herat today? Hajji inquired. He talked about his beloved motherland that was now being ravaged and raped by nonstop fighting for over two decades. But Hajji had other concerns on his mind. For over three thousand years, blue glass was blown here using the same old natural formula and technique used over the centuries.

But today, there was only one surviving glassblower who knew and practiced this ancient skill. He was getting old and was in poor health. Hajji took me to meet Saqui, a skinny man who looked liked the Hunch Back of Notre-Dame. His shop was primitive, and Saqui, because of his illness, squatted with his head bowed down, a shoulder hunched forward, and blows glass with nothing more than the plain and utilitarian fire, water, and a blowing tube.

The heat was intense, and the furnace was so archaic that I became immediately concerned about the safety of this sole surviving craftsman. Oblivious of the fact that we were watching, he finished blowing and doused his work of art in a bucket of water fashioned from an old truck tire. He then fished out the glass object from its bath with an old pair of tongs and placed it on a bench next to him.

The fading sunlight that filtered through his shop radiantly highlighted his works of art. Their color reminded me of the clear blue Herat sky, and I marveled that this artist could create such a beautiful objects under such primordial conditions. But as a trader, Hajji was concerned about what would become of his lucrative blue glass trade once Saqui passed away. This ancient skill and institutional knowledge would be lost forever. I understood the logic of his argument and reasoning, which even though valid presented no alternatives. I returned home sympathetic and fully acknowledging the long-term impact if this cultural heritage was lost.

In a letter home, I voiced concern that this ancient art would soon be lost, and immediately I received a response from a family member who had recently visited the Corning Glass Museum in New York. On display was a collection of original Herati hand-blown blue glass. She was astounded by the beauty of the work and spoke to the curator of the museum, Dr. Robert Brill.

I wrote an e-mail to Dr. Brill, explaining the prevailing situation, and solicited his advice. As luck would have it, Robert Brill told me that he did his PhD on the blue glass of spell Herat in the early 1960. He was familiar with the situation and understood the difficulties and the problems faced under these trying circumstances. Without hesitation, he committed to doing all he could to sustain this ancient art form. Robert said that he would raise the necessary funds and come to Afghanistan to assess what could and should be done immediately to safeguard this primeval skill.

I had discussed this issue with the governor of Herat, Emir Ismail Kahn. He agreed that that glassblowing could be taught as an extracurricular subject to boys who were interested. My concern was the hazards posed by the furnace to young people. Dr. Brill had of course anticipated this problem.

Shortly, he informed me that he would travel to Herat accompanied by Mr. Bulichi, the foremost, noncommercial grassblower in the United States. They had consulted with engineers at MIT and had come up with a design for a wood-burning furnace that would present minimal risk to young people.

We all went to the airport to welcome our honored guest. It soon became apparent that Robert was flabbergasted with the destruction and the plight of the people. Mr. Bulichi was astounded by what he saw. He displayed a feeling of sadness that in this day and age, humans can be forced to exist under such appalling conditions. He had the good grace not to express his views or emotions in public.

Hajji and Robert had known one another in the 1960s and were extremely pleased to see one another again. Hajji asked me to buy the sheep to celebrate this reunion. I was glad to do this, and we all gathered in our UN compound to watch the sheep being slaughtered according to principles and values that govern Islamic behavior. We later gorged ourselves with pounds of delicious *sashlick*. As we sat around a bonfire, most of the conversation centered on the glorious days of the past. Nobody wanted to dwell on the horrors of the present. It was a brisk, cool Herat evening, with a full moon and clear pale-blue skies.

But the mood was dampened by the story Fazal, the UN guesthouse manager, told our guest. The feared KHAD, the Soviet intelligence services, used this house not so very long ago. They tortured people here, killing them and then dumping their bodies down our well, which is our only source of "fresh" water—not the best of notes to end what had been and enjoyable and relaxing evening.

At a breakfast of green tea, leveled bread, and yogurt, Robert announces that he had a solution to the problem. They had brought with them a special low-tech wood-burning furnace that would present minimum risk to the young people using it. He also had the funds to build a prototype and to carry out some basic training.

In retrospect, I must admit that this was a distraction from my regular duties. But the fact was that there were so many children living on the streets, and UNICEF was mandated to ensure child survival and protection. I saw this intervention as doing just that.

I spoke with my colleague who was in charge of the World Food Program in Western Afghanistan. Eddie agreed to provide us with a daily food ration for all the kids who attended to glassblowing training under WFP food for education program. With this incentive, we had street kids lining up to join. We fed them all but only selected a few to be trained by Robert and Dr. Buluchi under the watchful eye of Hajji.

We were all saddened to see Robert and Dr. Bulichi leave. They had brought not only hope but also stability and some normalcy into our lives. I was pleased that this antediluvian craft would remain alive and hopefully flourish. That night I felt at peace with myself and fell soundly asleep.

Word of this initiative generated global media attention. At this time, all the news about Afghanistan painted a pragmatic picture of doom and gloom. This was the first sign of the country returning to "normalcy." It was a ray of hope that carried the promise of a brighter future. Soon we had an influx of international media correspondence wanting to cover this story of hope and recovery. This international exposure not only gave me an opportunity to solicit additional funds from Donors for my projects, but it also gave the world an insight into Afghanistan and a glimpse of the plight of the Afghan people.

The best way to predict the future is to invent it - Afghan saying

I was informed by my headquarters in Kabul that these international correspondents would only spend twenty-four hours in Heart. I wanted this to be a constructive visit that would highlight not only successes but also failures of some of our endeavors. Based on their nationality and interest, I designed a comprehensive itinerary to satisfy their individual story needs. Their interest was varied depending on the medium and country of origin. The majority, however, wanted to have lunch in a traditional Herati restaurant. Well, there were no restaurants in operation at the time, so I decided to take them to a kebob shop owned and operated by "Hajji Kababi."

This eating house had an excellent reputation among the locals, and depending on their disposition, some foreign aid workers frequented it too. Located in the old town amid scores of bombed-out buildings and destroyed Soviet tanks was this traditional mud structure with a dome-shaped roof. One could smell the kebobs a block away. The dirt road leading to it was rutted and full of potholes, a sure sign that it was constantly used by tanks and other tracked military vehicles. The neighborhood was littered with garbage, and wild dogs foraged in the mountains of garbage that were everywhere.

Living in Herat, we had become accustomed to these surroundings. However, my guests appeared to be taken aback by what they saw and also by being exposed to the realities of Herati life. Through a narrow passageway, we entered the "restaurant." It was dark except for a shaft of light that came through a hole in the domed roof. This hole also acted as an exhaust for the smoke and the aroma of the cooking. Hajji Kababi sits cross-legged by his wood-fired grill, sticking chunks of meat and fat on metal skewers. The eatery had no furniture, so we sat in a circle on a handwoven Herati rug and waited for the food to arrive. I only drank green tea as the water was boiled. Freshly baked naan was tossed onto a plastic sheet in the middle of our circle, and some of the journalists appeared a bit apprehensive at this unusual way of serving food. The more seasoned ones took it within their stride and were looking forward to the meal.

In the darkness, we noticed a number of black turbaned men sitting on carpets on the floor and eating their lunch with their hands. They spoke in whispers and were obviously surprised to see us here. They were from the villages and not used to foreigners. As we waited, I looked at the vent; the upward draft sucked up the smoke that had a hue of gray with a tinge of blue. The scene was almost biblical. This mud building was constructed in the traditional style that has been used for hundreds of years. Here we were men and a woman from different parts of the globe, in a strange world under difficult circumstances, sitting on the floor, waiting to break bread together. To my perception and imagination, this could have been the Last Supper.

It was impossible to tell what we were being served, but it smelled and tasted delicious. The rays of sun filled with smoke formed a halo around our meal, and it gave me a feeling of peace and tranquility. The fact that my guests were in unfamiliar surroundings threatened some of them. They were forced to rely and depend on us and were happy that I provided the leadership. We began to bond and were no longer strangers to each other. They empathized with us and understood our feelings, pain, and frustrations. These were extremely difficult circumstances to work in. Security is of constant concern, and we were witness to so much death and destruction. They would tell the world our story in a warm and passionate way.

The factual accounts of the events, the problems, and the suffering imposed on the Afghan people received worldwide coverage, and this generated support for UN programs in distant capitals. We were of course delighted, but this euphoria was soon eclipsed by the tragic news that a French journalist was killed in a land mine accident a few days later. This media visit resulted in stories ranging from war to culture, refugees, rehabilitation, education, health care, and an assessment of UN emergency interventions and programs in the Region.

One feature story highlighted our efforts to ensure the survival of the skill and the traditions of ancient blue glass blowing.

About a month later, I received a communication from the Museum of Man in Paris informing me that they were impressed with our blue-glass initiative. They went on to say that in the past, young boys in Herat used to do embroidery and that all the original and very old Herat patterns were now stored at the Museum of Man in Paris. The museum would return these to Herat if we could guarantee their safe custody and proper use.

As I knew nothing about embroidery, I went into the bazaar to check out what was available. I also spoke to Hajji. My conclusion was that women were now doing this handicraft and they were using Iranian patterns. In a subsequent meeting with the Emir, I discussed the communication from the Museum of Man and the possibility of reteaching young boys this skill.

Ismail, the emir was an old mujahideen commander and a very traditionalist. He certainly did not think that boys should be thought what was now considered a woman's skill. I saw no point in making a persistent attempt to advocate for the preservation of this ancient craft skill and a traditional cultural heritage.

I was aware of, interested, and cognizant of the fact that Herat was once on the old "Silk Road" where the merchants were rich and famous. There was a sizable Jewish population, and the city and the ancient tradition was a culture of tolerance and understanding. Numerous religious texts in both Arabic and Hebrew mention the "Land of the East" that was inhabited by sizable Jewish communities. What was then known as the "Land of the East" encompassed what is now Western Afghanistan, Mashad in Iran, and parts of Central Asia.

These people were ethnically connected with the people in Iran. In around 1978, four synagogues were identified in a part of Herat that formed the old city. This area was known as "Majalla-Yi-Musahiya," or the Jewish neighborhood. I was taken to a synagogue, which I believe was called "Yu Aw." By and large, it stood in its original splendor and still retained most of its original distinctiveness and was now being used as a Muslim primary school for boys.

I was told that in those days, the Jews dressed the same as their Muslim neighbors, apart from the fact that all Jewish men wore black turbans not dissimilar to those worn by the Taliban today. Jewish men were mainly involved in the cotton and silk trade, and their specialty was dyeing using natural dyes. This discolored their hands, and the rest of the community viewed this as a religious characteristic. It is estimated that in 1930, the Jewish population in Herat was around thirty thousand. Most of them migrated to Israel in 1951 when they were permitted to leave.

Afghanistan has the unenviable status of being one of the most heavily mined countries in the world. The biggest scourge to the population is the antipersonnel mine. These indiscriminate weapons of destruction are designed to maim and not to kill. The contention is that you would tie up more enemy resources caring for a wounded soldier then if he was killed outright. It is a well-known fact, however, that in modern warfare soldiers are well protected. They engage in combat driving in armored personnel carriers or tanks.

Land mines have, over the decades, been planted haphazardly all over the country, polluting the region with a deadly and destructive weapon that cannot distinguish friend from foe. Mines continue to be one of the major obstacles to repatriation, rehabilitation, relief, and development in the country. Broad estimates suggest that over seven million square meters of Afghanistan are still polluted by land mines that continue to maim and claim the lives of innocent civilians.

We were constantly aware of this unseen threat that exposed us and made us vulnerable to harm, injury, or loss of life. On mission, I therefore always drove myself. All roads or tracks were avoided because these were usually mined. Traveling cross-country took its toll on both humans and vehicles. But I firmly believe that to a certain degree, it kept us out of harm's way.

We were returning to Herat from a mission to Islam Kalah on the Iranian border. The road was surfaced, but I chose to drive cross-country parallel to the main road. This upset the national staff who were traveling with me. They were tired and felt that we could go much faster and have a smoother ride if we used the road. I have always followed my instincts and was in no mood to debate the issue.

Suddenly there was a massive explosion on the road just in front of us. Clouds of dust, smoke, and debris filled the air. The minivan traveling in front of us overloaded with people and cargo had driven over an antitank mine that was planted on the road earlier. Were we the intended target? I cannot find words to describe the death and destruction that unfolded under our very eyes. Bodies and body parts speckled the road and the surrounds. There was panic, confusion, with children screaming, and women wailed in anguish as they became conscious of the loss of those near and dear to them.

I rushed to the scene, followed by the medical doctor on my team. He examined the injured but soon came to the conclusion that in this remote area, there was nothing he could do to save lives. This was a lost cause. My senses were numbed by the cries for help from the people in pain and by those who realized that they had only a few minutes to live. We offered the injured some water. That's all that they wanted.

I have mentioned the resilience of the Afghan people. True to form and after pulling through the trauma caused by this unexpected event, the men started digging shallow graves by the roadside to bury the dead. I was taken aback by the fact that after so many years of war, most Afghans were no longer sensitive or susceptible to the emotions that relate to death. This had to them become a reality of life. Every person or family whom I met had lost relatives in this war. This incident struck the very core of my being. I had flashbacks of torn and tattered bodies and bore the guilt that we were unable to do anything to mitigate the suffering of those injured.

Friday in the Islamic world equates to Sunday in the Christian world. In Western Afghanistan, all government offices shut down by twelve noon on Thursday. We, however, continued working until sunset. I was therefore surprised when I was informed at 3:00 p.m. that the director of health for the region wanted to meet with me immediately.

It transpired that there was a serious outbreak of cholera in six villages that near Herat to the north. A number of people had died, and the government was amazed at the rapid spread of this infection. As team leader of the UN in the region, I was requested to assume the role of spearheading government's efforts or organize and guide the immediate response to this emergency. I was also requested to take whatever measures were necessary to stem the spread of this epidemic.

Cholera is an acute intestinal infection that is typified with profuse watery diarrhea and vomiting that rapidly leads to acute dehydration and death. However, even in severe cases, patients respond to a very noticeable degree and often with surprising suddenness to proper case management. I immediately summoned the regional management team that consisted of representatives from all UN agencies and NGOs active in the area. The French NGO, MSF, or Doctors Without Borders had the most in-house expertise and the trained medical staff to deal with this outbreak. This NGO had extensive experience in dealing with cholera contagions in Africa and Asia.

We agreed that all patients and those with symptoms should be immediately quarantined in a camp set up by the UN on the outskirts of Herat. WHO and UNICEF would provide whatever medical supplies and operating funds were needed to run the camp, the World Food Program would be responsible for providing the food to feed the patients, and MSF would be accountable for the provision of medical and technical support. Initially, we decided to make provision for fifty patients.

The distinctive symptoms cholera are extremely serious, severe, painful and copious diarrhea. If not treated immediately, it results in rapid weakening and death. Rehydration is therefore the foundation to treatment. Oral rehydration salts, intravenous fluids, and electrolytes must be administered in a timely fashion to ensure survival of the patients.

The camp we established was basic. Stretchers perched on brick blocks with holes cut out for the buttocks allowed the patient to defecate easily, and the excrement flowed into a bedpan directly under the hole in the stretcher. This method of patient care was simple but effective.

In the first week, five of our patients died. Perhaps they had passed the point of no return. I don't know. But from then on, we had a 100 percent rate of success. Despite the fact that the patient loads rapidly increased to three hundred inpatients. That the international community was able to control this epidemic so efficiently and effectively greatly enhanced our credibility with government.

As I write, I feel that I am only painting a picture of doom and gloom. This is not my intent, and this was certainly not the reality. One Thursday, just before we started our weekend, my financial assistant, Shukhrat, invited me to his home for dinner. He was a man in his midfifties who showed the scars of pain and suffering. I have seldom seen him smile and often wondered what was traumatizing him so.

I was honored to be invited to Shukhrat's home, but I was also profoundly surprised.

I got Malhia to discreetly find out the reason why Shukhrat wished me to socialize with his family. Apparently, Shukhrat's son from this marriage spoke good English. Ali was eleven years old, and I was unsure as to who would have taught him the language. To me, this was something out of the ordinary, and it therefore keyed up my curiosity and also concern.

Because of the dusk-to-dawn curfew, we went over to Shukhrat's home at 4:00 p.m. It was obvious that a great deal of preparation had gone into this visit. A plastic sheet serving as a tablecloth was neatly spread on the carpeted floor. It was bedecked with fresh fruit and salads. Having done a cost of living survey, I knew that the family had spent a great deal of money on this meal. It embarrassed me as I felt it to be unnecessary. But now it was time for the main event of the evening. Ali was going to sing for me in English.

The whole family was excited and closely watched me for reaction. Ali sang a very nice song in what appeared to be English, but in fact, it was not. It was a collection of English-sounding sounds that were joined together in harmony to create a melody. I clapped and praised Ali for his effort. I was also troubled by it. Here was a kid who was eager to learn, English in particular, and there was nobody to teach him. I have often heard fond and nostalgic stories about the American Peace Corps. They worked in Herat in the sixties, and many were English teachers. In fact, most of the older Afghans who spoke English were taught by members of the Peace Corps. When will they return? I was often asked.

At long last, the time had arrived for me to go back to New York on home leave. I was excited but also afraid. I had been away from home for almost a year. So many things had changed, and I was tormented by the fact that perhaps I could not be "normal' again. Living on my own for a year under such adverse conditions had turned me into a hermit. Could I socialize again?

I spent a few days in Kabul, writing reports and collecting my outstanding allowances. In those days, there were no banks in Kabul. All financial transactions were conducted by Afghan sheiks from the money market on the banks of the Kabul River. We were given a check drawn against a bank in Pakistan, and we got these cashed in the money market. The rates of exchange varied but the system worked, and millions of dollars were traded in this market each day. I had received a check for $1,400 in respect of allowances and cashed this at the money market. I happily stuffed the fourteen $100 into my wallet and thought nothing further about it.

When I got back to Manhattan, there were numerous chores that needed to be done, including payment of the utility bills. I walked to the Chase bank where I had an account and presented the cashier with two $100 bills. The cashier politely asked me to wait for a second, and the next thing that I knew was that my hands were cuffed behind my back and I was led to a security office at the back.

I was stunned at being treated like a criminal and inquired why I was being treated in such a humiliating way. As I was strip-searched, the officials said that they were going to charge me with possessing and passing counterfeit money. They opened my wallet and removed the remaining $1,200, which were also forged.

This put me in a very difficult position. I was a "preferred" customer at the bank, so I asked to speak to the manager. I had met him previously, and he understood that the explanation I had offered was genuine. After a very lengthy discussion, it was decided that the bank would not pursue criminal charges against me, but they would confiscate the $1,400.

I was unhappy but my options were limited. But I had to return to Afghanistan, and when I got to Kabul, I went to the chief of finance to seek reimbursement of the $1,400. His reaction was curt. I had received a check, which I had cashed and received the money. If the currency was counterfeit, I would have to take up this issue with the money market. I decided to bite the bullet and return to Herat as soon as possible.

As the UN team leader in Western Afghanistan, I had always felt that it was important that we maintained cordial relationships with all parties in this conflict. The muijhadeen controlled all the rural areas, and over the years, I had become friendly with many of them. In the spring and summer, like all the people of Herat, they loved going on picnics into the hills to breathe the air that was sweet and clean.

Daud was a Tajik commander in his early forties with no formal education. He was tall, charismatic, a born leader who had a following of sixty fighters all willing to give their lives for him. Besides, he appeared well funded. His men were well armed, they had plenty of ammunition, and their vehicles were relatively new.

As Daud spoke some English, we were able to directly communicate and enjoyed each other's company. On the following Wednesday, he sent an emissary into Herat and invited me to go on a picnic with him and his men. I consulted with Katibi, and he felt that that because Daud was such an influential Tajik commander, we were obliged to go.

Before dawn on Friday, our guide gently pounded on my gate. Kamal, AK-47 at the ready, charged to the gate. He recognized this clandestine emissary and ushered him in.

After breakfast of green tea, naan, and yogurt, we set off on foot. The easiest way to get to Daud's village was crossing a minefield that ringed Herat. We could have driven, but that would involve traveling forty miles north and then another eighty miles south. My national entourage was not happy with this arrangement, but nevertheless, we proceeded.

It was not yet dawn, and in the dark, I realized that it was not an easy to task navigating through this minefield with no light to properly see in what under normal circumstances to identify. But our guide was not only an expert but was also cautious, and I certainly respected him this. The final obstacle was the river. It was fast flowing, not very deep but cold. I have always had an aversion to water, having being dumped into the ocean at age ten and not being able to swim.

Once we reached the far bank of the river, Daud, resplendent in his silk turban and traditional garb, greeted us, and his body was bedecked with weapons. His warriors, who were also dressed in their Sunday best, accompanied him. After the long, warm, and somewhat repetitive Afghan greeting, we walked to a brick and clay house not far from the river. This was a place for men. Daud's family lived in an entirely different compound. I enjoyed the cold, fresh morning breeze as we sat on the roof to watch the sunrise. After the morning prayer, we all sat down to breakfast that was more like a banquet.

Being out of the city and with rural folk was an experience that was invigorating, liberating, and very satisfying. There was a festive spirit in the air, and I understood the fact that all of us humans must have a time to shed our worries, concerns, and sorrows and just relax. This was such a time. But then time and tide waits for no man, so on Daud's command, his men jumped up and start preparing for the picnic.

I had no inkling that this was going to be such a major event. A live sheep was loaded into one of the vehicles, as were many other items of intrigue. But Daud was not concerned with the detail or the logistics. His troops would take care of that. He asked Katabi and me to ride with him. We got into his new turbo Toyota Land Cruiser and drove into the hills, hotly pursued by his bodyguards who crammed into the back of a Toyota pickup.

The sun had risen and cast a warm glow on the meadows that were ablaze with color from the wildflowers—mainly poppy.

As we raced along this dirt track, I was amazed to see so much wildlife. There were birds, hares, mountain goat, and some deer. They all appeared to flourish despite the war that engulfed their domain. This experience led me to believe that Daud did not really know how to drive. It was a case of learn as you go. Finally we got to an elbow in the river where the banks were wrapped in green grass. This was our picnic spot. I was glad to feel mother earth beneath my feet again and was fascinated how clear the water of the river was, so translucent that one could clearly see all the fish swimming by.

Daud did not understand why I looked for such a long time with a fixed stare into the water. The fish, the fish, I said. He immediately understood that I wanted to catch some fish, and in a flash, he grabbed a hand grenade from his belt and was just about to toss it into the water when I stopped him. This angered him as he was just about to disseminate a whole school of fish that were swimming by. This was certainly not the time to raise the issues of conservation or to sow and spread ideas about a green earth.

As I had deprived Daud of the excitement of blasting fish out of the water, he now looked for alternatives. Soon he floated the idea of a shooting match. A target would be placed two hundred yards away, and we would use Daud's AK-47 to shoot at it. I was immediately cognizant of the implications of such a competition. The AK-47 was the tool of Daud's trade, but it certainly was not mine. The last time I had fired a rifle was during my military service over forty years ago. Besides, I knew enough about small arms to understand that the sights of a rifle must be zeroed in to the vision of the user. However, under these circumstances, I just could not back down from this challenge.

As I was the guest, Daud asked me to go first. I declined by stating that as the commander, it was his right and privilege to shoot first. He did and stepped up to the mark and sprayed the target with automatic fire but without a hit.

He was amused and said that any enemy in the vicinity of the target would be killed in any case, coming under such a hail of gunfire. I am sure that he was right. He gave me his rifle and a fresh magazine of ammunition. I loaded, took aim, and fired. My first round hit the target. Daud immediately wanted to know what I was trying to prove. The explanation was simple. Now that I have eliminated the enemy with one round, I therefore had lots of ammunition to deal with any further threat. In retrospect, I understood that I had overplayed my hand. I had humiliated Daud; the only saving grace was that most of his men were not around.

I was often called to Peshawar in Pakistan for consultations. Getting out of Afghanistan was always a welcome break. After our meetings, I was told to drive to Kabul and then catch the UN plane to Herat. I loved taking this road trip. It took you through the scenic and historic Khyber Pass that overlooked Afghanistan.

We got to Jalalabad, the winter capital of Afghanistan, without incident and stayed in the UN guesthouse. So far, the journey, although long, was uneventful, and I felt relaxed and secure. From Jalalabad, we motored through the rugged hills that were the graveyard to so many Soviet soldiers.

The road was corrugated and full of potholes, a testament to the many Soviet tanks that once used it. The going was slow, backbreaking, but at least one had the comfort of knowing that the road was mine-free. Burned out tanks, trucks, and armored vehicles bore witness and proof to the intense fighting that took place along this stretch of road. These relics are a testament to the courage and effectiveness of the mujahideen against the might of the well-equipped invading Soviet Armed Forces.

There were numerous checkpoints along the route, manned by various commanders. The commanders levied a toll for passage through their territory, and nobody had the audacity to challenge them. The UN had right of way, and we were never stopped.

Before getting to Sorobi, a town near the high dam, I was warned that the area was under the command of a ruthless mujahideen commander who obtained money from all travelers using force, threats, and other unacceptable practices. I was told that he had a human dog that was unleashed on travelers who did not pay the toll.

I had to see this for myself. When we got to Sorobi, we went directly to the commander's compound. I cannot say that we were welcomed in the traditional Afghan way. The commander was indifferent, and his men just glared at me. Undeterred, I raised the question of the unique human dog.

He proudly walked me to a cage where a human on his hands and knees growled at me like a wild guard dog. I was speechless and almost vomited when I saw this person/animal unleashed on a traveler who could not pay the toll. The creature attacked the individual like a hyena, bighting, tearing flesh, and lapping the blood. This phenomenon was demeaning and depressing and disgusting. I subsequently learned that this commander had fled to England with millions of dollars and now ran a lucrative pizza parlor there.

It was stimulating working in Herat. Despite the trials and tribulations, we were able to make a difference in more than one way. When the fighting escalated and the situation became really untenable, the UN team was evacuated to Peshawar. We stayed at the Perl Continental Hotel. Staying there was like taking a vacation in paradise. The rooms were comfortable and clean, the beds were covered with fresh linen, all the rooms had running hot water for baths or showers, there was a swimming pool, but most importantly, the hotel had two excellent restaurants with an à la carte menus.

War zones are not famous for their cuisine, and Herat was certainly no exception. Then there was the shopping, daily newspapers in English, foreign magazines, no restrictions on movies, and a local population whom we could socialize with. We certainly recharged our batteries during our shot stays at the PC, as it was fondly called. Most international humanitarian staff working in Afghanistan treasure very fond memories of this hotel. I got a lump in my throat when I learned that the hotel was destroyed today by a vehicle bomb. Sixteen people were killed, including two UN international staff members.

Central Asia—Lifting the Iron Curtain

I had served in Herat for four years, and now it was time to rotate to another duty station. I received a communication from New York informing me that I had been posted to Bishkek in the Kyrgyz Republic. I had never heard of this country, and nobody else even had the faintest idea, except for the fact that it was in the former Soviet Union. Looking at a map, I found the Kyrgyz Republic but could not find the capital, Bishkek. The Soviet Union had just collapsed, and UNICEF decided to open country offices in the five Central Asian republics, which were Kyrgyzstan, Kazakhstan, Uzbekistan, Turkmenistan, and Tajikistan. We affectionately called them the "five Stans." Little was known about the European part of the former Soviet Union, but even less was known about the Asian part, the Stans. I later discovered that Bishkek was known as Frunze during the Soviet era and appeared on all maps as such.

But how was I to get there? Because of the war, the airspace over Afghanistan was closed. Depending on the security situation, the UN operated a few flights in and out of Herat. I was informed that it was most important that I report for duty in Bishkek as soon as possible. I was instructed to drive. It was a very long way to drive, and I was unsure what sort of logistic support would be available en route. When I inquired, I was told not to be naive. "This was the former Soviet Union," yelled my boss over the radio. "They were a superpower, as you know, and therefore, all the in-country facilities will be super." I have since learned that one must never take the boss's words at face value.

By nature, I am comfortable with taking calculated risks, so to mitigate the circumstances, it was imperative that I planned the road trip very carefully. I treated it like a military operation by making a situation analysis and examining every possible scenario. The project vehicle that I would use for the journey was a new Toyota Land Cruiser. It had twin fuel tanks, giving it a range of about five hundred miles; it also had a roof rack, which increased its load carrying capacity. There were two spare wheels, and the vehicle was fitted with HF and VHF radio. I had maps, food, water, and cash, US dollars.

The entire journey would take four days if I drove twelve hours a day and if everything went according to plan. Unfortunately, I could not take my Afghan driver along as he did not have a passport, and even if he did, he would not be granted visas to enter the "Stans."

Just before I departed, I did a radio check, and all systems were working and in good order. I felt that this would be an exciting and educational journey into the unknown. The drive from Herat to Murray on the Turkmenistan side of the border was uneventful, and I was able to cross the border with no problem. What I had not realized was that I would be functionally illiterate as soon as crossed the border.

All the road signs were in Russian and written in Cyrillic. My maps were in English, and as I did not speak Russian, I therefore could not ask for directions. I felt that my planning was not as my meticulous as it should or could have been. But the problem had another dimension to it. Very little was known about the Soviet

Union in the West. We had vague ideas and some information, but most of it was outdated, distorted, and did not reflect actual conditions on the ground. But my options were limited, so I navigated as best as I could.

At the end of the first day's drive, I needed to refuel but had not seen a single gas station during the entire day's drive. Toward dusk, I stopped at a police checkpoint and, using sign language, indicated that I wanted fuel. The policemen were amused; they had not heard of the UN and were surprised to see all the communication equipment in my vehicle that also bristled with antennas. I had repeatedly tried calling our radio room in Almaty in Kazakhstan but was unable to reach them because of the extensive distance between us. At long last, my newly made Turkmen police friends decided to help and led me to a metal shed behind a house.

This was the local gas station. Two forty-four-gallon barrels stood in the shed. One had diesel and the other petrol. But there was one problem—they only took local currency. I had wanted to change money but could not find one bank en route as the whole banking system was in its infancy and banks did not have branches. Credit cards were unheard of. The police commander who accompanied me understood American dollars and agreed to pay for the fuel in local currency if I gave him two hundred dollars in advance.

I wondered how he arrived at this figure. What none of them knew was that I had twin fuel tanks and hoped that there was enough diesel in the drum to fill both tanks. I subsequently learned that the actual cost of the fuel was only $25 but was happy that I did not have to spend days stranded in the town, waiting for the next shipment of fuel to arrive.

It was getting dark, and I was tired and hungry. I just realized that I had not eaten all day. So using sign language once again, I asked for directions to a restaurant and a hotel. At the time, there were no hotels in small towns, and travelers rented beds for the night from the local town people. But this was not an issue, as I had made provision to sleep in my vehicle. I was then taken into the only State restaurant in town. The dining area was large but the place had no patrons. The only people there were the entire restaurant staff seated and eating dinner on the next table. I waited for service, but the policemen who were familiar with the situation pulled out a bottle of vodka from a plastic bag and started to drink. After about an hour and a half, a waitress nonchalantly sauntered to our table and asked me what we wanted.

Using sign language, I indicated food. "Netu," she responded. There was no food left as the staff had eaten it all. "Net problem," declared my police friends, who were finishing off their second bottle of vodka. They knew a place where we would find food. As this was the first Toyota Land Cruiser they had ever seen, they were fascinated with its looks; the interior and its performance impressed them. In assertive tones, they demanded to be allowed to drive. "Net," I responded politely. So without further ado, they directed me to a wooden shack on one of the side roads. I was taken aback by what I saw, so I wound down my window to take a better look. The aroma of fried meat was inviting even though the circumstances were not.

We entered a dingy small dimly lit room that appeared to serve as a restaurant, bar, and brothel. The tables were bare except for cans that served as ashtrays; the air was filled with tobacco smoke, the whiff of fried meat, and the stench of vodka and human sweat. I ordered some meat and bread, and my companions ordered more vodka. They had long forgotten their police checkpoint duties and were now all set to party the night away. Their boss asked me for another hundred dollars to pay for the food and drink. I was at their mercy and was not going to argue, even if I had known how to.

The food was served unceremoniously on metal plates. The meat appeared to be deep fried, and the bread was fresh—well, sort off. As no knives or forks were provided, one ate with one's fingers.

But I was quite used to this custom, having lived in Afghanistan for so long. My mouth was watering, so without further ado, I grabbed a chunk of meat and took a bite. Wow. This was not meat but a chunk of deep-fried pork fat. What an anticlimax. I guess eating lumps of salty deep-fried pork fat washed down with gulps of vodka is definitely an acquired taste. After my dinner of dried bread embellished with salt and pepper, I decided to call it a day.

I parked by the only street light that was working, pushed down the seats to form a bed, rolled out a sleeping bag, and was lulled asleep listening to the BBC World Service. This was my only lifeline to the world that I was familiar with. I was too stressed to really find sleep and wished that I had a few shots of vodka with my Turkmen police buddies prior to calling it a day. As soon as it was light, I woke up. I started to get ready to hit the road again.

I was startled to see a young boy with a bundle wrapped in a sheet balancing on his head, peering through the window. The fragrance of freshly baked bread floated in the air. He only knew local currency but also knew how to barter. He pointed to a Dubai Duty Free plastic bag and indicated that he would give me two naan for it. I came to learn that in those early days, soon after the collapse of the Soviet Union, a foreign plastic bag was a prestige item. People paraded them like we would a designer handbag.

My compass really saved the day. I had worked out in what direction I had to travel, and this succeeded. On the second day, I entered Kazakhstan. It was much more developed, and at nightfall, I was directed to a government "dacha," where I was given a room with clean linen and hot shower and invited to dine in the restaurant. The other guests were senior government officials who were accustomed to foreigners. The food was good, and after "thto gram" (one hundred grams) of vodka, I had an excellent night's sleep.

Reveille was at first light, and I was elated to find the restaurant open for breakfast. Before checking out, I was presented a bill for twenty dollars. This covered the cost of the room, drink, and all meals. Just before I departed, I tried calling on the HF radio our base in Almaty. I was pleasantly surprised that they responded immediately. They knew exactly where I was as they had been informed by the intelligence service, and they would continue to closely monitor the rest of my journey. With great excitement, I hit the road again. My Land Cruiser was turbocharged, so I normally drove at 80 mph. Most of the Soviet vehicles cruise at about 50 mph max and the trucks are much slower.

En route I got flagged down by the police. When I stopped, they immediately opened the driver's door and grabbed the ignition keys. I did not understand a word of what they were saying, so I called Almaty on the radio and asked for help. The UN Radio operator spoke to one of the police officers and all was well, but I was also asked to observe the 60 mph speed limit. On the outskirts of Almaty, I was met by a Kazak driver who spoke a little English. He drove me to Bishkek and then returned to Almaty by bus. This gave me the opportunity to relax and take in the countryside.

We got to Bishkek in the afternoon of the fourth day, and I checked into the only hotel in the city, which was government owned and operated. The building was uninteresting, and the establishment looked dowdy and tired. The lackluster attitude of the staff was unwelcoming and condescending. Each floor of the hotel was watched over by an old Russian woman known as "babushka." I am not certain what their exact function was, but I guess that they eavesdropped on all activity on the floor and had keys to every room. I soon realized that they also acted as pimps to augment their measly wages.

My room was very small and cramped, but I was glad that I had made it safely to my new duty station. After a shower, I was surprised to hear the phone ring. The voice at the other end said in English, "Beautiful little girl for you." I slammed down the receiver and was certain that the babushka had given this hooker my room number. Either business was bad or she felt that a foreign client pays well. Whatever was the case, she showed determination and was persistent in her approach. In the end, I just left the phone off the hook.

Before I fell asleep, I locked the door and made sure that the security chain was in place. I was woken up suddenly by the smell of cheap perfume. My door was ajar, letting in some hallway light. Standing next to my bed and getting undressed was this woman. I turned on the light, screamed, and she took off. It was obvious that she had a key to my room, but I still don't know how she was able to get past the security chain. This invasion on my privacy made me furious. I complained to the Kyrgyz hotel manager, who faked being surprised. He went on to say that she must be Russian, as their women are all prostitutes. I did not want to participate in this racist tirade and kindly requested that the lock on my room door be changed immediately. I was assured that it would be. It never was.

There were numerous challenges and constraints to establishing a new UNICEF country office in the Kyrgyz Republic. The local officials did not understand how the UN worked. Under normal circumstances, the host government provides quality office space to the Agency at no charge. With the collapse of the Soviet Union, all the kindergartens that provided free day care for children of working parents were shut down.

The government offered these vacant buildings to the UN and other international organizations wishing to establish a presence in the republic. At one stage, these were fine buildings. Neglect over the years, however, caused them to fall into disrepair. It would take vast amounts of money to rehabilitate them. I therefore decided to ignore this option. There was ample vacant space in other government buildings, but all were unacceptable as structurally, the buildings were dilapidated, the toilet facilities were appalling, housekeeping was terrible, and the security services flawed.

I accidently stumbled into a gated compound with four duplexes that were unusual. They were in excellent condition even though the external structure did not look extraordinary. I was told that during the Soviet days, the most senior members of the Communist Party, including the president, lived in this complex. Recently, the state privatized this building, and units were sold to the occupants for $25 apiece. As we looked around, one of the owners came out and inquired what we were doing. Through a translator I explained, and he said that he would be willing to rent his unit to us at $1,500 per month. The inside of the duplex amazed me—six bedrooms with hardwood floors through, three bathroom/toilets, all in perfect condition. This was exactly what I was looking for.

We drew up a standard UN lease agreement but had great difficulty explaining the document to the owner and his lawyer. Eventually, the deal was done, and we rented his fully furnished apartment, including Persian carpets and rugs. The next step was to recruit national staff. It was imperative that they were fluent in English.

I was swamped by applicants. Unemployment was extremely high, as most of the state-owned factories and plants had closed, the collective farms were in shambles, and the private sector was in an embryonic state. The government was the only other employer and was cutting staff even though they only paid paltry wages. I initially hired three people, and all of them spoke English. What concerned me was the fact that they were all physicians who were being hired to fill logistics and administrative positions. I had reservations about taking away these professionals from the health care system and discussed this issue with the minister of health. He did not share my concern.

This would be my last night in the hotel, and I looked forward to moving. I had informed the front desk of my morning checkout on the way up to my room. It was a long and exacting day, and I was glad it was over. Back in my room, I got out of my suit and put all my money and valuables on the writing desk before going down to the front lobby to buy my customary dinner, which consisted of a piece of bread that masqueraded as a pizza and a bottle of beer, which I brought up to my room. On my way down, I noticed the babuskha eyeing me in an unusual way. Striding behind her was a young man who ducked into her room as soon as our eyes met. They must know about my morning checkout. I was away for not more than ten minutes, but when I returned, I found that my room was ruffled and the $7,000 in cash that I had on the desk was gone.

I immediately called the Ministry of Foreign Affairs to complain. The desk officer on duty was polite but unconcerned. "Rudy, you know that even though your hotel is owned by the government, it is controlled by the mafia. You must move out from there in the morning."

"But what about my loss?" I inquired. "Oh, just claim it from your insurance. In America I am told that insurance pays you for whatever you lose. We do not as yet have this system in Kyrgyzstan." So the MFA knew about my morning checkout as well. Boy, news in this part of the world travels fast!

I now understood why UNICEF wanted to program in Kyrgyzstan. The children and women were among the most vulnerable segments of society. The infrastructure of the country had collapsed, and people who were disoriented and afraid were all of a sudden left to fend for themselves. In Soviet times, every need of the individual from the cradle to the grave was provided for by the state.

The state made available subsidized food, housing, health care, education, recreation, and employment. This robbed the population of their ability to fend for themselves because that had never done it before and just did not know how. In this society, people had their distinct roles and were told exactly what to do—with no questions asked or expected. There was no need for individuals to think autonomously. As Soviets, everything was done collectively as ordered by the state. The presumption was that there was no hierarchy as all Soviets were equal.

This indoctrination started at preschool. All the children had to dress exactly alike, and their day was regimented, including when and what they ate, when they slept, and for how long. The older kids went to pioneer camps, where they learned the virtues of being a Soviet, the advantages of communism, and the malevolence of capitalism. They sang songs in praise of Lenin and felt strong and secure because of the military might of the Soviet Union. In the summer, all older children were sent to work as volunteers on state farms and factories.

My translator said that she clearly remembers the period when the Soviet Union collapsed. She was afraid, felt exposed, and was petrified because she and her family and were unprotected against the evils of capitalism. I felt certain that she did not understand the true significance of entrepreneurship. Their unawareness coupled with years of Soviet propaganda made them anxious and vulnerable in a realm that was now different and unfamiliar to them. She asked me to explain how such a catastrophe could have ever occurred.

The masses felt betrayed and abandoned by their former leaders. I did not have the answer but could only surmise that the Soviet model was not sustainable in the milieu of the modern world. In Africa, people knew that if the rains failed, they would starve unless they found alternative ways and means of sustaining their families. This certainly was not the case in the Kyrgyz Republic.

When people lost their jobs, it was like a death sentence. They had never experienced this trauma before. Why me, what did I do wrong, and what will my neighbors say—that I am a failure? In their eyes, this was the worst thing that could ever happen to anyone; it was unknown and unthinkable. It was a personal stigma on the individual that branded them as misfits for life. These are proud people who always worked hard and gave their best, but now they were being robbed of their pride and esteem.

In order to conceal their predicament from their neighbors, they got dressed in the morning and left as usual for work. Many of these people told me how painful it was to spend the day out of sight, sitting in the park, being unproductive. They sustained themselves by liquidating their household assets. When I walked the streets of Bishkek, I saw many people standing on the sidewalk, trying to sell what little they owned. It was truly an awe-inspiring experience. These people were physiologically ill prepared to cope with the trauma that they now faced. Many were desperate, but the majority just could not deal with the situation. Many of the girls and women were forced into prostitution.

It was sad, and I blame the international community for exposing these helpless people to such suffering. My colleagues in the World Bank and the International Monetary Fund always used the term of this being a "transition" economy. I understood "transition" as being a process in which elements in the environment undergo a change and pass from one state, stage, form, or activity to another. But what were the indicators that this evolution was actually taking place and in fact working? Regrettably, I was unable to get an answer to this question. So we soldiered on, the blind leading the blind.

The mountains of Narin in Kyrgyzstan must be among the coldest on earth. But now the infrastructure that was designed to mitigate these harsh conditions had collapsed, thanks to the transition. The people were exposed to the extreme elements and could no longer cope. Homes were no longer heated, insulation was poor or nonexistent, only a few people had any winter clothing or footwear, and the overall nutritional status of the population was poor.

UNICEF had an extensive program to prevent acute respiratory infection (ARI) in the area. We provided technical expertise and the drugs to support this intervention. However, I felt that our actions were not far-reaching enough. The children did not have proper clothing or footwear and had to walk miles to school in bitterly cold temperatures. Once they got there, they were forced to sit more than six hours in a freezing cold classroom. Being malnourished worsened their predicament.

In order to reinforce our AIR Program, I felt that UNIICEF would have to supply coal for heating and winter clothing and boots to all children in need in Narin Province. My budget was limited, which ruled out me using the traditional UNICEF supply chain. I had to figure out ways and means to stretch my dollars by trying to reharness the existing but dormant capacity. Most of the coal mines were state owned, but production had ceased because all the equipment was in disrepair because they did not have operating capital. There was a huge market for the coal, but the people were so impoverished that they could not afford to buy it.

During the Soviet times, the state operated transport cooperatives that owned large fleets of heavy-lift cargo vehicles. These operations had now shut down as there were no funds to pay wages, and because of lack of maintenance, most of the vehicles were now unserviceable. So it would take innovation to get this show on the road again. I met with government officials and argued that if they supplied the coal at no cost, UNICEF would pay the transportation cost to get it to the remote villages.

The next step was to meet with the leaders of the transport cooperatives. I offered drivers wages and funds to buy fuel if the vehicles were repaired at no cost to us. The drivers were eager to get back to work and to demonstrate how skilled they were at what they did. So they repaired the required number of trucks by cannibalizing parts from other vehicles. These were hardworking, industrious people, and I learned to have great respect for them.

I crunched the numbers and concluded that there was enough money in my budget if all went exactly as planned. There was no margin for error or cost overruns. This was a massive logistic operation in difficult terrain and in extreme winter conditions. The risk and potential pitfalls were massive, but I drew consolation that I had navigated through some treacherous minefields in Afghanistan, and as long as I kept my cool, this operation would succeed. I was nervous and often wondered if I had bitten off more than I could chew. However, I understood that it was too late to turn back now. The winter turned out to be brutal, with well-above-normal snowfall and extremely cold temperatures.

I established an operations center in Narin high up in the mountains. One wall was covered with a large map of the area showing all the schools, the roads that we would use, and the coal mines that were designated by government to supply us the coal. We would use one hundred by twenty MT transporters, and we had established five mobile fuel stations that would supply the fuel to our trucks. I put a mechanism in place to ensure and prevent fuel being stolen.

Two days before the operation started, all vehicles, drivers, mechanics, and monitors assembled at an airfield in Narin. I held detailed briefings so that every player knew exactly what to do. I drew heavily on my experience and lessons learned when I was director of a very large UN humanitarian trucking operation in the desert in Northern Sudan. The only difference was that here you substituted sand for snow and lots of it. At the end of the first day of operations, I debriefed my managers. There were lots of hiccups, but eventually, the coal started to flow. We did not achieve our target, but I was encouraged that the team were adjusting to the challenges and adapting to the harsh weather conditions.

On the second day, I joined the team with the most difficult assignment. Their coal mine was high up in the mountains, and the approach road was narrow, unsurfaced, and had not been used for years. It was cut into the side of the mountain so that there were vertical drops on one side. It was snowing heavily, and therefore, it was difficult to determine where the road was. Mine was the lead vehicle, so I asked my driver to walk in front with a pole and direct me accordingly. The going was very slow, the surface was slick, and I was very concerned about going over the side. It took us four hours to cover the ten miles to the mine.

We all were delighted and relieved to reach the mine, but sadly, our troubles were not over. It was so bitterly cold that the mechanical loading shovels had frozen. We were forced to make an unplanned night stop at the mine. We had emergency rations but no sleeping gear. Some of our truck drivers were experienced mechanics, and without being asked, they started fixing the mechanical shovel. The caretakers at the mine said that they would sell me a sheep and some home-brewed vodka. I settled for the sheep, and the men cooked on an open coal fire.

Once we had eaten, our spirits got higher, and this was stimulated by the vodka that most of the men drank. I spent a very cold night, trying to sleep in my vehicle, which was more like a refrigerator. We were up before dawn, and the mine was a hive of activity. The mechanical shovel was back into action even though its capacity was limited. Slowly but steadily, the trucks were loaded. By noon, we were ready to make the descent down the steepest part of the mountain. The loads made the trucks more stable but put a tremendous strain on the engines. It took us three hours to reach the first village, and we arrived there just as it was getting dark.

The villagers were all energized and awaited our arrival with great anticipation. They could hear the screech of our engines for miles and wondered why it took us so long to get there. There had been no vehicular traffic in the area for years, and all their travel is done on horseback or on foot. On arrival, we were greeted by the villagers as heroes. It was a joyous occasion and a time to celebrate. After unloading 40 MT of coal at the school, I asked the chief where we could park our vehicles for the night. "Leave them where they stand," he responded in Kyrgyz. He cut a dashing figure dressed in a "chapang," a traditional overcoat, and a "kalpak," the traditional hat. It was pitch-dark, there was not a star in the sky, and the high winds were gale force and blowing snow, causing a whiteout. Proceeding in the dark would be death-defying. As I settled into my vehicle for the night, I reflected on the day.

So far, we were behind schedule by two days, but at least we had made our first delivery. I worried about the other teams. Although they were operating in less hostile terrain, their progress was very much slower than ours. However, I took comfort in the fact that all the vehicles and crew were safe. Because of the penetrating cold, I just could not find sleep. I wandered over to a coal fire, where the men sat huddled, chatting and drinking home-brewed vodka. They offered me a drink, and in the local culture, refusal is deemed to be an insult. But the home brew is real firewater, so I went to my vehicle and poured myself a shot of whisky. On returning to the fire, I took a swig, and the whisky tasted like nectar that would sustain by body and soul. It also acted like antifreeze, and once more, I could feel my blood flow.

At first light, we set off again. Because the going was so rough, we drove for two hours and stopped for ten minutes. During this time, the crews relaxed, decompressed, and smoked. I knew that we had been working long hours, and after so many days on the road, I was keen that the team does not lose focus. After delivering 400 MT of coal to twenty villages, we returned to base exhausted.

Just before I took a cold shower, I was told that the "hakim," governor of the province, was here to see me. It was an honor and privilege, but at this stage, all I wanted to do was sleep. But protocol demanded that I welcome my honored guest. The hakim was rapturous in his acclaim of our coal operation. He had numerous delegations from tribal elders admiring him for having such prudence and the audacity for formulating and carrying out such a daring but decisive operation that saved the lives of hundreds of people especially children.

I was happy to let him bask in the glow of adoration and glory. I was not going to tell his people that he profited from the operation and provided us with little or no support. But my greatest relief was that this part of the mission had now been accomplished. The next part of the equation was the purchasing of winter coats and boots for the kids. To short-circuit the process, I had a meeting with the Chinese ambassador in Bishkek. He undertook, and he assumed all responsibilities to make relevant arrangements in China. The following day, I flew to Urumqui, the capital of Xinjiang in China. On arrival, I was greeted by a bevy of very senior officials, but I cannot definitively say who or what role they played.

My government-appointed translator was a young Chinese woman. I was amazed at how outspoken she was. At dinner one night, she attacked me by saying, "Rudy, you Americans preach to us about human rights and democracy, but what do you actually do to nurture it in China? I would like to travel but do not have a passport. I am only given one when the government approves of my itinerary. Is this respecting human rights and dignity?" she inquired. "We are your biggest trading partner, but yet you ignore your principles and values in my country."

I shared her sentiment, but after what happened in Tiananmen Square, I feared for the safety and well-being of this young and courageous woman. However, I did not feel at liberty to engage in this conversation as I did not know whether she was in fact a government informant just trying to inveigle antigovernment reaction from me. I forced a smile and let the conversation drop. In retrospect, I am uncomfortable with this decision, as I feel that I did not cope with this challenge in an honest and honorable way. It took courage for this young person to speak to me in such a free and unfettered way.

Was she was candidly looking for support from the West in her quest for liberty and freedom? Or was I just being used by her?

The following morning, I met with a group of manufacturers. They listened and asked me for the exact specifications for the winter coats and boots. I wanted every garment to have a label to indicate that it was provided by humanitarian assistance and therefore could not be sold. But on reflection, I felt that it would humiliate the kids wearing these garments, so I dropped the idea. I learned a great deal from this visit. In the States, we often say that people speak Chinese. But in fact there is no Chinese language as such. Or we talk about Chinese food, and once again, this is an aberration. There are a numerous different cuisines in that country, and all of this are contingent to where in China you actually are.

I was amazed at how quickly the factories were able to respond to our inquiries. The entire order would be shipped in ten days. Now I would have to work out a distribute plan when I returned to Bishkek. But it was the weekend, and so I decided to travel to Kashgar. This historic Islamic city was famous as a political and commercial centre and was at one time mostly populated by Uighurs. The Uighurs are a Turkic-speaking people who are mainly Sunni Muslims who were the preponderant ethnic group in Xinjiang, the largest oil-rich administrative region in China.

Kashgar was also on the was the most traveled route from Gandhar in what is now Pakistan to Jalalabad in Eastern Pakistan. Kashgar's Old City is renowned as being the best conserved example of a traditional Islamic city in Central Asia. This celebrated nucleus of the Silk Road on which caravans transporting silk and jade from China converged with traders from Central Asia, transporting furs and spices, will soon vanish because it is slowly being bulldozed by the Chinese government in the name of modernization. But perhaps the main reason for this is that Xinjiang is a hotbed of Islamic fundamentalists who are agitating for an independent homeland.

Over the years, the Communist central government has been flooding Xinjiang with the Han, the main and most influential ethnic group in China. This has generated ethnic tensions in the region, and during my visit, I became acutely aware this was potentially an extremely explosive situation.

He who loves without discipline dies without honor - Central Asian saying

Kyrgyzstan is famous for its mountains and its heavy snowfall, but I am only aware of one operating sky slope just outside Bishkek. On evening, I had a few local guests over, and during the course of the conversation, I said that I intended trying out the local sky facility. A Russian single mom asked me if I would take her son along. He was born in Siberia and loved skiing but had not had the opportunity to do so since they came to Kyrgyzstan. He was twelve years old, and I decided to take him along.

I was suited up in my Canadian ski gear but was startled to see young Andrei dressed in cheap polyester tracksuit and canvas shoes. His mom was with him, so I did not comment. We got to the slope, and I was amazed at how antediluvian the lift equipment was. Open chairs conveyed skiers to the top of the mountain. There were no safety belts or, for that matter, any other safety device to ensure the safe passage of the skier.

I was nervous and looked at Kimerbeck, my driver. He had a huge grin on his face and said "Sovietkiisky." So Andrei and I jumped in our bucket as the lift did not stop at the station but kept rotating. The view was spectacular as we started our ascent up the mountain. My experience is that in most mountainous regions, the weather is unpredictable, and I could see gray storm clouds, but the wind was slight and I was reassured that there was no cause for concern.

However, I decided that we would only take one run down and then call it a day.

The tranquility was suddenly shattered by a pulverizing sound followed by an unnerving stillness. We were no longer moving but just dangling in the air. I glanced down and noticed that we were a long way from the ground. On top of us, there were several steel cables, which would make it impossible for a helicopter to rescue us. I had to smile as this was archetypal of me to start planning for a worst-case scenario before the occurrence. Andrei sensed my discomfort and said that it was normal for Soviet lifts to stop midway. There was probably a glitch in the system that made us stall, but it would be fixed and soon we would be on our way again. I so much wanted him to be right. I enjoyed the panorama from our suspended perch, but now, after one and a half hour, I started to get concerned. A cold wind had picked up, and it was clear that we were in the path of a threatening winter storm. Andrei had started to get blue from the cold, and he shivered all over. I knew that this was caused by not only the cold but also by fright. I wrapped my warm down-filled parka around his frail body; this gave him comfort. He gave me a charming and appreciative smile and rested his head on my arm. But now the wind had started to pick up, and our chair began lurching around like a drunken sailor. In a way, it felt to me like a ripe mango, ready to drop off the tree at any moment. It was also getting dark. I glanced upward and noticed the people above showing signs of desperation. They were flimsily dressed and were jumping up and down to try and keep warm. I said a prayer in silence, and no sooner had I finished than we started to move again after being stranded for three hours.

When we got down, Kammibeck rushed to our gondola and shouted, "Rudy, are you OK?" He had two blankets with him and immediately draped one around my shoulders. Andrei's mom was hysterical as she was certain that her only child had frozen to death. Then Kammibeck told me the story. When he saw the lift come to a standstill, he rushed to the operator and asked him what was the matter. No power was the answer. On our way up, he had noticed a power station and, looking down the mountain, the lights emanating from it. "But they have power," retorted Kammibeck, pointing to the lights in the distance. In a nonchalant manner, the operator said that they had been warned that if the outstanding bills were not paid immediately, the power would be shut off.

Kammibeck jumped in his Land Cruiser and sped down the mountain. He demanded that that the power to the ski lift be turned on immediately. But they did not have the keys to do this as the manager had taken them with him when he left. Kammibeck grabbed one of the workers and hustled him into the vehicle. "Take me to the manager's house," he roared as they sped off to the village. After banging on the back gate for a significant period, the gate was opened by a young boy. "Where is your father?" Kammibeck demanded in an authoritative voice. "Drinking vodka in that house" was the response. Storming into the house, they grabbed the manager, who was half-drunk, and dragged him out. Kammibeck intimidated him by saying that there was a very senior foreigner stuck on the lift, and if he did not turn on the power immediately, he would be banished to the Gulag for life. As soon as the power was turned on again, Kammibeck raced back to the lift station, leaving the drunken manager to fend for himself. I had hired Kammibbeck because he was an officer in a Soviet tank battalion. As an ex-soldier, I am so very glad that I did. But then, all is well that ends well.

Iodine-deficiency disorders posed a substantial public health problem in the Central Asian republics at the time. This insufficiency causes needless mental impairment, goiters, and cretinism. A simple and inexpensive remedy is to add iodine to salt. Public health experts in the Central Asian republics were conscious of this fact but could do little to bring about change because of the related cost. All the salt used in these countries is harvested from the Aral Sea. It is therefore cheap and sold unrefined for use by humans and animals.

The most efficient equipment for iodizing salt was manufactured in New Jersey on the outskirts on New York. I sent an e-mail to the manufacturer, and they would offer us the equipment at a very preferred price. However, they warned that the transportation cost would be exorbitant. At a reception, I explained my quandary to the American ambassador. She did not react, but I was satisfied that she understood the significance of this initiative and was very supportive of it.

About a week later, the ambassador called. "Rudy, I have a solution to your problem." She went on to explain that that Burnham and Bailey circus in the USA had chartered a cargo aircraft to fly from New York to Bishkek to pick up some Kyrgyz horses and their riders. They were willing to donate the entire cargo capacity of twenty tons to UNICEF for the trip New York to Bishkek.

But there was a catch. The cargo had to be at LaGuardia the following day. I called New York but was informed that the lead time was not enough. The equipment had to be packed before transportation. It was Thursday and the start of a long weekend. I made a frantic call to the president of the manufacturing company. I explained to him the urgency and the opportunity that he and his business had to bring about instant change in the former Soviet Union. He was of course sympathetic and eager to make the deal, but unfortunately, he was not a miracle worker. I searched for options, but there were none. Late on Thursday, I received a fax from the producer informing me that the equipment had been packed and would be available for shipping early Monday. This information was of little consolation as this would not meet the deadline.

On Saturday morning, I received a fax from the charter operator saying that their aircraft had become unserviceable just before takeoff and that departure from LaGuardia had now been rescheduled at 1300 hours Eastern Time on Tuesday. If our cargo was delivered to their hangar no later than 1100 hours on Monday, it would be transported to Bishkek. I sent an urgent fax to the company and received confirmation that they would comply and deliver the equipment by 0900 hours. My team was ecstatic with the news, but it was premature to celebrate just yet.

Now I had to find a salt supplier with a large-enough production capacity to productively utilize the iodizing equipment. Once iodized, the salt has to be immediately packed into 1 kg plastic bags and sealed to prevent evaporation. I immediately ordered specially printed plastic bags from China together with the appliance to seal the bags. Both of these items were inexpensive and would be delivered in days thanks to the congenial relationship we had developed with the Export Committee of Xinjiang Region.

There was a large salt-processing plant just outside Bishkek. They crushed the Aral Sea salt then bleached it and retailed it across the country in brown paper bags. The director was a progressive middle-aged man who was enthusiastic about partnering with an international organization. It took time, however, to convince him that he could no longer use the brown paper bags as they would leak the iodine. Besides, if his salt was marketed in plastic bags, the consumer would be able to see the quality of his product, which would increase sales. He was impressed with this line of reasoning but did not like my assertion that the cost of iodized salt must remain the same as ordinary salt as all additional cost would be absorbed by the UN. He was fast learning to be an entrepreneur and was not content at giving up this opportunity of making an extra buck.

A few days later, the equipment arrived, and it was immediately installed and tested by an American technician. For the first time, salt was being iodized in the Kyrgyz Republic, and this was a major public-health step forward for the nation.

But we were not out of the woods yet. We faced the challenge of creating public awareness to the importance and advantages of only consuming iodized salt. Social marketing was a new notion in this infant republic. Winning over traditional former Communist officials and getting them to accept new Western ideas was no straightforward task. These people were set in their ways and, as Soviets, were habituated to doing what they were told without thinking or questioning. Not being used to this mentality, I had to ponder on how to harness this suppressed energy.

In a short period, I was able to establish an excellent discourse with the chief national physician. It took little persuasion to get her to agree to be the nucleus of our public-education campaign. Being ethnic Kyrgyz, she spoke the national language, was educated and trained in Moscow, and had achieved national eminence. Similar campaigns had been tried and tested by the UN worldwide, so all we had to do was to adapt an existing ethnically analogous promotion to meet indigenous needs. With excellent local talent, this was easily done, and our crusade received wide national coverage at no cost on the state-controlled mass media. A few years later, I was delighted to see salt that was iodized in the Kyrgyz Republic being sold in other Central Asian republics.

The whole country lies on a major fault line and is therefore very prone to earthquakes. Just before dawn one day, I received a call from the duty officer at the Office of the President. A major quake measuring 6.2 on the Richter Scale had just occurred in the mountains, doing serious damage to a village, with loss of life. The president was going to visit the affected area and asked that I accompany him. I got to the presidential helicopter pad at the appointed time and was delighted to see my colleague, the country director of the World Bank, also there. Also present were five government ministers and other officials. As soon as the president arrived, we all shook hands and boarded two Soviet Mi-8D helicopters. The president and his most senior officials were in one machine, and the rest of us climbed into the second. I had never flown in a Soviet aircraft before and was appalled at how indefinite things were. We were seated in canvas netting seats, and my seat belt did not work. There were two large drums of fuel in the passenger cabin, with rubber hoses connected to them. I surmised that this was the auxiliary fuel tanks. When the engines were switched on, the sound in the cabin was deafening, and the fumes from the engines were intoxicating. If anyone lit up, we would be charred toast. I later learned that this helicopter was the most massively produced helicopter in the world, and I now understand why the manufacturers disregarded passenger safety and comfort. The only consolation was the fact that these were technically sound machines.

Presidential security dictated that we were not informed of our final, destination but when we landed, the village appeared familiar to me. The destruction caused by the quake was indeed massive. A gigantic rock slide buried all the homes in its path, hence the heavy toll on life and property. We were high up in the mountains, and the weather started to change. A cold wind blew from the north, and I regretted being dressed in a business suit.

The entire village had turned out to greet the president, and this was probably the first time that they had ever seen their head of state. So despite the death and destruction that surrounded them, the overall mood was festive, and I have no doubts that this was stimulated by a few shots of vodka. The bottom line is that these are resilient people who have long learned how to cope with adversity despite overwhelming odds. Being an introvert, I shunned the limelight and decided to hang back and go with the flow.

There was a folding table with four chairs perched precariously on a slope. It was covered with a hand-embroidered tablecloth, and an empty pickle jar served as a vase for some freshly cut indigenous mountain blooms. It was obvious that this would the president's perch. Like vultures, the ministers circled the podium to claim a place at the table of power. This was very understandable because the national media were present and had started beaming live pictures to Bishkek. But suddenly, the silence of the extraordinary mountain air was broken by a loud holler from the head of state. "Where are Michael and Rudy?" he inquired, and I smiled to myself to see his staff scramble. In short order, we were whisked to the front, and the ministers who were jockeying for positions of eminence were relegated to the second row.

This was the start of the formal ceremony. The village elder made the opening discourse in the Kyrgyz language, and his speech focused on flowery salutation for the president and his party, followed by an extensive wish list of all the things that he personally wanted and a few others for his people. In the rural areas of Kyrgyzstan, very few people spoke the then official language, which was Russian. My Kyrgyz-born Russian translator only spoke Russian, so both Michael and I were unable to follow the proceedings. The president spoke next. He opened his remarks in Kyrgyz and then switched to Russian for the benefit of his urban-dwelling people. Michael was then introduced. The World Bank was a major player in the development of this young nation, and the president was happy that the country director of the World Bank was present to see the damage and the need for the provision of emergency assistance to help the people. The audience rose to their feet and cheered; this was quickly followed by pleas for help. I did not comprehend either as my translator only spoke the official language, which was Russian. The head of state was now given the platform to address the nation. He started off in Kyrgyz and then introduced Michael. The audience all rose to their feet clapped and cheered wildly as they understood that Michael would leave them with a trunk full of money to pay for reconstruction.

The president then started to introduce me, but no sooner had he started to speak than he was brusquely interrupted by an "asakal" (traditional elder). He looked dignified with his white beard and weather-beaten skin. He was dressed in an elaborately embroidered traditional winter overcoat called the "chapang." Around his waist and acting as a belt was a brightly colored sash, and on this head he had a white and black time-honored wool headdress called the "kalpak." His trousers were tucked into knee-high black riding boots, and on his right shoulder perched a magnificent fully grown hooded hunting falcon.

He then let the president know that there was no real need to introduce me. I had visited the village twice before—once to deliver much-needed coal, and on the second occasion, we distributed winter coats and boots to schoolchildren. He did not say too much about the children's clothing but was drawn out in his praise for the coal delivery to the village school. I guessed that this was because he had misappropriated some of the coats and boots and did not wish to dwell on this issue. So no introductions were necessary as his people knew me well. Turning to me, the president said laughingly, "Now I know why my people call you 'uncle.'" I had to respond and undid the UNICEF tie that I was wearing and presented it to the president, saying that it would more appropriate if he wore it as the "father of the nation." He wore the tie on a number of subsequent occasions, and I felt that this was a very good advocacy tool for UNICEF.

We were then invited to lunch. The weather had started to change, and dark clouds now obscured most of the mountain peaks. A wind had also picked up, and I became concerned about our flight back home. The president and his ministers were unperturbed. The party had started, and the vodka was flowing freely. The old guards of Soviet leaders were well known for their capacity to drink, and the president was no exception. In Soviet custom, one had to make a toast before gulping down the neat vodka in one swig. Soon the speakers were becoming incoherent, so Michael and I excused ourselves and left the room.

In the courtyard, we saw the ethnic Russian helicopter crews walking back and forth with edginess. I asked my translator to find out if they were concerned about the weather that was fast closing in. They were, and if we did not take off immediately, we would not make it out of the mountains. Unfortunately, they were not in a position to convey this to the president. Michael and I decided that we would. We went back into the room and told the president that both of us were feeling poorly. It was due to the rare mountain air and the vodka. The president countered by saying that he understood. We were not Kyrgyz and therefore not used to the high mountains or the vodka. Everyone laughed loudly, and the joke was on us. But the point was made, and the presidential party rose to their feet and left the room. I was hoping that they would proceed directly to the aircraft and we would take off immediately. Not the case. Everyone needed to go to the toilet and have one for the road.

The crew was in their machines, and they were revved up ready to go. As soon as the last person staggered into the lead helicopter, the door was slammed shut and the engines started. I don't think that the crews did their pretakeoff checks because there was no time. Because of poor visibility and the lack of sophisticated navigation equipment, they ascended almost vertically in order to avoid slamming into the mountains. From the intense roar of the motors, the intense violent shuddering and throbbing of the cabin, and the strong smell of combusted jet fuel, I could tell that the aircraft were being operated at full throttle. Normally, there would be only two crew members in the cockpit. The engineer, the load master, and the second captain would be lounging around in the passenger cabin. This time it was different, and all of them were on the flight deck. I went forward and noticed how anxious the crew appeared. It was obvious that they were struggling to gain height. We were now at sixten thousand feet, but I don't know how much higher they could coax the aircraft to climb. It was noticeable that we were in trouble. Visibility was down to a few feet, and the strong crosswind worsened matters. I returned to my seat in the cabin and noticed that all the nationals were fast asleep and oblivious of the peril they had placed us in. In a way, they were fortunate that the vodka had sedated them. Michael, who was sitting at the back of the cabin, gave me a thumbs-down sign, and I responded similarly. There was nothing that we could do, and our faith was in the hands of the Lord. As it struggled to gain height, I felt that the airframe of our helicopter was being put under so much pressure that it would shatter. The only consolation was that we were still flying and had been airborne for about two hours. The outward journey had taken two hours, so we should be reaching our destination soon, I surmised.

After what appeared to be hours, we started a very rapid descent. Soon, I could now see the ground a road and a large body of water. We were over Lake Issykul and out of the mountains. I saluted the crew for their superb flying despite the numerous constraints. Their skill ensured that we will have the same number of landings as take-offs. When we got to the helipad, I was greeted by my very agitated driver. "Rudy, I was afraid that your plane was lost in the mountains. This is not weather that you should be flying in." I dared not tell him the whole story.

A real man must keep his word, as every lions roar is heard - Uzbek saying

The disintegration of the Soviet Union in 1991 was without a doubt a historical event. Newly independent republics emerged in Central Asia, and their leaders appealed to the people to embrace the unity of the past to guide the infant nation through a doubtful, difficult future caused by the painful disengagement of their countries from the of Russia economy. This resulted in the collapse of the national economy and infrastructure, and as a consequence, there was mass unemployment and poverty, and all of this eventually transformed into to despair. Communist philosophy ridiculed nationalism as being disruptive to their principles, and the Soviet Government did whatever it could to stamp out ethnic languages, culture, and traditions and, in its stead, promote the concept that all nationalities should be proud of being Soviet. In the early 1930s, the Soviet government started a campaign to get rid of "The Epic of Manas" from school curricula, and certain parts were falsely interpreted to undermine Kyrgyz nationalism.

To try and restore national pride and patriotism, the government decided to hold an elaborate international Manas one thousandth festival. I personally felt that despite the very valid reasons for wanting to restore patriotism, the timing for this manifestation was wrong. The country was bankrupt, there was massive unemployment, and even those who were fortunate enough to have jobs were not getting paid. Besides, the 22 percent minority Russian population were appalled that so much money was being spent to manifest something that was so very abstract. This view was shared by the other minor ethnic groups like the Jews, Germans, Koreans, Chinese, etc. They all felt that this event was designed to promote ethnic tensions and create a split in a society that existed in perfect harmony during the Soviet era.

For the many Kyrgyz Muslims, their faith in Manas was based on the belief that he was a Muslim and that it was through him that Islam was spread. As with other great larger-than-life stories, there is an enormous difference in opinion as to whether the events in the tale actually happened and if Manas himself is, in reality, a real historical figure.

Despite my skepticism, I drove in convoy with the American ambassador to Talas, which is about 250 miles west of Bishkek, to officially participate in the festivities. When we arrived at the Manas showground, I was amazed at the profligacy and excessiveness of this undertaking. On entrance, each delegation was assigned a separate yurt, which would be their home from home. The yurts, magnificently decorated and manned by a Kyrgyz family, dressed in their brightly colored traditional costumes. It was all very festive and certainly convivial. At the entrance stood a young maiden resplendent in her traditional garb. She performed a custom of offering us naan and salt. This ancient custom demonstrated honor and respect for one's guest. We were then led into the yurt and in accordance with local ritual and then invited to be seated on richly embroidered felt carpets on the floor. A banquet of traditional Kyrgyz cuisine was laid out in the middle of the yurt, including fresh fruit, juices, and vodka. I was very interested in who was paying the bill and asked my host. To my surprise, I was told that individual families were. They had no choice. They were selected by the "hakim" (governor), and that was that. This family had to sell some precious livestock to pay for this wingding. This news disgusted me, and pretending that I had an upset stomach, I refused to eat or drink anything. After a while and accompanied by our host, we toured the showground.

I was astounded to see the whole area fenced off. Hundreds of Kyrgyz villagers stood on the outside, naturally wanting to get in and participate in the celebration. I was informed that today's event was for foreigners only.

As we walked the beautiful pavements of the Manas village that was designed to reflect Kyrgys weavings, I once again contemplated on how imprudent this undertaking was. Millions of dollars had been spent to inject a resilient mix of history, independence, patriotism, and self-determination into the hearts and minds of the Kyrgyz people. Yet they were not permitted to be spectators and witness this manifestation intended to glorifying Manas and his contemporaries.

We watched hundreds of costumed performers bring to life "The Epic of Manas." The Kyrgyz people are superb horsemen. Both men and women start riding at a very early age. Dressed in detailed period costumes, they mounted an incredible horse show, and now I knew why Burnham and Belies wanted them in their show. The culmination of the performance was Manas's victory over the forces of evil. For me, this was an action-packed day, full of excitement, drama, spectacle, and entertainment. But I cannot justify the spending of millions of dollars on an event that does little to diminish the hunger and poverty that so many people have to contend with in their daily lives.

Having served in the country for almost three years, I was coming to the end of my tour of duty in the Kyrgyz Republic. Over the years, I had many friends in government and was in a privileged position that I could go and see the president when necessary. In addition, I had a cordial relationship with the ministers and regional governors whom I worked with. We had helped form and train and supported nongovernmental organizations that worked to provide support in the best interest of children and women and had advocated vigorously that the Kyrgyz Republic ratify the convention on the rights of the child, which they did. During my twenty years of service with the United Nations, I have come across and worked with many volunteers of the American Peace Corps. Without exception, they have been excellent ambassadors of our country. They are hardworking, are committed, speak the local language, are respected, and live with the communities in which they serve. In most cases, they emerge as the leader of the village, and locals seek their guidance on many diverse topics.

In the Kyrgyz Republic, some of the Volunteers helped with the implementation of some of our programs. For example, we had a major campaign to promote breast-feeding. A lactation expert who had just retired after an extensive hospital career in America was now a volunteer in Narin Region high up in the mountains. She gladly agreed to provide technical support to the Regional Health Director on lactation, and this tremendously improved the quality of our programs. This experiment worked so well that I expanded it to other areas, and many volunteers subsequently wrote to me, saying how rewarding their time with UNICEF was.

My birthday was few days away, and I must admit that I have never celebrated the occasion before. But in Central Asia, the customs are clear. Birthdays were a significant event worthy and warranting a whooping celebration. The staff party was organized by my secretary. There were balloons, a live band, food, drink, dancing, but strictly no presents. In addition, I was going to have a special lunch party for some youngsters at the new Pakistani restaurant that had just opened and was the talk of the town. I went to the café and met with the owner. I wanted a buffet for thirty people with all the house specialties, including sweets. "Sahib, I am honored. Your patronage is most welcome, and I will ensure that this party will be very special. Oh, what will you all drink ?" I told him that as my guest would be young people, he was to only serve juice and pop.

Back in the office, I met with Gulsana, my child-protection officer. She had been working with a group of thirty street children. The majority were Russian and boys. She was amused that I wanted to invite these kids to such a fancy restaurant. After all, society's behavior toward these children is one of derision. They are treated like vermin, and nobody wants anything to do with them. But this was just my point. These kids were forced to live on the streets through no fault of their own. They are certainly not misfits but rather survivors because they were exposed to and had to cope with awe-inspiring impediments in their daily lives. On the day, I wanted all of them to be at the Lenin statue in the main square next to the restaurant.

Despite their tattered and dirty clothing, all of them had washed in a nearby fountain and were sparkling and very excited. Passersby wondered why this foreigner was talking with these outcasts. Gulsana led the way to the restaurant, and when we got there, the jaw of the owner dropped. He was certainly not expecting to be feeding and entertaining these vagabonds. But my guests were all very well behaved, they waited to be told where to be seated, and then Gulsana explained how they should serve themselves at the buffet. They could take what they want, eat as much as they liked, but no food should be wasted. As an example, Gulsana and I started off, and they followed us in a very orderly fashion. They were amazed at the variety of food available but appeared hesitant to pick and choose. Back at their tables, none of them had started to eat. Gulsana said that they were intimidated by the environment, and none of them knew how to use a knife and fork. "Tell them to use their fingers." Now they felt more comfortable and started to enjoy themselves. A group of them had rehearsed a song that they wanted to sing, and I was touched by this gesture. At the end of the meal, one of the older boys came up to Gulsana and asked about the leftovers. They would like to take it for their friends who were not here. Each of them had a doggie bag, and as they left, they came up to me individually to say thank you. When they had all gone, I went to pay the bill, and the owner said, " Sahib, I am shocked. These are normal children and so very well behaved. Today I learned a lot, and we as Muslims are required to be benevolent, and at the beginning, I was not. I am ashamed."

A few days later, I was sitting in a sidewalk café, drinking a beer, when I heard a young voice in the bushes say "Rudy sashlik." It was one of my lunch guests. He had to hide because they were not allowed to come anywhere near. I walked over with my translator, and Igor said that he wanted to buy me a stick of sashlik because it goes well with beer. He dashed off and, a few minutes later, returned with a stick of sashlik wrapped in a grubby piece of newspaper. I reached into my pocket for some money, but Igor flatly refused because this was his treat. It made me think. In order to give, you must have, and this is a great source of pride to humanity.

My next assignment was in Uzbekistan as head of an office in Tashkent. Although it was a lateral move, this was going to be a difficult assignment because the present relationship between the government and UNICEF was strained. To my mind, no UN agency can function effectively without the full cooperation of the host government. But before I transferred to my new duty station, I was nominated to represent the UN at an international conference that would review the progress being made in dismantling the old Soviet Union nuclear test facilities at Semipalatinsk, located on the steppe in northeast Kazakhstan. I was surprised at being given this assignment as my knowledge of nuclear disarmament was rather limited. When I queried my participation, I was told that it was important for the UN to have a diplomat attend these gatherings as an observer. We flew to Almaty and then drove to Kurchatov City, named after Igor Kurchatov, the leader of the initial Soviet nuclear program. This was once a very beautiful municipality located on the Irtysh River. In its heyday, the city was a hive of activity and the home to the best physicists and scientists in the Soviet Union. Being a top secret Soviet installation, it was only known by its postal code, Semipalatinsk 21. For the best part, the scientists, their families, and all the workers were confined to the city. Therefore, the facilities, living conditions, and quality of life were excellent. However, today the town is drab and rundown. Most of the buildings were empty and in the state of decay. There was garbage all over the place, and the concrete apartment buildings were almost vacant and crumbling. In 1947, Mr. Beria, who was head of the Soviet atomic bomb project, carved out vast chunks of steppe for use by the project, and Gulag labor built the facilities. The first Soviet atom bomb was exploded in 1949 from a tower at the Semipalatinsk Test Site, causing fallout that rained down on villages in the vicinity. Dwellers were not warned and had no idea about the health risks they were being exposed to.

Subsequently, a further 100 above ground explosions were conducted in this area. In the days of splendor, the city and the test site was heavily guarded by the Soviet Army, and acres of obsolete tanks and MiG fighters bear testament to this. I was intrigued to see some Pakistanis and Iranians shopping in a bazaar on the outskirts of this facility. When I inquired who they were and what were they doing here, I was informed that they were trying to recruit Russian scientists and were offering them up to $3,000 per month to work on the nuclear programs in their home countries. In local terms, this was an extremely attractive offer. They were also shopping for nuclear material, military spare parts, and ammunition. Because of poverty, and out of desperation, military officials were willing to sell anything. No questions asked. As these scientists were unemployed, bored, and broke, many took whatever they were being offered. However, the best and brightest scientists were recruited by the CIA and sent to America.

At dinner that evening, we met with many of the permanent staff of the test site. I sat next to a Russian general who was the overall commander of the facility. He was dressed in his full military dress uniform, and his chest was covered with medals and decorations. After consuming a great deal of vodka, he became very lucid and outspoken. He lamented that he and the entire staff at the test site had spent their whole life working on this project and developed a nuclear arsenal that made the Soviet Union a superpower. "We were respected and feared by the imperialists. Our people were happy and safe. Everything was available, including work, food, health care, education, and recreation. The Soviet Union dominated the Olympic Games, and we held our heads up high. After all, it was the Soviet Union that sent the first man into space from Baikonur Cosmodrome, which is not far from here. But you capitalists have succeeded in destroying our world and have brought nothing but pain and suffering on our people. I have to witness the destruction of the very facility that kept us safe and proud." I felt empathy with the general. He viewed us as vultures feasting on the carcass of their lifelong work.

The Semipalatinsk test site was of immense interest to the West, especially the United States. Of specific interest were the explosions that were carried above ground and 340 underground explosions known as borehole or tunnel shots. Research was also carried out in this facility to develop a nuclear-powered spaceship. We visited the radioactive "hot spots" and viewed clean operations and were told that all the enriched uranium had been successfully transferred to the United States.

The "Man of the Year" salutation was a very special event on the Kyrgyz political and social calendar. A panel of experts chaired by the president chooses one national man as "Man of the Year." This is in recognition of their outstanding service to the nation. This year it was different. An expatriate, a colleague, and head of the UN Country Team, Ercan, was selected. This was a tremendous honor for Ercan, who had given tirelessly to the Kyrgyz people, and we in the UN family were thrilled. I delayed my departure to attend the ceremony that was presided over by the president. After all the accolades were read and sung, Ercan was presented with a superb Kyrgyz stallion and a hunting falcon. UN rules require that all gifts are reported to New York, who would issue disposal instructions. At coffee next morning, I asked Ercan what response he got from the secretariat. He said that they were delighted but wanted nothing to do with the stallion or the falcon. We laughed before we parted.

I was no stranger to Tashkent, the capital of Uzbekistan, and have visited the city often. This is an impressive cosmopolitan metropolis with its tree-lined avenues, the streets are clean and safe, and there is a highly efficient subway system, with theaters, museums, art galleries, sidewalk cafés, and a host of cultural activities, including world-class ballet at twenty-five cents a ticket. I was excited that this was going to be my home for the next few years. Besides, the winters are less harsh than in Kyrgyzstan. I was able to rent a large traditional-type house that was surrounded by a high perimeter wall, it had a central courtyard, and there were a number of fruit trees in the garden. The building was owned by a Jewish individual from the ancient city of Bukhara, and as he was in the process of migrating to the United States, he demanded that the rent be paid in dollars into his New York City bank account. In this way, he circumvented currency-control regulations and also avoided paying all local taxes. As a foreigner, it was easy to rent a house for a reasonable rental rate if one paid in dollars. As my salary was being paid into a Manhattan bank account, this arrangement suited me fine.

The city of Tashkent was the center of Soviet industrialization, starting in the 1920s, but the pace picked up significantly during World War II. This was because all major factories were repositioned from western Russia to safeguard the Soviet manufacturing capacity from the invading Nazi armies. At the same time, ethnic Russians were also moved to the more secure environment of Tashkent.

My first task was to mend fences with our government counterparts. I adopted a strategy of listening and learning. The source of the antagonism soon became clear. The Uzbeks do not like to be preached or dictated to. To bring about change, one had to gradually get them to accept a concept and then adopt it as their own. Using this philosophy, the government's attitude started to change. They moved unhurriedly in the initial stages but nevertheless progressively. We had now established a free and frank discourse, and they understood and accepted the fact that the UN acted as a conduit to the global experience, but it was entirely up to the government to adopt and accept what models they choose.

The regime requested that our programs be concentrated in the Karakalpakstan Region. At the time, I did not understand the implications. But this is a region that surrounds the Aral Sea and is mainly populated by ethnic Kazaks. Many of them wanted the territory to secede to Kazakhstan. But the Aral Sea basin is purported to be rich in mineral resources, including oil and gas, so the Uzbek government did not hinder migration from Karakalpakstan into Kazakhstan, but the breakaway of the province would not be tolerated. Karakalpakstan was a "closed area" during the Soviet times, so entry and exit was tightly controlled.

The Aral Sea is often described as an environmental catastrophe, and it was depressing for me to witness the reality of the situation. It is obvious that this vast sea will soon disappear. Already the waters are infinitely polluted as a result of Soviet weapons testing, the dumping of manufacturing waste into the sea, and the substantial runoff of chemical fertilizers used in the cotton fields. The widespread problem is that the wind now blows salt from the miles and miles of dry seabed into populated areas. This destroys crops, and it pollutes drinking water and causes enormous public health problems for the people living in the area. On these grounds and despite the ulterior political and economic motives of the government, I decided to focus some of our interventions in this region because the need was so great. Our assessments indicated that interventions were urgently needed, all designed to provide protection to the most vulnerable women and children.

But what caused this environmental catastrophe in the first place? In 1918, the two rivers, the Amu Darya and Syr Darya, which fed the Aral Sea, were diverted by the Soviet government to irrigate a desert to enable them to grow cotton, or "white gold" as it was called at the time. This policy made Uzbekistan one of the largest exporters of cotton in the world today. The problem was that the irrigation canals that were constructed were of inferior quality, and in some cases, over 75 percent of the water was wasted. From the early 1960, the Aral Sea began to shrink. Fishing, which in the heyday employed over forty thousand people and produced one sixth of the Soviet Union's total fish catch, completely vanished. Nukus was a harbor town with a number of fish-processing plants. But today, the nearest stretch of water is more than 150 miles away. In addition, the Soviet government built and operated a very large biochemical weapons research and test site on Vozrozhdeniye (Renaissance) Island in the Aral Sea. At this facility, extensive experiments were conducted using extremely dangerous toxins such as anthrax and radioactive materials, and as part of their biological warfare program, they experimented with microbial agents of the plague, typhoid, and smallpox. Recent tests have shown that there is now a passage of the buried material to the surface. The island also served as a depository for large quantities of spores for the bacterial agent of anthrax and other disease-instigating bacteria and viruses.

Since being decommissioned in the early 1990s, the facility was abandoned and remains unprotected, unmarked, and risky. As the waters of the Aral Sea recede, it will so be possible to walk from the mainland to the island on a peninsula, giving easy accesses to the tons of bioweapons that were disposed off in a hurry by being buried on the island. The biochemical weapons material is now easily available to plunderers and terrorists. There are reports that rats, rodents, and other animals have made their way on to the island, and this creates an immense possibility of an animal-sustained pandemic.

A former Soviet paratrooper named Juma Namangani formed a militant Islamist group called the Islamic Movement of Uzbekistan (IMU) in the midnineties, and they have operated with the Taliban in Afghanistan and Pakistan. The IMU has grassroots support in the Fergana Valley of Uzbekistan, and I believe that trying to retrieve some of the bioweapons may one day be an attractive proposition to this terrorist group—that is, if they have not done so already.

I worked closely with the minister of health, developing health-related programs. He obtained his medical degree in Moscow and was a refined and cultured man who was very interested in what was going on in the world. When I was in Nukus, he always invited me to his home, and we spent hours discussing global politics and the state of the union. His wife, who was also ethnic Karakalpak, obtained a doctorate in fine arts from Moscow University. My knowledge of art is limited, but it gave her great pleasure telling me about famous national and Russian artists. In the course of a conversation, she mentioned that she was the curator of the Nukus Art Museum. I did not know that one existed, so she invited me to visit.

The museum opened in 1966, and it houses the largest collection of Russian avant-garde paintings in the world. It is home to a collection of eighty two thousand pieces of Central Asian and Russian artists, all stored in a cramped, moist basement. The Russian painter, archeologist, and collector Igor Savilsky first visited Karakalpakstan in 1950. He made it his home and started collecting ultramodern paintings of Klimet Red'ko, Iyusov Popava, Ivan Koudriachov, and Robert Flak. These painters were already well known in Western Europe, but their works were banned in the Soviet Union. So Savilsky figured that because of the inaccessibility of Nukus, the collection would go undetected and therefore be safe. Needless to say, he ran the risk of being detected, and if and when he was, he would be branded an enemy of the Soviet people, sent to the Gulag for the rest of his life.

As stated previously, I know little or nothing about art, but I was amazed at the quality of the works, was astounded at the commitment and dedication of the poorly paid staff, and appalled at the primitive conditions under which these treasures were stored. But it was all a question of money, or rather the lack of it. But this was a hidden treasure concealed from the world for so many years. Surely there was an opportunity to raise much needed money for the museum and for the children and women in Karakalpakstan. I floated an idea to our

Geneva office and the sister of Sir Bob (of "We Are the World" Band Aid fame) came back with a proposal. She had discussed the issue with Sir Bob, and he said that we should host a worldwide exhibition of a selection of these works. British Airways was an interested sponsor. We would get a panel of experts from the Metropolitan Museum of Art in New York to select the pieces that would go on display, and exhibitions would be held in Stockholm, Copenhagen, Frankfurt, Paris, London, New York, Los Angeles, Toronto, Tokyo, and Sidney. Entrance to the exhibition would be only $10 per person. British Airways would fly the exhibit free of charge between the cities, and the display would be staffed by Karakalpak women in their traditional costumes. They would also have the opportunity to talk to visitors to the exhibition about Karakalpakstan and the challenges that are faced by people living there.

I was keyed up by this plan and excited by its immense potential. The UNICEF National Committees in the various countries we intended to visit would assume all the administrative and logistic arrangements, and they all endorsed it as a tremendous fund-raising vehicle. The government of Karakalpakstan were very accommodating but made it clear that the central government in Tashkent would have to make the final decision. Back in Tashkent, I hit a brick wall. This national asset was the contention, and therefore, all income generated from this exhibition would have to go to government. They, and only they, would decide how the proceeds would be disbursed. For me, this was the final nail in the coffin. This was indeed the end of the road as I felt certain that none of the funds would go toward meeting the needs of the most vulnerable.

One morning in February 1999, my national program officer and I set off for a meeting with the minister at the Ministry of Health in Tashkent. It was a bright and sunny winter's day. I felt stress-free, blithe, and eager to get a resolution to some long-standing issues we had with the ministry. I had a strategy, and I was optimistic that today's meeting would determine most, if not all, the unresolved issues. I drove into the ministry and parked in the rear as I normally did. There was a reserved visitors' parking at the front of the building, but I felt that we would be less conspicuous if I parked out of sight. My national officer started to explain why we should park up front. "Rudy, as a VIP, you must park in the front. This is Uzbekistan, and status matters a great deal." On arrival, we were ushered into the minister's private conference room and were soon joined by the minister and his entourage. After being served with tea and cookies, the meeting started. Suddenly, our calm morning mood was smashed to smithereens by an enormous explosion that threatened to blow in all the windows. The minister asked my opinion of the reverberation. "Your Excellency, that was a bomb explosion," I responded. Having served in Afghanistan for so long, being able to distinguish a detonation became second nature to me. The minister and his staff all laughed at me contemptuously. "Rudy, you are obsessed. This is Uzbekistan, a safe country where the peace, stability, and security is pledged to our people by my government." This was a very sensitive and contentious issue that I did not wish to discuss. So I smiled back in acknowledgement. No sooner had he finished this sentence than there was a second explosion that rocked the capital and sent massive shockwaves through the air. This time, the windows shattered and were blown in, scattering glass, wood, and dust all over the conference room. The space soon filled with black smoke and fumes of high explosives. In a flash, my Uzbek counterparts had dived for cover under the tables. Then it was deadly still. I was pondering how lucky we were that nobody was hurt, but then the minister yelled hysterically and frenetically, "Rudy, what should we do now?"

"Get out of the building as quickly as possible," I responded as I did not know who or what was being targeted. Everyone dashed for the two doors, and there was pandemonium and panic in the hallways. Some ministry staff received cuts from flying glass. Shukhrat, my assistant, stared at me like a hare caught in the headlights of a car in the dark.

"Stay cool and follow me," I tried to reassure him. As we descended the rear stairway, there were two further blasts, and these were nearer and much more substantial than the previous ones. The blasts caused tremors that caused plaster from the ceiling to rain down on us. There was panic in the streets, people were streaming out of their offices, and the situation was aggravated by the fact that nobody knew what was going on. Then another blast shattered the frenzied environment, but it was further away. Nevertheless, people started to run in all directions, screaming as they did. People were driving frantically as if the end of the world was at hand. The sirens of emergency vehicles could be heard everywhere, enormous plumes of black smoke were clearly visible from that part of the city that housed the majority of government offices, and police cars rushed around in apparent disarray. I decided to go back to the office to make sure all my staff was out of harm's way. Because of the commotion and terror on the streets, I took the longer back way. As we exited the ministry, I noticed that all the vehicles that were parked in the VIP parking at the front of the building were badly damaged by the blasts. Once again, my intuition paid off. I drove slowly and defensively as most of the other drivers on the road appeared to be in a state of shock and therefore drove recklessly. Many of the streets were now cordoned off, and this contributed to enormous traffic jams. I received a phone call from UN security informing me that all arteries out of the city were also closed. The staff at my house called to inform me that the last explosion was close to where I lived, and they were petrified. I instructed them to remain in the house, lie on the floor away from any windows and doors, and not to let anybody in.

On reaching my office after a great deal of difficulty, I discovered that the staff had evacuated the premises, leaving everything open. Being concerned about their safety, I called each one of them individually to reassure myself that they were safe. They were afraid and bewildered, but nobody was injured. I then called our headquarters in Almaty in Kazakhstan to report what was going on and to inform them that our team and property were safe. Later I was bombarded by calls from Geneva and New York, all wanting to know what was going on in the country. All I could report was what I saw. The state-controlled media blacked out all information and only reported that the president was safe and was in command of the situation. Judging by the size of the explosions, I felt that the damage would be extensive, that there would be numerous fatalities and casualties. Unfortunately, I could not be more precise. Now that the danger had subsided, I decided to sit in the office garden and eat my packed lunch. Just as I started, my boss called again. "Rudy, what are you doing?"

"Eating my lunch," I responded.

"What the hell, when the world is crumbling around you." I knew that he was concerned for our safety and also understood that his bark was louder than his bite. The conversation ended there. It was now 4:00 p.m., so I decided to lock up and head home. Besides the army and the police, the streets were deserted. A block from where I lived was a post office and major telephone exchange, and it was one of the targets. The front of the three-storied building was entirely smashed by a detonation. It was only because I had diplomatic plates on my car that I was allowed to go through the army roadblock. Most of the houses in my block had windows shattered. The high brick wall around my residence spared us from any damage. My cook and the housemaid were glad to see me was glad to see me, and on reassuring them that the worst was over, I drove them home as all public transportation had been suspended.

Slowly I was able to piece together most of what happened. The story was that this was a well-planned and coordinated attempt on the president's life. The official version was that six car bombs exploded near government buildings, causing extensive damage and killing fifteen people and wounding 150 others. My sources in the hospitals told me that the figures were much higher. Whatever was the case, the authorities exploited these circumstances by cracking down hard on anyone who opposed the president and his policies. In this environment of communal panic, the government detained human rights activists, independent lawyers, and journalists. There are some skeptics that say that these events were staged by government to give them the opportunity to eliminate members of the growing opposition to the president's autocratic rule. I felt that this was only the beginning and that there were more forbidding things to come.

I had never been to Urgench, and when invited to visit by the "hakim" (governor), I gladly accepted. Most of the factories and "kolkhozy," or cooperative farms, in the region had shut down soon after the collapse of the Soviet Union. The majority of people were now subsistence farmers who were also obligated to work on state-controlled cotton plantations where the production quotas were mandated by the government. I explained to the governor that as most of our recourses were already committed, any intervention in the province would have to be small-scale and restricted. During the course of the day, I met with five women who had all sustained major disabilities in farming and domestic accidents. Because they were now unable to work as hard as they did before, they were discarded and divorced as being valueless by their husbands who immediately wed younger women. Eviction from their homes followed, and with their children, they were now destitute and compelled to do whatever was necessary to feed their offsprings. They all wanted to know what the UN would do to alleviate some of their affliction. I felt that it was inappropriate to discuss the role of the UN at this point.

In conversations with the women, it became obvious that besides their farming and housekeeping skills, they were all good seamstresses who enjoyed embroidery. I suggested to the governor that we assist these women by helping them form a sewing cooperative. "Ah! Kolkhozes," she said. Our thinking on the topic was, however, poles apart. In the old Soviet model, a cooperative was compulsory and state supported. The members therefore had no autonomy, and all their actions were dictated to by the state. They were in fact indentured labor. I was thinking of a cooperative where the members would have autonomy and be egalitarian. But this was just semantics. To get the project started, we needed a building. It would have to be government owned, be made available rent-free for a period of five years, and all the utilities paid for by the governor's office for the first year. The governor conceded because I had a feeling that she wanted a favor in return. She then asked what we would offer. I immediately said five sewing machines, cutting boards, and all the tools and the initial resources needed to purchase fabric, furniture, and basic essential items, and we would also support the establishment of a day care to look after the children while the mothers worked. I estimated that on the outside, our cost would be about US$30,000. We looked at five structures, and I selected a traditional-type building close to where the women lived. It had a central courtyard surrounded by a high perimeter wall and a water well with ten rooms. On the outside were two vacant retail spaces.

But I had a further prerequisite. All the medical staff in regional hospitals wore white gowns. As a startup gesture, as a show of solidarity, and as a token of goodwill, these women should be awarded the contract to produce these garments. After all, today was being celebrated as the International Day of the Women in Uzbekistan. The local media were present, and the governor seized on this opportunity to show her benevolence. She immediately called up her director of medical services and issued a string of orders. As subordinate, he had no option but to agree and humbly asked what the price would be per item. I would develop a business plan when I returned to

Tashkent and provide him with the information he needed. I then drafted a simple memorandum of understanding in English, which my translator fashioned into Russian for signature. The deal was done.

On return to Tashkent, I called our suppliers in China. They were very familiar with what we wanted to do and immediately faxed me suggested equipment and ancillary supplies that we would require. The cost was well below what I had projected. Delivery would be in a week. Based on the cost I got from China, I was able to quote 10 percent below what the province was currently paying for the gowns and still generate a 25 percent profit. I had spoken to a Peace Corps volunteer working in the village, and she said that she would shepherd the project forward. Under her leadership, the women opened a beauty salon and a Turkish bakery in the vacant outside bays, and these were busy. Ann, our American volunteer, used to call me regularly to keep me posted of progress. The cooperative had expanded from the initial five disabled women to thirty single mothers with disabilities.

I decided to go to Urgench and was delighted to see real vibrancy in our community, so much so that other abused women wanted to join. But when I asked members how they were doing, they all said that they enjoyed the work but none of them had been paid because the coop had no money. They had been in operation for eight months already! When I looked at the books, they were owed by the province eight million soms. Suddenly the penny dropped. These women knew nothing about business, about accounts receivable, billing, and balancing a budget. I felt perturbed because I had let them down. I had failed to see this important building block in the whole equation. That night, I invited Ann and her boyfriend, Tom, for dinner. Ann had done such an excellent job, and I wanted to show her my appreciation. During dinner, I explained my dilemma, and Tom immediately said that his dad owned a grocery store in Wyoming. He was therefore familiar with the running of small businesses. He volunteered to oversee the business aspects of the operation. I was relieved, and the women were thrilled. The province immediately paid all the outstanding receivables, and the director of health said that he was very pleased with the quality of the product. Tom decided to put 50 percent of the money he received from the province into a reserve account and a further 20 percent into upgrading the facilities. The rest of the money was distributed equally among the women. They were dumfounded as they had never seen so much money in their entire lives. The money was so much that many could not count how much they had. Ann rented a local bus to take them into the city shopping. Word spread quickly in the village, and all the husbands were now scrambling to reclaim their ex-wives.

At a reception back in Tashkent, I learned that the UN in Afghanistan wanted to locally purchase children's winter clothing. The contract was valued at around $500,000, and it was suggested that the Urgench women's cooperative should submit a bid. The bid documents were e-mailed to me, and after doing a quick costing, I gave them to Tom for completion. A week later, I was informed that Urgench had been selected as a supplier, and an advance payment of 20 percent of the contract value had been deposited into the coop bank account. With the Afghan contract, the cooperative expanded to one hundred women and was now the only booming industry in the region. I received calls from other provinces asking us to replicate this venture. But the risks were high, and providence played a big role in making this venture a success. Besides, I was due to assume my new appointment in the South Pacific soon. I got great satisfaction from the fact that we had demonstrated that they should stop concentrating on the disability of an individual but rather value their ability.

The Convention on the Rights of the Child forms the moral fiber of all UNICEF programs, and therefore, country offices have an important role by advocating for compliance by state parties. Local legislation is the only way to actually ensure that the rights of children are recognized, respected, and protected. To move these processes forward, I felt that it would be beneficial to take a high-level Uzbek delegation to Europe to witness best practices. The Danish Refugee Council offered to host and pay for a delegation to visit Denmark. I consulted with the deputy prime minister, and she suggested that the delegation be led by the minister of interior, accompanied by the chief justice and the head of police. I felt that this was a commendable delegation that could really bring about change on their return to Uzbekistan.

The deputation received an excellent reception on arrival in Copenhagen, and the Danish Refugee Council was an excellent host. At the end of each day, we met informally in the hotel room of the minister of interior. They had brought along plenty of preserved food and vodka. So we sat around and nibbled at the Uzbek goodies and drank some vodka. What was important to me was the fact that I was getting to know each of them on an individual basis, and in many ways, we were able to connect. These settings were informal and relaxed, making bonding possible. One evening, the chief justice said that he would like to visit a jail for young offenders. Our host was taken aback by the request. That afternoon, we went to a juvenile jail just outside Copenhagen. The facilities were excellent, but the minister of interior, in a very somber voice, said to me, "Rudy, these people are racist. Why are the entire inmate population people of color? They are all of foreign origin, and I do not see a single Danish convict. Is it because white people do not commit crimes in this country, or is it because the Danish system does not offer equal opportunity to all young people, thereby forcing young immigrants into crime?" This was a philosophical statement that I had to agree with. I am afraid, however, that it totally negated the rationale for our visit.

I was astonished when I was told by the government's chief medical officer that in Central Asia, abortion is considered an important method of contraception. In fact, most women have at least three or four abortions in their lifetime. To accentuate this reality, a lady friend told me what actually happened to her. She married at age sixteen and soon became pregnant. Her husband, however, did not want the child and instructed her to get an abortion. She refused, left, and got divorced. She delivered a son and had a very difficult time raising him as a single mom.

When I met Emir, he was a strapping lad of sixteen. We got on well together, and he often wanted to talk and seek my guidance. His girlfriend, Olga, was an ambitious, bright young woman who wanted to study law. One evening, I got a call from Emir. He seemed distracted and was not his normal effervescing self. I messed about, trying to put him at ease, and we laughed together and at each other. Then like a pent-up volcano, he got off. Olga was pregnant, and they were considering abortion. He had not told his mom and wanted my advice. I started off by saying, "Emir, firstly, thank you for sharing this news of great consequence with me. Please be rest assured that I will hold this tête-à-tête in the strictest of confidence. I know that you now accept the fact that you are no longer a boy but a man. Therefore, you are obliged to do what is right. Remember the time when your mom was pregnant with you. Your dad did not want a child and ordered her to have an abortion. She refused and ran away and gave birth to you. Today you are a fine young man. Any decision that both of you make will have long-term repercussions. The bottom line is that I cannot tell you what to do. You must decide, and may God bless you both."

Three weeks later, I was invited to Olga's and Emir's wedding. I was out of the country at the time, so I was unable to attend. When I returned, I met the young couple and their beautiful baby daughter. Young Lena has brought so much pleasure and joy into their lives.

Many years later, Emir thanked me for saving his daughter's life. I did not, but he did.

Kind words can be short and easy to speak, but their echoes are truly endless - Saint Teresa

After the coalition invaded Afghanistan to oust the Taliban, it became apparent that because of war and drought, Afghanistan was confronted by a massive humanitarian crisis. Over seven million people were at risk, and thousands of tons of relief supplies were needed immediately. Currently, all relief supplies had to be transported by road over long distances from Pakistan at an enormous cost. Besides, this route was tenuous, there were numerous delays, and convoys were often ambushed and plundered. Uzbekistan shared a long border with Afghanistan, and in 1980, the Soviets built the "Friendship Bridge" to span the Amu Darya River and connect Uzbekistan with Afghanistan. The bridge also carries a railway line, and in the town of Termez on the banks of the river, there is a well-equipped river transportation system that uses 500 MT barges to ferry supplies across the river. On the Afghan side, the port of Hairaton can handle a vast volume of cargo. This was, after all, the main supply line for the Red Army fighting in Afghanistan.

Soon after the withdrawal of the Soviet forces from Afghanistan, the border was sealed and the area declared a military zone, and the army were ordered to shoot to kill all infringers. The UN had already started preliminary discussions with the government regarding opening the border to allow the flow of relief supplies from Uzbekistan into Afghanistan. Because of my amiable relationship with the minister of interior, I was asked to lead the consultations with the Ministry of Interior, the intelligence services, the military, and the police. Many of the issues were sensitive, and it was impossible to predict the outcome as it was imperative that we ramped up our staff structure to sustain a large relief operation, and it was also important that we immediately started stockpiling supplies for cross-border shipment. For these reasons, I was being coerced by my headquarters to give them a valid assessment of whether the border would in fact open. They did not want to act on speculation as startup costs in Uzbekistan would run into the millions of dollars. I constantly agonized about whether we would be successful getting the border opened. Out of desperation, I decided to draw on my amity and request a private meeting with the minister of interior. He invited me to his residence for dinner. During the course of the evening, I was reassured that once all the details were worked out adequately, the government would agree to reopen the river transportation system for a limited time only, but with the proviso that only UN-certified cargo would be transported on the barges. Besides the UN, other donors played an important role in the relief and rehabilitation efforts in Afghanistan, and the NGOs were an important component. I was not happy with this stipulation, but we had overcome the initial impediments, and I wanted to maintain the momentum and move forward. Based on this meeting, I informed my superiors that the border would open, and I was told by them in no uncertain terms that I would suffer the consequences if it did not.

I then had a staff meeting and clearly delineated how the office would function. The country staff would continue with program implementation, and I would recruit additional staff to run the relief operation. We rented separate offices in Tashkent and Termez, and I recruited short-term staff from neighboring countries. We rented warehouses on the river in Termez and placed an order for ten 30 MT Russian trucks and trailers. Subsequently, I met with the head of the national airline to discuss the charter of their gigantic Antonov cargo aircraft to lift materials from our supply division in Copenhagen to Tashkent. I felt that this gesture would assuage the government as the airline was state owned. We arranged two such flights, but the Uzbeks were unable to match the price of their competitors from the Ukraine.

The relief generated tremendous global media interest, and at the peak, we had 120 members of the internatonal media register with us to cover the story. I valued this interest because it made fund-raising easier. Our staff started piling blankets, foodstuff, and emergency drug kits to the ceiling in our warehouses in Termez. The municipality started laying fresh asphalt over the potholed road leading to the port, and the barges and tugboats were being serviced and tested to move thousands of tons of supplies to help the needy. We held daily press conferences, and although the president of Uzbekistan had formally agreed to allow the barges to ferry supplies across the border, we were still not given a definite date when the operation could start. This made me apprehensive and also caused some concern with members of the media..

After a few days, we were told that we could load one barge with 500 MT of cargo, and this capacity would equally divided between the different UN agencies. This would be a test run, and if things went smoothly, the operation would pick up cadence. I was asked to represent the UN on the first barge accompanied by only one camera crew. The barge would fly a UN flag, and besides, the crew would have no other passengers. I arranged to fly to Termez on the early morning flight, but at the evening press briefing, I shared the government's ruling on press coverage. There was an outcry and outrage at this decree. The journalist threatened to rent boats and follow the first barge or swim across the river to obtain firsthand coverage. This I understood, but what was also apparent was that any unilateral move by them could place the whole operation in jeopardy. I appealed for calm and begged indulgence. As a consolation, they could select whoever they wanted to accompany the first barge, and pool arrangements would apply.

When I got to the port in the morning, I noticed a fully laden barge tied up in front of the one we were going to use, the contents of which I knew were non-UN, but more importantly, the owner of the consignment was also unknown. The manager of the facility was embarrassed that I had detected this irregularity, and he pertinaciously evaded the issue. He repeatedly said I had nothing to worry about because the UN barge would be the first across. But I pointed out that the government had stipulated that only UN-endorsed cargo would be ferried across to Afghanistan. I said that I would raise this issue with the minister of interior. We then walked over to the barge. It was loaded with sugar, flour, cooking oil, and vodka. It belonged to an Uzbek warlord from Afghanistan, and the shipping of this cargo had been sanctioned by very senior local officials. Once again, corruption raises its ugly head.

But then, at last we got the final word. We could set off in the morning, and I had to be at the wharf by 6:00 a.m. I asked my driver to pick me up at 5:00 a.m., and frankly, I was unable to sleep at all that night. I had wagered so much at being able to pull this off that if it had failed, I would be dead in the water. I cannot recount the poignant feeling that consumed me when we cast off. I felt that there was excitement but also trepidation among all the well-wishers who saw us off. The engines of the tugboat coughed and spluttered but then gained steam, and we were on our way. Along the Afghan banks of the river, there were hundreds of people waving green branches at us and cheering. They certainly were in jubilation at our appearance. Once we docked at Hairaton Port, I was met by my UN colleague, and I handed over responsibilities for the cargo to him. He wanted to drive me to the bridge so that I could walk across, but I wanted to be left alone. I walked down a dusty path out of the port and suddenly was seized by the pangs of hunger. I had not eaten today, and already it was 3:00 p.m. Outside the port area, I was met by the local cab. It was an ancient Russian vehicle that had so many transplants that one could no longer identify the original make of the car. The driver, who was in his teens, knew exactly where I wanted to go. As soon as I got into his louse-infested vehicle, he started to play a scratchy old tape of Hindi music. "You see, my friend, we now have music, and

I want you to enjoy. We are free." He turned the volume up to full blast, but because of the poor quality of the tape and the dilapidated state of his sound system, one only heard transitory sounds of music. But it was the first music that he had heard for a very long time as playing music during the Taliban era was banned. This was progress. As I walked across the bridge, I could not help thinking about the 160,000 Red Army troops that only made a one-way crossing of this bridge from Uzbekistan to Afghanistan. That was the number of Soviet troops that were killed during the Soviet invasion and occupation of Afghanistan.

When I returned to Tashkent, I received an e-mail from my ex-wife, Karen, who lived in Manhattan. She was single and desperately wanted to adopt a child from Central Asia. Would I help? I contemplated the question with concern and decided that I would in every way I could. But first I had to figure out how to make her goal achievable. I called the office of the president in Kyrgyzstan and spoke to his chief of staff. He laughed and said, "Rudy, forget about ex-wives. You just marry a beautiful woman from here and have a child, problem solved." After this banter, we got down to the nitty-gritty. According to Kyrgyz rules, foreigners cannot adopt, and the notion of a single parent was not recognized. In any case, if a Kyrgyz couple wanted to raise a child of other biological parents, the processes would take five years at minimum. A thorough evaluation of the parents-to-be and their state of affairs would have to be made first. As the conversation continued, I felt that this was a no-win situation. In angst, I asked if the president could be consulted. In ten minutes, I got a callback from the office of the president. As a special concession, the president had agreed to facilitate but only if I appeared as the father on the records and with a further stipulation that the child could not be ethnic Kyrgyz. With relief, I conveyed this news to Karen in New York. I owned an apartment in Bishkek that Karen could use at no cost as her base. I then called the minister of health as the ministry had a big orphanage on the outskirts if Bishkek. The minister said that he would notify the director and there would be no problems. Karen and her support team arrived in Bishkek a week later. They rented a car and driver to get them around, and they frequently called to say how excited they were to be in this strange but exotic land on a quest for a daughter. They visited many orphanages in the city but were most impressed by the Ministry of Health facility.

One afternoon, they made a courtesy call on the American ambassador. She was not positive about the prospects, but when Karen told her about my involvement, she said, "Oh, that stallion, he can jump over any obstacle." After a week of agonizing about which child to select, Karen decided on a six-month-old Russian girl who was severely undernourished and underweight. But now came the difficult part, and they wanted me in town. So I took a week off and flew to Bishkek. Before the director would release the baby, she demanded a fee of $50,000 as reimbursement "for food and upkeep of the child." I called the minister, and that was the last we heard of that stipulation. The adoption papers were now sealed and certified, and Karen, in tears, collected her daughter. I thought it would be a simple process to get the child on her mother's passport and they could leave the country. But this was not possible as the child was not an American citizen. Well, she would have to get a Kyrgyz passport, but this too was unlikely as in Kyrgyzstan passports are not issued to anyone younger then sixteen years old. I once again called on the good offices of the president. We now had a passport but, to our dismay, discovered that there was a need for an exit visa. To get a visa, one has to have an approval stamp from the agency that used to be the KGB. But they could only do background checks on people sixteen years and older. It was clear that I was creating a lot of precedents, and it made me concerned that I was becoming too much of an imposition on the office of the president. But at last we had overcome all the hurdles bar none. The baby would have to be taken to Moscow to be medically cleared by the American Embassy there before allowed to travel to the United States. I was told that this could be a nightmare and could take weeks as Russian doctors did the examinations and carried out the test, and they were very difficult to deal with. The preferred way would be to travel through Germany, where the service was efficient, courteous, and quick. But this would require state department approval. The ambassador helped, and in a week after the adoption papers were finalized, Karen and her daughter arrived in Manhattan. Kathrin is now a thriving eleven-year-old American girl who lives with her mother in Manhattan.

Are You My Wantok? - Papua New Guinea pidgin statement

My next posting was to Papua New Guinea in the South Pacific. The country was notorious for its violent crimes, rape, poor national capacity, and dire infrastructure. But then, I have never been to this part of the world and therefore looked forward to the assignment. The country is composed of numerous islands where the inhabitants are laid-back, sociable, yet aggressive, unpredictable and live from one day to the next. Theirs is a leisurely life where anything and everything can wait till tomorrow or the next day. Having lived in Manhattan, this cadence was fundamentally different, but in order to cope, one had to listen and learn. The culture and traditions of these charming people is based on a "wontok" (one talk) system, and in this ethnicity, members from the same family and village who all speak a similar language pool and share their resources. This arrangement influences every level of society. Every Papua New Guinean is obligated by convention to duties and obligations to their wontok, and in return, they receive reciprocal payback. For example, when my national staff got paid, all their unemployed wontoks lined up to receive their share of the salary. In this beautiful country that is endowed with fertile lands, superb climate, an abundance of fish, and a profusion of mineral resources, the wealth is shared by just a few, and the majority of people live in abject poverty. Regrettably, the elected leaders use their positions for personal gain and unfortunately invest most of their ill-gotten gain in Australia and elsewhere. The churches have been long established as wealthy and influential and play an important role in people's lives. German missionaries were the first to arrive in this part of the world. There are eight hundred different languages spoken in this relatively small country, with English being the official language. However, Tok Pisin (pidgin English) is most commonly spoken and serves as a bridge so that the people of PNG can communicate among themselves.

But the day had arrived. The curtain was up, and for better or worse, I must face my new challenge. I wish that I could have shared this apprehensiveness with someone else. But alas, I was alone. Overdressed and out of place, I boarded the flight in Bangkok. Most of the passengers were Australians. The carrier was Air Niugini, the national airline, and I was a bit uneasy. So much of this was strange to me. It was difficult to decipher the Austrialian accent, but I was determined to look and learn. Before takeoff, the passengers ordered double shots of gin, vodka, and whisky, but it was early in the day. All of this made me apprehensive. Could I settle in, adapt, and be productive? I have always had the good fortune of having the privilege of selecting my management team. But on this occasion, there were no takers. But life goes on, and this is certainly not the end of the world.

It had been a long flight from New York, and I started to doze, only to be suddenly woken by a stewardess asking me what I wanted to drink. In my sleepy haze, I was startled to see that she and all the other cabin staff had shining red-stained teeth and lips. I wondered what caused this. I later learned that the reason was that people chewed green betel nut not only socially but as part of their everyday life. Betel nut is carcinogenic, acts as a stimulant, is addictive, and is believed to enhance attentiveness and block out the pangs of hunger. On arrival at Jacksons International Airport, we were exposed to chaos and confusion. This is a small airport, and therefore, word travels fast. A few minutes earlier, armed bandits staged a holdup and escaped with a large amount of cash. Shots were fired, but apparently, nobody was injured. I was told that one should not get alarmed as armed robbery is an everyday occurrence. On the way to the office, my predecessor started briefing me on the prevailing conditions in the country. The Economist Intelligence Unit had rated Port Moresby as the worst-ranked city in the world to live in out of 130 cities it assessed because of the high level of rape, robbery, and murder. Large areas are controlled by "raskol's" (rascals), and these districts are out of bounds to foreigners. The unemployment rate in the city fluctuates from 60 percent to 90 percent, not very encouraging news for a newcomer, but I was certainly not deterred by it. In fact, I felt that these constraints would present opportunity. We then made courtesy calls on a number of government ministers, and I was taken aback at how rundown the government buildings were from long-term neglect. When we drove back to my hotel in the dark, I noticed an entirely naked man with a bow and arrow walking around the perimeter fence of the hotel. "Who is that guy?" I asked my driver. "Oh, the night watchman" was the reply.

My first priority was to rent a place to call home. All foreigners lived in compounds that were ringed by high barbed wire fences and guarded by armed security guards reminicient of Afghanistan. Rents were very high as all properties were owned by Australians or government ministers. I rented a house on a hill overlooking the ocean and hired a "house mary" (housekeeper) called Navy. She was a delightful plump young lady who enjoyed talking with herself. With her flaming red lips and teeth, she was gregarious and ready to do everything but really did nothing, not dissimilar to the baddies we have in New York. I don't know whether it was the effects of the betel nut or something else. What I do know was that dear Navy believed in some mumbo jumbo that guided her in life she could never explain exactly what this was, but it was out there, maybe in the ocean, the sand, or the wind. After all, it's difficult explaining something celestial. Despite her having worked as a housekeeper for several years, I felt that her dexterity was somewhat limited or even lacking. Perhaps it was because of my inability to "Tok Pisin" with her. Every day Navy looked forward to one event, and that was "mumu" (lunch). She dived into the refrigerator and piled everything in sight on her plate, mountains of stuff, but I never knew if she ate all of it or took some home to her kids. One day, Navy asked me for some money. "What for?" I inquired. "Oh, I need to buy a 'susu cover'" (bra). Getting to more serious stuff, the talk of the town today was the national elections. I asked navy if she had voted, and she replied that she had—ten times in all. One of the candidates had given her and her wontoks half a pig to vote for him as many times as they could. Very few people register births and have birth certificates or ID cards. Therefore, voter register rolls are of little or no use.

There are two clubs where expatriates could socialize. I joined the upscale Yacht Club not because I sail but because the clubhouse was a modern facility with a full restaurant, exercise room, patio bar, and a fishing club. But most importantly, the club owned all the land around the bay, and this was enclosed by a very high fence and patrolled twenty-four hours a day. As it was not safe to walk in the streets of Port Moresby, many of the foreigners walked around the bay, and this is where I tried to exercise daily. Almost all the members were Australians who had spent a lifetime working in Papua New Guinea. In many ways, they had lost touch with reality as they lived relatively isolated lives in such ghettos. But it was important for me to get to know them as they had the wealth and were powers behind the throne. However, the setting of the club was idyllic, the atmosphere relaxing, and I soon made many friends. As I was sitting on the veranda, the vista over the marina was captivating. Yachts sailing the South Pacific docked here. Their crews were intriguing and their tales alluring. Listening to them made me want to sail. I love the sea but am in a way afraid of it, which does not bode well for being a sailor.

Having spent a month in Port Moresby, I decided to undertake my first field mission to the island of Bougainville. This semiautonomous island endured years of civil war that destroyed its infrastructure and left the people impoverished and exposed. In the early 1970s, Rio Tinto, the Australian mining giant, started harvesting the island's vast resources of copper. All staff at the upper echelon were Australian, with a sumptuous untroubled lifestyle in this Garden of Eden. Their towns were modern, with schools, clubs, shopping, and superb recreational facilities. It reminded me of the White Highlands in Kenya during the colonial rule. However, very little of this wealth trickled down the native islanders who lived in primitive villages with no power, water, or sanitation facilities and performed menial work. This stirred discontent and resentment against the foreigners, which resulted in the outbreak of a civil war in 1990. The PNG military, aided by mercenary forces from Australia, used horrendous force to try and quell the rebellion that resulted in the deaths of twenty thousand islanders. Over this period, the expatriate population abandoned the island, and all mining and economic activity ceased. The infrastructure soon started to erode and disintegrate. It was not long that the tropical rainforest started to reclaim the land it had lost to civilization. The island became autonomous in 1997, but despite the wealth in latent but untapped mineral resources, the government lacked the capacity and the resources to provide even the most fundamental goods and services to the people. In meeting with local administration officials, I soon realized that they lacked the vision and had no plan for rehabilitation and reconstruction. Without credible counterparts, it makes our task in program development and delivery very difficult. The road network on the island was ruined, which made it enormously difficult getting around the island and reaching the scattered fishing communities along the coast.

Providing basic health care was an urgent but daunting problem. Perhaps a floating mobile clinic would be a way to bring urgently needed health care to the people. But this was an expensive proposition, and there were serious questions about sustainably. I approached the ambassador of Japan about donating and equipping a boat for this purpose. It would have to be large enough to accommodate the crew, a doctor, and a nurse and be able to remain at sea for at two weeks at a time. Because of their experiences in the South Pacific during WWII, there was a lot of sympathy in Japan for the people of the region, and there were economic implications too. The ambassador, who was a man of vision, liked the idea and would pursue it, provided that UNICEF paid the operating cost for the first year. According to my calculations, the cost of the crew and the medical would be the most expensive items.

I approached the New Zealand ambassador about funding the crew and medical staff for the first year, and although he was conducive, he was not entirely swayed because of visibility. Perhaps all these people could volunteer, which would reduce the cost. But this was not the concern. Donors do not like sharing high-visibility projects with others as they cannot claim full credit for it. I realized that this idea would not gain traction, and besides, I knew the government of the island did not have the resources to take over the project after the first year. I dreamed about the idealist lifestyle the crew would have cruising around a beautiful South Pacific island in a modern, well-equipped vessel bringing urgently needed health services to the people and fishing for supper.

Climate change is having a devastating effect on islands in this Region. Carteret is an atoll island of Bougainville, with a population of 1,500. Over the years, the sea levels have been rising, inundating gardens and causing coconut trees to die and fall. Villagers have had to relocate to higher ground, fresh water sources are becoming polluted, and the people are fast losing the ability to continue existing on Carteret. They are being told to evacuate the island, but despite their lack of enthusiasm, the government lacks the resources to make this happen.

Early one morning, I heard long and sustained gunfire coming from a village on the outskirts of the city near an army barracks. This was unusual, and shortly afterwards, one of the main costal roads that serves this area was closed to all traffic. Later that day, I met with the minister of social services, an ethnic Australian who was married to the chief justice, a Papua New Guinean. I asked Lady Carol what was going on, and she said that some soldiers had picked up some young women from the village the night before. When they were dropping them off at the village in the morning, two of the soldiers were killed by villagers. When word got back to the barracks, a band of armed soldiers returned to the village and started burning and looting in revenge. The situation was tense and out of control. The army was unable to rein in these rogue soldiers, and the police washed their hands of the whole affair. Public opinion was that the only person who could mediate and restore order was Lady Carol. "But Lady Carol, you are not really thinking of doing this?" I inquired. "Reports indicate that the soldiers are drunk and out of their minds."

"Rudy, these people are in my constituency, and therefore, it's my obligation to ensure that there is no further bloodshed. I will travel there as soon as we finish this meeting." The afternoon news reported that Lady Carol had met with the rascal soldiers; they had laid down their arms and returned to barracks. The situation was back to normal. This report reminded me of a description of gang rape that I was told about but at that time found it impossible to believe. The local men called it "lineup" and had no apprehensions about it. After a party, the men would find a victim, and then they would all line up to rape her one after the other.

One morning, my secretary came into the office in shock and unfocused. I immediately sensed that something was wrong. Amy was travelling to the office in a bus. Two stops before her destination, a man boarded the bus with a bush knife. There was nothing uncommon about this, as these long knives were commonly used for agricultural purposes. But then, without any warning, the man went up to a woman sitting in front of her and in one fell swoop decapitated her. She was his wife. This was "payback" for something she had or had not done.

At a Japanese-government reception one evening, the ambassador of New Zealand came up and asked me what UNICEF was doing about the unaccompanied juveniles being detained on the island of Nauru. This was double Dutch to me, as I had no inclination of the issue. During the course of the conversation, I was able to glean that there were over sixty unaccompanied minors in detention on the island. Nauru is a tiny South Pacific island in the middle of the ocean that is barren and desolate. It served as a naval base during WWII. Back in my office, I started to scrape together the specifics of what actually took place. In August 2002, a small fishing boat set sail from Indonesia carrying 438 Afghan asylum seekers on a trip to Australia. After paying large amounts of money to the traffickers, the refugees were told that the crossing would take less than two days. However, after the first day at sea, the motor stopped and the vessel started to drift and take on water. By the fourth day, many of the passengers were ill, weak, distressed, and hungry and were hunkered down on deck, exposed to all the elements. In the early morning mist and by the grace of God, they noticed a ship approaching. It was the Norwegian oil tanker *Tampa*. These dejected people were ecstatic and started to pray to Allah for their redemption. Meanwhile, *Tampa* had radioed a distress call to the Australian mainland, requesting authority to take on these shipwreck travelers. In no uncertain terms, the ship's captain was ordered not to enter Australian territorial waters. So they dropped anchor and awaited further instructions. Twenty-four hours later, the fishing boat sank, and the feeble asylum seekers waved frantically and pleaded to be rescued. The *Tampa* crew waited till the fishing boat was almost underwater before fishing out of the water the frail and dying would-be refugees. Under the international rules of the sea, the captain decided that this was an emergency and started to steam without authority to the nearest Australian port. But the drama was yet to unfold. Before entering territorial waters, they were met head-on by an Australian naval destroyer. In a flash, the Tampa was boarded by Australian Special Air Service commandoes. Without a word, they transferred all the Afghans to their mother ship, and the vessel set course for Nauru. The rest is history. In these warehouse conditions, these boat people had no legal recourse and were allowed no visitors.

I was told that the camp was operated by the International Organization of Migration (IOM). I had worked with this organization in several countries and held them in high esteem. I understood local politics, but what was termed as the "Pacific solution" turned out to be an absolute nightmare for so many innocent people fleeing from the hazards of war. Because this was an issue affecting children's rights, I called IOM in Nauru and asked to speak to the officer in charge. He was very evasive and said that he could not give me any information and suggested I contact the Australian Ministry of Foreign Affairs in Canberra. I did and was told that as Nauru was an independent country, and therefore, I should communicate directly with that government. I was obviously not making any progress and in fact was being deliberately jerked around. Being aggravated, I contacted my headquarters in New York for advice and support. Australia is a major donor in the Pacific, and therefore, this was a sensitive issue that everyone wanted to shun. "Rudy, as our country representative, you must decide on what to do and act accordingly." I should have known better, but then, one lives and learns. In conjunction with my colleague from the United Nations High Commissioner for Refugees, we wrote a letter to the Australian Ministry of Foreign Affairs requesting permission to visit the detainees. In response, we were invited to attend a meeting at the Ministry of Foreign Affairs in Canberra. Wow, things were looking good, and we were at last making progress. At the meeting the Ministry was represented by a battery of high powered Lawyers. They all sat opposite to us and from the superior look on their faces, I became aware that this was a setup. In succession, they bombarded us with legal arguments supporting the Australian government's contention that they were in compliance with all UN and other international guidelines. There was a long-established process for immigration to Australia, and it was the government's obligation to ensure that these rules were not circumvented. The people who were being detained had violated Australian law, and the government was desperately seeking a compassionate way of dealing with these people but at a same time sending a strong message to other would-be asylum seekers. All very legitimate and understandable, but my concern was that these were unaccompanied minors apprehended on the high seas, and their imprisonment was detrimental to their physical and mental well-being. Besides, this was a violation of articles of the convention on the rights of the child to which Australia was in agreement with.. The meeting then ended, and the next day, all the local papers carried articles about the Australian government meeting with officials of the United Nations to elucidate misunderstandings about the asylum seekers. Disillusioned, I recalled Jugay's paramount advice to me as a kid: "Never let yourself be exploited, nor should you ever exploit another human being." But on this instance, I failed on both counts.

HIV (AIDS) was a growing problem in the country and one of the major challenges that we faced. We chose and adopted a strategy of prevention through education. This, however, was easier said than done. This was a land of diverse cultures, customs, and a multitude of varied languages, and therefore, interventions would have to be pinpointed. I once sat down with a group of teenage girls to discuss prevention. They were told by some older women in their clan that if they only had sex with one man, they would get pregnant. So in order to avoid conceiving, they should only have sex with a multitude of different men. This was the crux of the high rate of infection. We used traditional performing artists to convey simple preventive measures in a nonthreatening way to teenagers. The messages were very specific to the local culture and traditions and achieved some measure of successes.

Don't soil a well after having a drink - Papua New Guinea pidgin statement

Bennie, who was the governor of the central bank, was a friend, and we socialized often. He came from Walis Island, and his description of his village made it sound like paradise. He invited me to visit, and I had every intention of doing so. In the morning of September 8, 2002, I received a call from the chair of the National Disaster Preparedness Committee informing me of a major earthquake followed by a tsunami that had caused considerable damage to some coastal villages. Because of the remoteness of the area, the information was vague, but the government had sent out an assessment team to the area, and he would have a comprehensive report in a few days. A few days later, Bennie called to say that Walis Island was badly damaged and all the freshwater wells were now dry. Without water, the eight hundred families who lived on the island would have to be relocated. This was catastrophic news for the villagers, who were seafaring people. Could I do anything to help? Looking into the matter, I learned that government intended to relocate these people in a virgin jungle with no infrastructure and miles away from the sea. It was obvious that this was not a viable solution. I consulted with Keith, a water engineer from New Zealand, and he agreed to go to the island and make an assessment. He warned, however, that it was remote, which would make the logistics complicated and expensive. In the interim, the villagers were harvesting small amounts of rainwater to meet their immediate needs. On his return from Walis, Keith's report stated that the earthquake caused a strong surge that persisted for some hours, flooding many vegetable gardens and forcing the villagers to seek shelter on higher ground. There was damage to many houses and structures, but to him, the quake uplifted the island, thereby causing the water table to drop considerably.

The solution was to dig deep wells, but this would require a drilling rig that could only be transported by barge or landing craft at colossal cost. The PNG Navy had two landing craft, and although I had never seen them put to sea, I assumed that they were seaworthy. I met the navy commander and discussed the possibility of using one of his landing craft on an emergency relief mission. He would be glad to help, and besides, many of his sailors had not been to sea for over a year. The problem was that the navy did not have the money to buy fuel for the vessel. I had done a costing, and chartering a commercial ship would be much more costly then purchasing fuel, so I told the commander that the UN would purchase the fuel. They would be ready to sail in forty-eight hours.

I then met with Keith as the German government had given me $80,000 to make this intervention. That's all I had. This would barely cover his cost, but in the spirit of "harambee," Keith signed the contract and mobilized the resources to undertake the task. I will not go into the details, but the PNG Navy had problems delivering, and Keith's team ran into some serious complexities in drilling, but a week later, they reported that four of the deep wells had struck water.

That evening, Bennie and I went to the club to celebrate. The islanders were ecstatic. Besides the four wells, they also had four rain-harvesting catchment areas. Under these, they would conduct classes for primary children. There was going to be a big celebration on the island, and I was the guest of honor. I met Bennie on the government jetty, where a boat would take us to Walis about two hours away. I did not recognize Bennie as he was dressed in traditional garb. His face was painted, he had beads and shells around his neck, and a large garland of shells that he wore indicated that he was a person of great importance. I felt overdressed in my slacks and tie, and I immediately got rid of the tie. I so much wished that I could have worn shorts. It was a crystal-clear cool morning, the wind was blowing from the south, there was a slight swell, and the sun, with its deep-orange halo, had just started to rise in the east as we sped toward Walis. The steward on board offered us some alcoholic beverages, but I was content gazing in ecstasy at the wonders of the South Pacific. There were seagulls flying in a clear blue sky, the dolphins gracefully frolicked not far from our boat, and the flying fish were enjoying the dawn as we did. I mused, *Am I really getting paid to do this?* As we approached the island, we were confronted by canoes whose crews were all dressed in their traditional form of undress. They were naked but for a sort of loincloth around their waist, their bodies were painted, and they carried bush knives and bows and arrows. As they circled our boat, our captain cut off the engines. This certainly did not appear to me to be a welcome, and the belligerent attitude of the welcoming party made them look more like head hunters. Bennie explained that custom required the island warriors to put to sea as soon as an unknown vessel approached their shores. Their mission was to determine whether the visitors were friend or foe. Two warriors boarded our boat and placed garlands of fresh flowers around Bennie's and my necks, and they sang and beat drums as we headed to shore.

The whole village was on the beach to greet us. The women and girls with painted faces were bare breasted but wore grass skirts. The ambiance was carefree and festive. They sang traditional songs and performed dances of welcome. The children, the poultry, the pigs, and the dogs raced around in excitement as if wanting to join in the celebrations. But first I wanted to see what had been done. Keith had dug four deep wells all strategically placed. In addition, he had also four wide roofs to harvest rainwater with large collection and storage tanks at each corner. These structures were now also serving as classrooms. I was very pleased with the outcomes and understood why the islanders were full of glee. Lunch was then served in the shade of coconut trees, and the blue sea provided a spectacular backdrop for to the occasion. We ate fish, lobster, prawns, pork, chicken, yams, rice, and tropical fruit, all washed down by a local brew fondly called "jungle juice." As part of the proceedings, I was made an "elder" of the tribe and presented with a magnificent shell necklace as a sign of this honor. As the sun began to set, we left the island and waved good-bye to its wonderful people. Wallis was truly paradise on earth, and it gave me great satisfaction to know that these enchanting people would not be relocated to some desolate virgin jungle with no infrastructure and no means for survival. But my time in PNG was coming to the end. I treasure the many fond memories that I have of that country and its people.

Deprivation in Dafur

Over the Christmas holidays one year, I was watching a documentary on the famine in the Sudan that had claimed the lives of thousands and forced over two million people to flee their farms, gardens, and homes and seek shelter in camps where they hoped to receive some humanitarian assistance provided by the United

Nations and nongovernmental organizations. They had lost everything, all their livestock, their crops, and most importantly, the water that sustained them and their animals in these harsh desert conditions. The focus of the story was about Canadian wheat that had been donated to feed the hungry but was instead being diverted to buy weapons. As wheat is a strategic commodity, the Canadian government appealed to people with experience in this part of the world to come forward and work with the government to ensure that our humanitarian assistance was not being misappropriated. On the urging of my children, I halfheartedly called the government number in Ottawa and was invited for an interview with the World University Services of Canada, a nongovernmental organization. They had received funding from the federal government to get involved in the famine relief operations and were looking to recruit a country director for the Sudan.

I was offered the position, and the mandate was clear and simple. Travel to Khartoum, the capital of Sudan, establish an office, and develop emergency plans to provide protection to the millions of internally displaced and starving people now living in makeshift camps in the desert. Although I was born in Kenya, I did not know much about the Sudan; however, I spoke Swahili, which was extensively used in Sudan. We arrived in Khartoum aboard a Sudan Airways flight from London, landing at 1:00 a.m. To our incredulity, the airport was in total darkness. None of the locals on the flight appeared amazed. It was only the foreigners who were taken aback. A few candles flickered on the immigration counters in the terminal building. The interior of the building was painted with dark-blue oil paint, which made it even more claustrophobic for me, but at least the light of the candles danced off the oil on the walls, which created a blissful feeling inside me. But the desert air was repressively hot, full of a fine, powdery dust, stifling, and reeking of sweat and urine. I was not surprised that in this environment, all the officials seemed agitated and aggravated at our arrival because it had woken them up from their slumbers. My passport was stamped within seconds, without the official even looking at it. Outside the terminal building, there were a few dilapidated cabs; the drivers dressed in long flowing white robes were fast asleep in the back of their vehicles. The perimeter fence of the airport was draped with empty plastic bags blown there by the wind. They appeared like a garland that celebrated our abuse of the environment and planet earth. There were goats all over, feasting on the trash like vacuum cleaners. The whole scene was disheartening, but it conveyed to me the feeling why I was here and the urgent need of what had to be done.

It took supreme effort to wake up one of the cab drivers; he mumbled, swore, and begrudgingly decided to accept my fare. On the way to the hotel, I was stunned to see so many people living on the side of the road. Families with young children just flopped in the sand, with nothing. The men appeared tall, with pitch-black skin, and their pearly white teeth presented a stunning contrast in the beam of our headlights. Despite my fatigue, my mind was racing, trying to bring all of this into prospective and understand where I was, what I needed to do and how and where to start, in light of all these odds. At long last we reached Hotel Acrapole located downtown, my bladder was bursting, and I was famished, tired, jet-lagged, and ready to drop after having being on the road for more than thirty-six hours. The hotel was owned by a Greek family. It was very old, primitive, but clean and safe. It surprised me to see that the hotel had power but the international airport did not. The ugly head of corruption once again prevails. Just pay off the right person and they will cater to your every need.

My room was on the third floor, but because of my heavy suitcase, I decided to take the elevator—a very bad decision. As we started to ascend, the power suddenly went off. We were abruptly plunged into total darkness, and the elevator stalled. I was stuck in absolute obscurity in the elevator shaft. In desperation, I started to bang on the iron grill that served as the door. This was an exercise in futility as I could not be heard and in any case nobody really cared. Before entering the elevator, I noticed the receptionist curling up like a cat and going back to sleep. Being stuck in a dark elevator was certainly and not exactly a preeminent welcome to a strange country. But I was not afraid and looked forward to this challenge with excitement and a feeling of adventure. As I overcame my initial night blindness, I quickly started to be focused and became more composed. Yes, this was unpleasant and discouraging, but then, I had not come here for a vacation. Despite the stifling heat and the airless milieu, I savored my little elevator. Yes, it was like being in a cramped jail cell; now, in my delirium, it felt like the Ritz. This was a place to relax and enjoy, so I was going to make the best use of this opportunity. The stench and fumes in the shaft were consuming, and I was sweating profusely. It was only then that I realized that I was still dressed in my warm Canadian winter clothes. To avoid fainting, I stripped down to my underwear, dumping my clothes on the ground, and then attempted to sleep. Despite being exhausted, I found it impossible to calm down. But then, at 7:00 a.m., the lights in the elevator abruptly came on and we started to move again. My mouth was parched and my lips had cracked; my eyes were puffy and painful. I oozed out onto the third floor, where a few housekeeping staff mingled. None were perturbed by my state of undress or by the fact that I just spent the night trapped in this cage. I concluded that this must be a regular occurrence.

Room 007 would be my abode for the next few days. It was small, scantly furnished, the walls were painted in a lime green reflective oil paint, and a bunch of plastic flowers adorned my bedside table. As there was no air-conditioning, the room was hot, unventilated, and smelled of disinfectant. To my utter surprise, I had to share a bathroom with three other guests. The heat was so stifling that I opened the shutters and looked outside. Was this hotel built in the middle of a garbage dump? There was rubbish everywhere, plastic bottles and bags, cardboard boxes, household waste was piled all over, abandoned dogs foraged through the reeking waste for scraps of food, and the scene was complete with flocks of goats eating anything and everything in sight including plastic bags. The air was filled with a fine red dust, and swarms of flies were everywhere. This was quite a change from pristine Edmonton in Alberta.

After a cold shower, I changed into some clean clothes and paid a courtesy call on the head of the United Nations in Sudan. He briefly outlined the humanitarian disaster that the country was confronted with and outlined the challenges faced by the UN in trying to feed the millions of starving people. He then introduced me to the country director of the World Food Program, the agency that was spearheading the relief effort. Alan was an Englishman who was also a graduate of the Royal Military Academy Sandhurst, so we connected immediately. Alan explained the dilemma that he faced. There was no lack of resources to cope with this situation. In fact, there were thirty-seven cargo vessels full of food anchored in mid-stream at Port Sudan, waiting to be offloaded. The cost of demurrage was extremely high and was around $7,000 per vessel per day. The government did not care as this was a tremendous source of revenue for them, regardless of the fact that millions of their people were starving to death and desperately needed to be fed. Some ships had been waiting at anchor for over two months. The problem was that the antiquated infrastructure of this country was grossly inadequate to deal with the generous response of the international community. Without any coordination, donors started shipping vast quantities of relief supplies to Sudan simultaneously prior to any mechanism to handle this vast tonnage being put in place. So what was immediately needed was logistics support to help unblock this vast logjam. The United States was focusing on the reconstruction of the railroad from Port Sudan to Khartoum, the European Union was working on the road between these two cities, and some other donors were involved with upgrading dilapidated port facilities and equipment. I needed to go to Port Sudan immediately to get a true feel for what the problems were and to figure out what role we could play to assist. Alan, who was also a pilot, said that he would fly me there in a single-engine Piper Cub.

The facilities at Port Sudan were archaic at best. Years of negligence had gnarled most of the port infrastructure, the warehouses on the pier had lost part of their roofs, and most of the heavy-lift cranes on the wharf were unserviceable. Mountains of wheat were piled on the dock, exposed to the elements, infested by rodents and exposed to pilfering. Only minimal amounts of food were being moved in antediluvian trucks that broke down every few miles and seldom reached their intended destination.

I decided to start up a trucking operation and used the seed money that I had been given to purchase ten Magirus Deutz 40 MT trucks. These all-wheel drive German-built vehicles were designed for work in the desert. They are very reliable, require little maintenance, and have a tremendous reputation. I contacted the manufacturer in Germany, and they informed me that ten vehicles were available for immediate shipping from Dubai. Alan endorsed the plan and said that he would give me whatever support that I required. I also realized that because the local experience base for this type of operation was limited, I would have to bring in seven Canadian experts to fill key positions. I quickly wrote a project document and forwarded it to my headquarters in Ottawa for approval. Next I started to look for office space and recruit national staff. The drivers and mechanics were the most important, and the supplier of the vehicles sent out a training team to run a driving/maintenance course for the ex-military drivers I had recruited. I was soon joined by the Canadian team of experts and was delighted with their caliber, commitment, enthusiasm, and willingness to work long hours. The IT expert set up a computer-based management system to track all cargoes and other management systems to track finance, administration, personnel, and donor updates. As soon as our vehicles arrived at Port Sudan, we loaded them up with 400 MT of wheat destined for El Fasher, a town on the far side of the desert and four days' drive away. I accompanied this convoy and was very pleased with the performance of our vehicles. The international community were amazed at how quickly we were able to deliver the cargo and turn around the vehicles. Our operation was slick and ran like clockwork. At long last, desperately needed food and other emergency supplies were now getting to where they were required. Certainly not in the quantities that were required, so I decided to double our lift capacity by having two crews for each vehicle and thereby doing away with rest and down time. We were fortunate to receive excellent international press coverage, and as a result, the government of Italy donated 250 additional Fiat bulk-transport trucks to bolster our fleet. In addition, they gave us ten mobile workshops and fuel boozers to enable us to establish mobile refueling points. Sudan is the largest country in Africa and among the least developed in the world. It has a harsh and inhospitable climate with no roads. Our fleet of last resort was now moving vast quantities of emergency supplies over an average of nine hundred thousand kilometers a month under some of the worst conditions on earth. Along the way, we encountered numerous pitfalls. Fully loaded trucks sinking in quicksand and having to be dragged out by camel power, trucks being washed away by floodwater, loads moving and causing the trucks to overturned, but mostly the rough terrain took a heavy mechanical toll on the fleet.

The operation had now grown into an enormous size. We had a staff of forty internationals and about three thousand nationals with operational bases in many strategic parts of the country. As most of our operational funding now came through the United Nations, a decision was made that we would be taken over by the World Food Program and, with immediate effect, would be called the United Nations Road Transportation in the Sudan. I was retained as the director but continued to perform my duties as country director of my Canadian NGO as well. I had two offices with different staff, which made the workday long and the nights short.

"I cannot alone change the World, but I can cast a stone across the water and create many ripples" - Saint Teresa

There was an ugly side to this famine, and food was now being used as a weapon to starve the tribes in the south into submission. As a consequence, they revolted and started an armed rebellion against the government. They legitimately felt exploited and discriminated against because they were African and non-Muslims. As the Sudanese military were having great difficulty in containing this insurgency, the government cut out all food aid to the south, hoping to starve the people into capitulation. This caused a global indignation, and the government was accused of genocide. Meanwhile, the UN was engaged in diplomatic talks with government to try and end this impasse to save thousands of innocent starving people. I was told that the Vatican was incensed by this persecution of Christians, and the pope had therefore decided to send Mother Teresa to Khartoum as a special emissary to mediate on his behalf of his famished people. I was nominated to meet Mother Teresa on her arrival and provide her with whatever logistical support that was necessary. She would be flying on Swiss Air from Geneva and was scheduled to land at midnight.

I felt a sense of intense unease starting to shroud me as I drove to the airport that evening. I considered myself inadequate to be in the presence of this hallowed person. Being baptized a Catholic, I consider myself to have some spiritual beliefs, but I certainly was not pious. I felt awkward in this role that was thrust onto me. I was uncertain about the correct way to welcome her and the way to speak to her and was oblivious of what she expected and would want me to do. When I got to the airport, I was greeted by the chief of government protocol and noted that the official government motorcade together with police motorcycle outriders were already in position. I was told that the state guest would reside in one the presidential palaces and that, as the leader of the UN party welcoming her, I would travel with her in the government limousine. It was now 11:45 p.m., and I felt restless, had butterflies in my stomach, and realized that I had forgotten to eat dinner. The international press corps was all over looking for a scoop and a story. All I could tell them was that Mother Teresa would hold a press conference at the presidential palace when she got there. It was a hot, clear evening with not a cloud in the sky. For a change, the air was free of the powdery red dust that blew in from the desert. The stars were bright and twinkled in the galaxy, casting a divine luminosity over the airport. There was apprehension among the officials of this Islamic state, and I knew that they would use the UN as a buffer if there was any lack of sympathy from their devout guest. The wait continued to unsettle me, so to keep engaged, I decided to go up to the control tower and get an update on the exact position of aircraft. When I asked the air traffic controller when the plane would land, he looked at me in utter astonishment. "This is Swiss Air, and at twelve midnight, their wheels would be on the ground as scheduled." Soon after, I noticed the aircraft approach in the night sky, its landing lights were on, and it touched down at exactly 23:59 hours. I dashed downstairs and took up my place with the welcoming party. I was required to proceed to the steps of the aircraft and welcome our eminent guest as soon as she set foot on Sudanese soil.

As the aircraft was marshaled to its parking spot, I moved forward in total trepidation. Once the aircraft doors opened, this tiny woman dressed in a blue and white sari emerged and came into view. In her hand she had an enormous staff with a crucifix at the top. Once on the ground, she lay on the tarmac facedown and, in a very loud voice, said, "In the name of my Father, I beseech you to let his people go." I walked up to her and with my palm on my chest across my heart I welcomed her to the Sudan. To my surprise, she had no luggage, so we walked directly to the motorcade. The parking lot sprung into life and was a hive of activity that caused quite a commotion. The press scrambled for pictures, the police escort revved up their engines, the blare of police sirens shattered the serene silence of the night, and flashing red lights pierced the darkness, indicating the imminent departure of this motorcade. Our guest was oblivious of what was going on around here. She appeared to be in a cocoon that insulated her from the rest of the world although I was convinced that she was watchful and in control.

In the car she sat hunched forward, saying the rosary in silence. So far, two things registered in my mind about her. How small, frail, unassuming, and vulnerable she appeared to be and, by the fact that despite being European, she spoke with a very strong Indian accent. However, I soon appreciated that she was a past master at politics, with a clear vision of who she was and where she wanted to go and a strong conviction that helped her achieve her goals. As we drove, her sari was draped low over her face, so I was not able to get a glimpse of her face, but now a feeling of tranquility embraced me. The fears and contradictions that I had grappled with previously were now all gone. As soon as we left the airport gates, Mother Teresa lifted her head slightly and asked, "Son, where are you taking me?"

"To the presidential palace," I responded. "No, I will not go there but will stay with the lepers in their colony in Omdurman." I immediately got on my radio and told the police escort commander to stop right away. I relayed Mother Teresa's message to the head of protocol. "But there is no leper colony in Omdurman," he replied in desperation. Soon another government official came on the air and said he knew of a place in Omdurman where some lepers lived in a sort of cage. But there were no facilities there, he protested. He then explained that the area was a small piece of desert enclosed by a high barbed wire fence with controlled accesses where the lepers were incarcerated. "They just sleep under the trees," he concluded. She had overheard this radio conversation and said, "Yes, that is the place where I will stay." She was insistent and said that she would not change her mind. We eventually got there, and I was aghast and sickened by what I saw. The headlights of our car picked up the outlines of people who were disfigured in a terrible way. They shielded their eyes from the glare of our bright lights as they melted into the darkness like hunted animals. Tattered rags draped their blemished bodies, and I felt shivers run down my spine. I knew that this highly infectious disease was known since biblical times and it can be cured if treated early. I felt a sense of indignation that these desperately ailing human beings were treated like wild animals and literally being starved to death. But then on contemplation, I did not have the courage, the compassion, or fortitude to spend a night with them as Mother Teresa choose to do. The government officials complained and rebuked me for permitting a state guest to spend the night with these untouchables. They were embarrassed as it faulted the Islamic virtue of compassion in them, and it conveyed a strong but subtle message about empathy to them. We agreed that I would wait outside the gate at 7:00 a.m. the following morning. Without another word, she disappeared into the darkness, and this made me feel even more remorseful for not spending the night there to ensure her safety. Now I think that I realize the reason for my initial misgiving. Was this her way of testing me? The images of the lepers haunted me all night, and I just could not fall asleep. In the morning, I met Mother as planned. Apparently, she was up at 4:00 a.m. and washed with water from a nearby well. After prayer, some locals gave her tea and bread, so she was all set to face the challenges of another day. I then dropped her off at the office of the head of the UN in the Sudan. He would accompany her to all the official meetings, and I was glad to get back to my regular duties. At about 2:00 p.m. that afternoon, I received a radio call informing me that Mother Teresa wished to talk with President Regan and that I should facilitate this. In those days, it was not possible to make international long distance calls from the Sudan. To overcome this, we registered our high frequency radio call sign as that of an aircraft in flight and made all our international calls through a radio relay station in Berne, Switzerland, where we had an account. The procedure was simple. We called up Berne on our high frequency radio, and they then patched our radio call into the international phone network. The service was not cheap, but there were no viable alternatives.

When Mother Theresa arrived, I ushered her into the radio room. I then called Bern on the radio and gave them the White House number. When I got through, I informed the operator at the White House that we were the United Nations in the Sudan, and that Mother Teresa wanted to talk to the president. He burst out laughing as he assumed that this was a prank call. Mother let her sari fall from her head, and then looking me directly in the eyes, she said, "Son, let me talk with him" Her stare was like a flash of lightning that struck me at the very core of my inner being. Her iceberg-blue eyes were piercing and penetrating. I felt powerless and felt that I could not verbalize or even breathe. When I recovered equanimity, I handed the microphone to her. But instead of speaking into it, she stuck it to her ear and she started speaking loudly at the radio. I could not help but find this amusing. But she soon got it right and spoke with the operator at the White House. His attitude appeared to have changed because I felt that he recognized her voice. In a very polite way, he asked us to stand by. In about fifteen minutes, another authoritative voice came on the air, and I felt certain that it was a member of the Secret Service. He asked Mother Teresa for three phone numbers from where she called the president previously. Without any vacillation, she recalled from memory the ten- to twelve-digit phone numbers from where she made these previous calls. Once again, he asked her to stand by. In about an hour, a female voice came on the air and informed Mother Teresa that an embassy car would immediately pick her from my offices and take her to the US Embassy. I tried to figure out why she wanted to talk with President Regan and then recalled that the president of the Sudan was scheduled to travel to New York the following day to address the UN General Assembly, an astute move by her to enlist the help of the most powerful man in the World to give support to her case.

Our guest was due to end her one-day visit and fly to Nairobi, Kenya, in the morning. As I wanted to ensure that she got there safely, I asked a staff member to accompany her. Departure was at 9:00 a.m., so I got her to the airport at 8:00 a.m. Peter, who would escort her, was there and, with his usual efficiency, had all the departure/arrival forms ready. It was a Swiss Air Flight, and I asked Mother for her ticket so that we could get her a boarding pass. She did not know what a ticket was as she has never had one for any of her numerous travels. Peter spoke to the Swiss Air Captain, and he was delighted to welcome her on board first class. But then we were faced with another dilemma. In order to enter Kenya, all travelers need to present a currency declaration form on arrival. Peter asked Mother how much money she had. The response was that she has had no money at all for more than fifty years! Before she departed, she told me that she was going to open a mission in South Sudan. Could I arrange for transportation for three of her Sisters of Mercy? I asked Mother for her autograph. One of her sisters had a calendar, so she tore out a page and inscribed on it, "Love others as Jesus loves you. God bless you. Teresa." She then took the rosary beads that she wore around her neck and placed them around my neck. I returned to my office feeling a strange consciousness within me. I certainly was left with a lasting impression that would henceforth serve as a prism through which I would view life. When I got back to work, I had to scramble to get caught up with the piles of stuff that lay pending. I asked my aircraft coordinator to arrange for a cargo plane to fly the three Sisters of Mercy and their furniture and supplies down to Juba in the morning. At dawn on the following morning, I went to the airport to supervise the handling of medicines and other perishable cargo that had just arrived from Europe. On the tarmac was one of our cargo planes that would fly the Sisters to Juba. It had a lift capacity of 20 MT, and I hoped that their cargo did not exceed this limit. Just then, I saw three sisters approach the aircraft. They were dressed in the same white and blue sari worn by Mother Teresa, and each of them carried a plastic shopping bag. I went over and greeted them and inquired where their cargo was. "What cargo?" they asked. "Well, the stuff that you will need to open your mission." Each of them carried all their worldly possessions in the plastic bag. I wanted to know where they were going to stay as they were entering a war zone and what funds they had to open their new mission. Their answer was that all they had was their faith, and the rest, God would provide. I instructed the captain of the aircraft to take off immediately and cogitated that there must be other ways to achieve one's goals.

It now appeared that there was a dramatic change in government policy and that they would lift the embargo to the south with immediate effect. I was given the task of making contingency plans for this eventually. I started the processes, but before I become fully immersed, I wanted to take a quick look at our Darfur operation to ensure that all was going accordingly to plan. As there were a number of internally displaced camps that I wanted to visit, I decided to drive. My driver, Abdullah, and I started the journey across the desert at 3:00 a.m. We wanted to cover as much ground before the sun rose and the temperatures rose to well above 100 F. We carried lots fuel as there were no gas stations around, some water, and food. Our first stop was two days away, providing that we did not get lost or break down. There are no roads or signposts in the desert, only tracks, wind, scorching heat, and blowing sand. With the help of a compass and maps, we were able to navigate without too much of a problem. After a sixteen-hour drive on the first day, we spent the night in the desert. It was eerily quiet. The full moon and stars reflected off the hot sands, and visibility was good. But we were alone in the vast expanse of wilderness and with no sign of any life. But the desert is full of living things. Snakes, insects, reptiles, birds, wild game, and scrub-like vegetation. This barren land was home to thousands of nomads who were perfectly able to coexist in perfect harmony with this harsh environment. The first day went without incident. It was depressing to see the barren landscape littered with the sun-bleached skeletons of so many livestock. I often fantasized about the vibrant, exciting, living desert, but what I was exposed to now was an unforgiving milieu that had already claimed the lives of thousands. We drove through deserted villages, wells that were bone-dry, parched crops that had withered from the heat and lack of water, mirages in the distance, the heat, and the swirling sand. We stopped on a rickety wooden bridge over a dry riverbed, and I asked Abdullah to change the air filters on the engine and refuel. The wood of the bridge provided us with some insulation from the intense desert heat, and the air flow under the bridge and our vehicle cooled things down. We would then have lunch, rest for half an hour, and then set off again. But then I heard movement and a rumbling sound coming from under the bridge. What sort of wild animal could it be? I grabbed a shovel as a means of defense if attacked. Then a totally naked woman and two children emerged from beneath the bridge. The woman was like a walking skeleton; her breasts were dry pieces of skin that lay flat on her chest. I could not judge the ages of the children because they were severely malnourished. Suffice to say that the older girl could walk, but the infant lay limp in her mother's arms. They were delirious but spoke in Swahili, which indicated that they were from the south. I immediately gave them our packed lunch, which the mother started wolfing down immediately. The little girl cried and wanted something to eat as well as she too was famished. But her mother explained that if she did not eat, she could not produce milk and the baby would die soon. I opened a can of chicken broth and gave it to the girl. She guzzled it down so quickly that I was afraid it would make her sick. Much to the dissatisfaction of Abdullah, I then gave this family all the food and water we had. I don't know how long it would last them, but it would improve their chances of survival and making their way south. I also gave the mother my "kikoy" (a length of cotton fabric that that I wrapped around my waste to sleep in) to cover and protect her naked body. Sadly, this was a clear example of the tragedy that was unfolding in front of our eyes this remote desert dictatorship. We drove for another day without food or water and chewed on pebbles to quench our thirst and prevent our mouths becoming parched. I kept my fingers crossed that we did not break down, for if we did, we would have been in real trouble.

My wife and three young children had accompanied me to the Sudan, and I was glad to have them with me. We rented an apartment in what was known as the "Korean complex" on the River Nile. It was a modern structure that was safe, clean, and had well-maintained tennis courts on the grounds. In fact, it was an oasis in the midst of the squalor of Khartoum. The Nile Hilton was our neighbor, so we had additional recreational facilities of the only luxury hotel in Khartoum nearby. The children were enrolled in the international school, and every afternoon, my driver picked up my wife from the apartment, and together they collected the kids from school. But this day was different. The car was late, and to make up time, the driver drove erratically at high speed. On the way home and in the vicinity of the palace, all traffic slowed down to allow a motorcade to pass. The Mercedes Benz 600 had a police escort and was obviously carrying a VIP. My driver refused to slow down and gunned his vehicle toward the Mercedes. This terrified my family as they were afraid that they would be shot if they got too close to the vehicle that was carrying the VIP. In extreme anxiety, my wife, who was sitting in the front seat, screamed at the driver to slow down. But he appeared lost in a world of his own. So she applied emergency hand brake, grabbed the steering wheel, and swerved the car off the road. Soon they were surrounded by police, and my driver was arrested for being under the influence of drugs. The passenger in the Mercedes was none other than Yasser Arafat, the leader of the PLO. Soon after this incident, a French cruise liner was hijacked off the coast of Sudan and the passengers held hostage by a Palestinian group. The UN felt that it was no longer safe for families to remain in Sudan, so my wife and children were evacuated back to Edmonton. They were never happy in the exacting atmosphere of Khartoum and were glad when they got back home. I was relieved that they were now safe and nothing terrible had happened to them in the Sudan.

The operation to start moving food aid to the starving people in South Sudan was called "Operation Rainbow." The overall plan to build an air bridge between Khartoum and Juba the capital of the south was conceived by my boss. He would be responsible for the political and press aspects of the operation, and I would oversee the management, logistic, administrative, and the programmatic side of things. The backbone of the operation was a Hercules C130 cargo aircraft chartered from Indonesia. The aircraft, with flight and support crew, had arrived from Jakarta, and we accommodated all of them in a large rental house in Khartoum. In this way, they could cook their own meals and make themselves as comfortable as possible in this strange and foreign land. Their plane was now loaded and ready to fly as soon as we received government clearance. Most media outlets from around the world had correspondents on the ground, waiting tolerantly but apprehensively to break the story. For reasons unknown to me, the government kept postponing the date of departure. This caused tremendous frustration among the press corps who were being pressured to file reports when there were no tangible developments to write about. Many did related stories, and one morning, Peter, my chief of staff, said that he agreed that ABC TV could do a story on the road-transportation operation and that they were sending one of their star correspondents do the story. They wanted me to be the central point of the story. Much to Peter's dismay, I flatly refused. I had no time for such things, and he was an excellent person to represent me. He protested and said that the USA was a major donor and in order to maintain American public support, we had to get our stories out there. This reinforced my opinion that Peter should act on my behalf. I thought nothing further of the matter.

One afternoon, Peter invited me to go to the Hilton coffee shop for a meeting with supporters and potential donors. I enjoyed getting out of the office, so I was quick to oblige. These informal meetings also helped resolve many issues in a relaxed and informal way. As we thrashed out some outstanding issues, we were joined by two Egyptians who Peter said were the advance guard of the ABC team. We did not talk about any specific issues, and I was pleased to meet them. The next to join us was this gorgeous blonde whom Peter introduced as the ABC correspondent. My initial instinct was to stand up and leave, but then, it would be ungracious of me to make a rash judgment based on a person's looks. Besides, I found Karen engaging, well informed, empathetic, and with an unadulterated concern for the starving and our contribution to alleviating pain and suffering of these destitute people. She said that she would like to visit the RTO and talk to me off the record. We had three subsequent meetings, and after each one, she wrote me a very demonstrative note about how informative the meetings were and complimenting us on the excellent work that we were doing. The network did a story on the RTO, but unfortunately, we did not have the opportunity to see it in the Sudan. Karen was then assigned to cover Operation Rainbow, and over time, we spent a lot of time together professionally and socially.

One morning, Karen told me that it was her birthday, and I felt that this called for a celebration. As Sudan was an alcohol-free country, the only drinks that we could buy was a limited supply that was smuggled into the country by camel caravans from Eretria. A few months ago, I had purchased a bottle of red wine on the black market and was saving it for a special occasion. I felt that this was it, so I invited Karen to my house for a glass of wine. When I produced the bottle, it appeared a bit worse for wear, but then it had come a long way, and I felt that the liquid it contained would be worth its weight in Gold. The liquid resembled red wine, but that was where the similarity stopped. But I had paid $30 for the bottle and therefore felt that it had to be drunk. But the taste was awful. More like vinegar than wine. During the course of our conversation, Karen said that the managing director of the Hilton Hotel was hosting a party for her at the owner's suite, and would I like to accompany her there. When we got there, I was stunned to see an extremely well-stocked bar with a whole assortment of French wines, beer, and spirits. I felt a bit of a fool for making such ado about my dismal bottle of wine.

Meanwhile, because of the high cost and the protracted delivery times, I was given the task of finding other food suppliers in neighboring countries. I knew that Zaire was a major agricultural country that was known to export large quantities of wheat and corn. So I decided to explore the potential there. We chartered a twin-engine Cessna out of Nairobi, Kenya, for this mission. Jim was a hard-drinking English bush pilot who had spent years flying around East and

Central Africa. I welcomed him on arrival in the Sudan and set a departure time of 6:00 a.m. the following morning. He immediately started to refuel and prepared the aircraft for an early departure. When I saw Jim at 5:45 a.m. the next morning, his eyes were bloodshot, his breath smelled of alcohol, and when I asked him if he was OK, he replied in Swahili that the night was short. We then took off and landed in Juba just before lunch to refuel. But Jim had failed to file an international flight plan, which caused a further delay in our departure, but we were eventually airborne at around 1545 hours. Our intended destination was a town in Zaire that was supposed to be two and a half hours away. But now it had started to get dark. I could see the strain on Jim's face, and because of his hangover, he was not functioning to the required level of competence. "Do you know where we are?" I inquired. He snapped back in exasperation that he did not. For hours we had been flying over what appeared a green velvet carpet of dense jungle. I could see no lights at all and concluded that the area was uninhabited and a virgin jungle. As Jim was not thinking straight, I suggested that he try and contact another aircraft flying in the vicinity and seek help. This he did, and the American pilot of a missionary aircraft responded in a very precise way, "If you are flying over the jungle and don't know where you are, I suggest you return immediately to the airport where you originated from." That meant Juba. But then the airport there closed at dusk, and because of the ongoing war, security is then handed over to the army during silent hours. From previous experience, I knew that the military was trigger-happy, and they would relish shooting us down as we came overhead. But to me, our choices were limited and bleak. Crash into the jungle, never to be found, or return to Juba and risk being shot down. It was now pitch-dark, and I had an eerie feeling in my belly. As the aircraft was on charter to the United Nations, I ordered Jim to fly back to Juba and suggested he made a low approach just above tree height and glide into a landing. I could not help but say a silent prayer as I knew we needed divine intervention to ensure our safety. Jim executed the landing with brilliance. This is a characteristic of bush pilots. When faced with a catastrophe, they pull out all stops and generally prevail. We approached the terminal apron without incident, much to the astonishment of the soldiers guarding the facility. I then radioed UN security to send a vehicle to pick us up and were thankful to be safe and grateful to spend a night in a comfortable bed.

The good night's sleep did much to restore Jim's vivacity, and after completing all the formalities, we were able to take off at noon the following day. This time, we tried to skirt the dense jungle areas, which made the flight path much longer but perhaps a whole lot safer. It was a lovely afternoon, clear blue skies, excellent visibility, and both of us were relaxed and enjoyed one another's company. As we ate our lunch, we were surprised to see a major airstrip in the near distance. The sun reflected on the tarmac, and the pitch-black of its surface was in stark contrast to the lush green jungle that surrounded it. As we circled overhead, we noticed the runway lights, which indicated that this facility could be used in the dark. However, it was not marked on any of our maps. Perhaps this was because it was recently constructed. But then, the civilian aviation authorities would know about it. Jim tried making radio contact with the control tower, but there was no response. So we landed and taxied to a parking area. When the engines stopped, the aircraft was surrounded by numerous men. They wanted to know who we were, where we were going, why we had landed, and who told us about this facility. The conversation was in Swahili, and I did most of the talking. This was a modern, well-equipped facility. Two very large Mercedes Benz generators would produce all the power that was required. There was a large hangar, and a few modern buildings stood in a compound that was surrounded by a high barbed wire fence. I then asked if there were any foreigners around but got no immediate answer. So I tried asking the question in a different way. If we bought maize and wheat from the farms in the region, could we use this airport to fly the commodities to Juba? If this was a possibility, with whom could we negotiate the terms and conditions? I would like to meet them now to get a better understanding of the situation. Also, as it was getting dark, could we spend the night here before returning to Juba in the morning? We were asked to sit by a picnic bench near the hangar. About twenty minutes later, one of the guys returned with some answers. Yes, we could night stop and were shown a room with two beds with clean linen. I was also told that there was no food in the area for sale in the entire region, and therefore, the need to use this facility did not arise. At sunset, we sat around a campfire and, in true African fashion, had a few beers. We spoke in Swahili, and in this informal setting, our hosts were more forthcoming with information. This was a secret facility built by the American CIA and was used to ferry arms to Angola during the war. At one stage, it was very busy with two to three flights a night, but now things had slowed down. We were told that we were not to mention the existence of this facility to anyone. We were soon joined by some soldiers who were drunk and disorderly, so we decided to get an early night. Reviewing the factors, I decided that this was not a viable option, and perhaps Kenya would be a good alternative source, and besides, the food could be trucked in, which would eliminate the need for costly airfreight.

Happiness is when what you think, what you say and what you do are in harmony - Gandhi

Asians in Kenya are immigrants. The majority was initially brought over from India as indentured servants to build the railroad. The Goans, however, differed in many ways from the bulk of the Indo-Pakistani community. They formed a homogeneous society in terms of religion, traditions, income, education, and way of life. Typically, they were civil servants and professionals rather then traders.

I was born during the British Colonial rule in Kenya, at a time when race, color, and creed determined one's permanent status in society. The barrier lines were clearly defined and demarcated. There was no flexibility, no fraternization whatsoever between the races that made up the demographic profile of society. The opportunity to capitalize on and perhaps harness the wealth and capacity of this multicultural populace was therefore frittered away. These prejudices ensured that there was no prospect for upward mobility, irrespective of how gifted or talented and individual was. I felt like a slave trapped in my own country and remember being acutely aware of the profound resentment I felt because of this unjust social order based on color.

The winds of change had started to blow. The prevailing vision of a postcolonial country was a nation that offered equality to its entire population, irrespective of their race, color, religion, or creed. I wanted to play my part and contribute in whatever way that I could to accelerate this stimulating and exciting transformation. The occupation of land by European settlers was the foremost point of contention. Most of the land that was appropriated belonged to the Kikuyu, one of the largest tribes in Kenya. This land was in the fertile central highlands, where the climate was cool and the rain fell in abundance. These injustices and repressive form of governance generated tremendous frustration and antagonized the oppressed.

Discord and antipathy between the white settlers and the native Africans would be the best way to describe the colonial experience that affected and changed so many lives. White settlers continued to be enticed to Kenya, lured by the offers of free land. They were encouraged to settle in what was nicknamed the "White Highlands." Harry Thuku, who was backed by many influential and revolutionary Asians, led the first nationalist movement. In 1922, Tuku was arrested and sent into exile. Jomo Kenyatta, a former water meter inspector with the municipality of Nairobi, stepped in to fill the void. World War II increased the discontent of the masses as African soldiers from the King's African Rifles fought alongside their colonial masters in foreign battlefields. They were exposed to an assortment of influences that initiated the perception that the white man was not supreme.

In 1951, the state of affairs in Kenya detroriated to such an extent that colonial government made a feeble attempt to put together minimal political concessions. However, these did nothing to appease the masses. By 1952, there was ample evidence of a plan for a rebellion that later became known as the Mau-Mau.

At the outset, oath givers were arrested, and Kikuyu loyalists were encouraged to denounce the struggle. Once the gravity of the problem was realized, the governor, Sir Evelyn Baring declared a state of emergency, bestowing sweeping powers to the police and army. This was deemed necessary at first, but it was later used as a pretext, for the blatant violation of basic human rights. This further spread and inflamed abhorrence for the British rule, leading to savage brutality, carnage, and death.

In 1959, freehold land titles were issued to Africans, new farm supports were put into place, and a major drive started to provide work for the jobless. The growth of the agrarian middle class had started to gain momentum. During this period, the trade movement also started to gain impetus and contribution. Mr. Mahan Singh, an Indian, was principal. Despite—or rather because of—this, he was quickly disposed of by the authorities and branded a communist.

The Mau-Mau revolt started in 1952 and ended in 1960. Members of the Kikuyu tribe formed the core of the struggle, supported to a smaller degree by members of the Embu and Meru tribes. The Mau-Mau was immediately branded as a terrorist organization by the British government, and although it did not succeed militarily, it created a rift between the powerful settler community and the British home office. The colonial strategy of divide and rule paid dividends as it succeeded in segregating the various tribes of Kenya and made it impossible for them to work in unison for a common cause.

There continues to be debate and disagreement as to the exact meaning of Mau-Mau. The most plausible explanation is that it is a Swahili acronym that, if literally translated into English, would mean "White man, go back abroad so that the African can get his independence."

At the onset of the emergency, the home office in London mobilized and dispatched thousands of British troops from the United Kingdom to Kenya. Crack Kalenjins, Wakamba, Samburu, and Turkhana soldiers of the King's African Rifles, with extensive combat experience in Burma, were also deployed into more hazardous regions, in the vast and desolate forests of the Aberdare Mountains in the Central Province.

I was seven years old when the Mau-Mau revolution started. From the beginning, the British Army had little reliable intelligence on the strength of the Mau-Mau. Senior officers felt that it was a minor event compared to the Malayan emergency that they had fought in. But the Mau-Mau carried out daring attacks on police stations, government offices, and settler farms.

As the army fought the Mau-Mau in the forests and with "pseudo gangs" composed largely of former guerrillas, the government instituted strict measures against civilians, detaining many people in circumstances that were similar in many aspects to concentration camps in Germany. Because of the intensity of the hostility, Britain was forced to deploy fifty thousand British troops during the course of this conflict.

My father Luis was of humble beginnings from the village of Cansalim that formed part of the Portuguese colony of Goa. His was a large family unit of subsistence farmers who were Catholic, deeply religious, and barely literate. Through hard work and dedication, Luis was able to obtain a good education. He spoke Portuguese, English, and was obsessed with the desire to elevate himself out of the vicious circle of poverty through hard work and travel.

Colonial Goa offered little or no real opportunities to the indigenous population. Like all colonizers, the policy of the Portuguese was exploitive and did not in any way cater to the aims and ambitions of the natives. Because of his upbringing and circumstance, Luis was serious in his outlook, and like a lot of people of his generation was reluctant to stray away from self imposed restrictive traditional values, and was intolerant to new ideas or changes. Why do we resist accepting that perhaps change is the only constant in our lives? He was most content with doing nothing that would disrupt the status quo.

I am not certain of exactly when he decided to set off alone on his foreign odyssey, but I believe it was around 1927. His plan was to travel to the Portuguese colony of Mozambique. The journey was long, arduous, and not without peril. At the time, passage was by steamship, on the crammed open deck of a creaky old vessel whose seaworthiness was questionable. There were no cabins, beds, and certainly no privacy. Passengers lived communally and made themselves as comfortable as they could in their austere environment.

On reaching Mombasa in Kenya, Father decided to jump ship. He had endured enough. He was unwell, seasick, and now wanted out of this marathon sea passage. He was fortunate to meet an old acquaintance who offered him a job in a bar in Mombasa. This was a positive start to his new life in an intimidating and primitive part of the world that was being unwrapped and tamed by adventurers, hunters, herders, pioneers, and fortune seekers. Luis gladly accepted.

Mother often spoke of being overcome by despair and enduring dire culture shock soon after arriving in Kenya. The environment she now faced was raw, rowdy, rudimentary, racist, and lonely. She was unable to speak the local language, which added to her sentiment of abandonment and isolation. The wives of the Indian neighbors were domesticated, uninformed, basic, and boring. They had brought their traditional India lifestyles along with them and on no account made an attempt to change or integrate. All things being equal, my early days were happy. I found myself growing to be increasingly independent. I precisely understood what my parents' expectations were of me and carefully avoided crossing the threshold of their tolerance. Therefore, there was no antagonism; I seldom got into trouble and started to make decisions at an early age.

The family cook was a Kikuyu gentleman called Jugay. He was not only a good cook, but in my opinion, he also was a very wise old man. I hung around him a great deal, and he, in his own quaint way, passed on to me a multitude of unconventional but essential life skills. Sitting on traditional hand-carved three-legged stools; he elated and educated me with fascinating tribal yarns that were designed to emphasize his lessons in traditional mythology.

I often sneaked in a meal with him. We ate in his dark little room that was dimly illuminated by a flickering kerosene lamp. I habitually noticed his eyes dance in the faint light as I gazed at him in awe. My favorite dish was "ugali." It was simple, cheap and was made from white maize meal. The texture was comparable to mashed potatoes; it was eaten with the fingers and dipped it into a soupy sauce called "sukuma-weeki" in Swahili (push the week) consisting of spinach laced with a few scraps of meat when Jugay's meager budget permitted.

One morning, my younger brother, Derrick, and I were at home with Jugay. It those days, the milk was not pasteurized but was boiled instead. Derrick yearned for the cream that formed on top of the milk once it was boiled. He used to stick his fingers into the pot and quickly scoop the cream directly into his mouth so as to go undetected. Jugay was concerned that Derrick would scald his fingers doing this. So on the day in question, the pot of boiling milk was placed on a high shelf in the kitchen, out of reach of Derrick. However, Derrick bid his time, and when alone, he grabbed a stool and reached out for the boiling milk. Somehow, he stumbled and the milk came crashing down on his chest.

On hearing the commotion, both Jugay and I dashed to the kitchen. Derrick was on the floor, wincing in pain, with boiling milk all over his chest. I will never forget the expression on Jugay's face. We tried taking Derrick's drenched shirt off his body. However, this was not possible as the fabric had fused with his kin. All hell was let loose when my parents arrived on the scene. I bore the brunt of their wrath. Not long after, I was told that Jugay had left and would never return. The reason we were told was that he had been threatened by the Mau-Mau for working for an Asian civil servant. I knew otherwise. To me, his departure was a profound loss, of a friend, a surrogate father, and a mentor.

Many of the people living in our neighborhood carried firearms, allegedly for their personal protection. My uncle Francis, who was a bachelor at the time and who lived with the family, also had a sidearm. To me, his pistol was more of a prestigious symbol. I was aware that Francis had never fired the pistol, and therefore, it was most unlikely that he would have been able to accurately hit a target. Francis, like his sister Charlotte, was a fastidious man. He always dressed impeccably and smoked using a long ivory and silver cigarette holder. He took great care of his person, played social tennis and bridge, and partied frequently at the Goan Gymkhana Club, where he was a popular member.

Francis was my first hero. He had just purchased a new 350 cc Norton motorbike. I just could not get my eyes off the machine.

It was black and chrome, and I very much wanted to learn to ride. Perhaps one day, I would be able to buy a bike of my own. For now, I had to be content with just polishing my uncle's machine for a shilling a week. As an added incentive, Francis would sometimes take me for a spin around the block.

Luis had now risen in rank and prominence in the British Colonial Civil Service. He was the senior administrator of of the government printing press, where he followed instructions without question. I once accompanied Luis to his place of work and had the unexpected privilege of being introduced to his English boss. The servile demeanor of my father astounded me as, at the time, I failed to appreciate the fact that the only way to getting a promotion was by being servile. I should not have been so quick to judge.

For his dedication and loyalty to the crown, Luis was made a member of the British Empire (MBE). The significance of this decoration was lost on me at the time, but I begrudged the fact that he was obliged to work long hours and well into the night, supervising the printing of top secret operational orders for the security forces. This made him very vulnerable to being attacked by the Mau-Mau, especially as he walked home alone through a swamp and on unlit streets. Nairobi was a dangerous place after dark. Despite the curfew, many residents were hacked to death with machetes in dreadful tribal rituals.

I never could find sleep until Luis returned home from work. One day he did, almost half-dead. He had been attacked and lashed with a whip made from the outer casing of a motor tire. He had huge welts on his back and chest and complained about having difficulty in breathing. It was past midnight, and without a car, we were unable to get him to a hospital. No doctor was willing to make a house call at that hour. I cannot recall what happened next, but I was thankful that my father was home alive.

This experience traumatized me. I could not put up with the thought of being subjected to a similar experience again. I therefore decided that for my own peace of mind, I would walk each night to the bridge where my father was attacked and accompany him home. I was twelve years old and never stopped to think what this would achieve. At breakfast the following morning, I told Luis what I had decided the night before. He did not comment, but I understood that he was glad to have the company.

My promise was easier said than done. I sneaked out of the house at 9:00 p.m. that evening. The streets were deserted and dark. I was alone and afraid and wished that Jugay was with me. He was Kikuyu; he spoke the language of the Mau-Mau. In the dark, I could easily pass as his son if only I kept my mouth shut.

Crossing the road on to a track that went through the swamp was real scary. Fear was new to me. The elephant grass was by far taller than I was, and it shut out most of the night-light. I was unused to being out so late and alone in the dark. The sounds of the night, the crickets, the bats, and the owls were alien, and the smell of the swamp was foreign and intimidating. All I wanted to do was pray. But I could not remember the words of the prayer I wanted to say. This added to my anguish.

As I approached the scene of the attack, the bridge over the stream in the middle of the swamp was barely visible in the muted light of the moon. I stopped and surveyed the scene. My ears and eyes wide open but unfamiliar with the sight and sounds. It was a cool night, but my body was covered in sweat, and I could not understand the shivers.

To my relief, I could discern no Mau-Mau on the bridge. Perhaps the gang was lying in ambush in the tall elephant grass? I was exhausted and decided to lie on my chest on the hard black cotton soil and observe. My misgiving was that I had told Louis that I would meet him at the middle of the bridge, but I was terrified of venturing forward. Then I began to wonder if there were any lions in the swamp. The boundary of Nairobi National Park was not far from where I lay, and on many occasions, prides of lions have strayed into the city, looking for prey.

Suddenly I saw a person sprinting across the bridge. The runner had the smoker's cough of my father. I could immediately tell that he was anxious. Knowing this gave me the audacity to spring up and run towards him. He was delighted to see me, and we embraced. This was the only time that I can remember my father showed me any real affection.

Compared to other areas in the country, our Park Road neighborhood was relatively safe. The local Home Guard unit made up of non-Kikuyu, who were armed with bow and arrows, machete, and a few Lee-Enfield rifles, were a fair deterrent. Despite the fact that all houses were purported burglar proof, residents lived in constant fear of being brutally attacked and ritually slaughtered. Horrendous stories of vicious attacks on the civilian population were reported daily in the national media, and although these mainly targeted the British community, there had been assaults against the Asians as well.

One night, as the whole family sat at the table having dinner, out of the blue, we head a loud clatter caused by a stick being moved against the corrugated iron security fence that enclosed the backyard. It drew our instant attention, and I saw a ball-like object with a lighted wick fall into the yard. I glanced at Francis and sensed alarm. We listened to the rapidly receding footsteps on the other side of the perimeter fence. All was now hushed both inside and outside. Francis and I went to investigate. We discovered a crude homemade petrol bomb and were grateful that it had failed to explode. Why was our family now being targeted?

The banking system was still in embryonic form, and therefore, all government salaries were paid in cash. It was the end of the month, and Luis's hip pocket was bulging with cash. As a matter of habit, he hung his trousers on a hook near his bed. My bed was near a window, and in the middle of the night, I was roused by a rustling sound.

Convinced that it was a mouse, I turned over and tried going back to sleep. But then I could feel a draft coming through an open window. This was impossible as I personally had made sure that all windows and doors were firmly secured before going to bed. I got alarmed. Were we being attacked? I could not hear any cries of pain or screams for help. Things appeared normal. This added to my restlessness. The best way of finding out would be to get out of bed and check. The prospect of being instantly beheaded with a machete was foreboding. With my head firmly covered with a blanket, I pretended that this too would pass away.

Then, as suddenly as it started, everything felt silent again. Falling asleep was out of the question, and I tossed and turned, trying to figure out what had happened. The ambiguity evaporated when Louis dashed into my room. He shook me out of bed, asking if I had taken his trousers. I looked at the window. Yes, it had been pried open with a crowbar.

Using a pole with a hook at the tip, the intruder fished Luis's trousers from where they were hanging and slithered them out through the window. With the pockets emptied, the trousers were dumped under a tree. The loss of an entire month's salary put a financial burden on Father, probably causing stress. Thankfully, this was not in any way passed on to the rest of the family.

Commotion was part and parcel of our daily lives. One evening, Francis returned home looking pale and worried. He had just lost his pistol. This was a criminal offence that carried a jail term, and he was rightly flustered. There were mitigating factors. He worked at the attorney general's chambers; he understood the law and knew he could avoid being charged if he could prove that the weapon was stolen and not lost.

I cannot remember the exact details but recall that he had a plausible explanation of how the pistol was stolen. That evening, Francis took me for a spin on his bike. We traveled further than normal and at high speed. I was ecstatic and felt the warm wind blowing through my hair with my eyes streaming.

Suddenly, Francis slowed down and, in a very serious tone, started discussing the implications of the forthcoming preliminary hearing into the theft of his pistol. I felt really uneasy when he asked me to substantiate his story by signing a written statement as a witness. I had no option but to sign. The very notion of the cool Uncle Francis being slung into jail sent shivers up my spine. Francis was cultured, well-read, and kind, and I loved him so.

My father was now entitled to a first-class sea passage for the whole family from Mombasa to Goa once every four years. The history of Goa can be traced back to the third century BC. In 1498, Vasco da Gama became the first European to set foot on Indian soil when he arrived by sea and landed at what is now known as Old Goa. The Portuguese objective was to grab absolute control of the spice trade from the other European powers.

In 1510, Portuguese admiral Alfonso de Albuquerque defeated the ruling Bijapur King and established a permanent settlement at Old Goa. Goa soon became the most important Portuguese possession in India, and it was therefore granted the same civic concessions as Lisbon. The Portuguese also encouraged its citizens to marry local women and settle in the country. After India gained its independence from Britain in 1947, Portugal refused to consent to surrender the jurisdiction of its enclave. Adjudication by the United Nations in 1950 ruled in support of self-determination for the people of Goa. In 1961, the Indian Army invaded, amalgamating Goa with India.

I really looked forward to our vacation in Goa, which lasted over a month. The voyage aboard the SS *Karanja* took eight days.

The ship was built in Glasgow and launched on March 10, 1948, and had a cruising speed of sixteen knots. It was owned and operated by the British India Steam Navigation Company of Glasgow and London and carried both passengers and cargo. I loved the vastness of the ocean, the scent of the sea, the spray, the sound of blustery weather blowing through the rigging, the quality of life on board, the entertainment, the food, but most of all, the freedom to be able to go anywhere without fear of being attacked by the Mau-Mau.

On board, I shared a cabin with my brothers Derrick and Tony, and they looked to me to set the daily agenda. Activities included playing table tennis, deck games, and wandering into the bowels of the ship to inspect the engine room. Sometimes we went to the back of the ship and stared at the foam that was churned up by the mighty propellers of the ship and watched the gulls follow in the ships wake. Older sister Hazel was of course excluded from these exploratory activities.

Luis owned a large house in Cansalum the village of his birth. There was an external verandah that wrapped itself around the entire building. It was adequately furnished but had no electricity or running water, and the pit latrine was strange and smelly. The house was situated on a large piece of land with fruit trees, flower bushes, and coconut palms. It also had its own well. Some fisher folk squatted on the land. The arrangement was they paid no rent but instead took care of the property in the absence of my father.

Local men who labored in the rice paddies wore a "khasti," which is similar to a G-string, like that worn by Tarzan in the movies. I fancied this form of dress and convinced one of my relatives to help me buy one. I donned it with pride, embellishing it with my Kenya hunting knife.

My Goan relatives were scandalized when they saw me appear in public dressed like a low-caste laborer. Caste and class were important in this traditional conservative society. Ignoring the protest, I pleaded to be taken to the beach at dawn to help the fishermen haul in their nets. The exercise was invigorating; the men hauled in the nets in unison, with the tempo being set by a simple chant.

The air was fresh, the smell of the sea stimulating, and the sensation of shale on my bare feet felt abrasive. The temperature of the sand that caressed my toes was starting to increase under the rays of the early morning sun as the waves twined with seaweed danced and crashed onto shore. Gulls circled the nets, shrieking in delight and anticipation, in reaction to being goaded by the fish trapped in the nets that caused numerous ripples in the water. Mackerel were the bulk of the catch, followed by squid and crabs. The owner of the boat and nets received the bulk and the pick of the catch. The remainder was then equally distributed among the fishermen, with the gulls feasting on the remnants. As a sign of goodwill, I was given two or three mackerel to take home for breakfast.

On the way home from the beach, I loved chasing sand crabs. They were small and would scurry down holes in the sand as I approached with my long stick. Part of the procedure was poking the stick down the hole that the crab had darted into. This was a futile undertaking that appealed to my fantasy.

One night, I was brusquely roused by the shouting, screaming, and barking of dogs. It was pitch-dark outside, and the house had no electricity. My first notion was that the Mau-Mau followed us to Goa, putting us under siege prior to slaughter. Once conscious, I realized that the people were talking in Konkani and not Kikuyu. I respectfully follow the family outside to find a number of the fishermen focusing their flashlights on a large cobra they had just killed as it tried to get up the steps to enter the house.

Everyone pointed their finger at me as being the culprit responsible for this near tragedy. Apparently, I had poked my stick down the cobra's nest. It had therefore followed my trail back home with the intention of biting and killing me in revenge. From then on, I quickly developed a total aversion to snakes, resolving never to mess with them again.

Hunting for sand crabs was now an anathema. Instead, I devoted my vigor to the brown ground squirrel. They were in abundance on the property and could be seen frolicking all over. They were majestic, unafraid, and exciting to observe. I fed them regularly and eventually became quite familiar with their behavior. Not long afterwards, a baby squirrel befriended me. With time, it grew bold and regularly ate out of the palm of my hand, not flinching even when I stroked it.

After a while, it became it became bolder and more aggressive, running all over my body and perching on my head. A sense of trust had developed between us, and we bonded. I called my new companion "Rafiki" (friend). We both looked forward to our daily encounters, and Rafiki would predictably be perched on the same coconut tree stump, waiting to be fed.

In retrospect, I regret the fact that I did not have a more robust relationship with my brother Tony as I would have liked to share these simple joys and pleasures with him. However, he was younger, different, and perhaps a little more introverted. Undoubtedly, I was the odd person out in the family. Was this a trait that I had inherited from Charlotte?

Our holiday was sadly coming to an end. I had grown to love Goa, its people, their strong Catholic beliefs, the food, and their uncomplicated way of life. Despite having so little, most Goans were content, uncomplicated, trustworthy, dependable, and happy. My only regret was that I was unable to communicate with my relations in their native tongue. To me, British colonial policy was to divide and rule. The Portuguese method was control through integration. Religion was intrinsic to their colonial policy. I am not able to discern which was more effective, but none were well liked.

With our imminent departure from Goa, I was growing increasingly concerned about what to do with Rafiki? He had become entirely dependent on me, and it was obvious that he could no longer fend for himself. The only viable solution was to take him to Africa. But how does one transport a ground squirrel to Kenya undetected? Firstly, he would have to be trained to travel in my trouser pocket. This appeared to be mission impossible. To my astonishment, Rafiki took to this approach like a fish to water. Once inside my pocket, he quickly fell asleep. I think that it was the warmth of my body that gave him a sense of security. The only snag was that when Rafiki started to dream, he would claw on my thigh—uncomfortable and bad for my trouser pocket.

Prior to our going away, I stocked up on peanuts. We all crammed into a vintage automobile for a high-speed, bumpy, and dusty drive to the port town of Marmagoa. Pigs squealed and dashed for cover, chickens squawked, the and water buffaloes gazed from a distance as we whizzed past in a cloud of red dust. Rafiki was not overtly happy in this confined environment, but I was thankful that he behaved and stayed out of sight.

In Marmagoa, we boarded a ferry for the short hop to Bombay. I felt a sense of calm as soon as we embarked on the SS *Kampala* at the start of our voyage back to Mombasa. The *Kampala* was a newer steamship than its sister ship, the *Karanja*. It looked sleek and majestic in its all-white trim, infusing in me confidence that it was able to tackle the high seas, come hell or high water. The crew was very friendly and lent a hand during boarding. This time we had three cabins, and I shared one with Derrick.

The *Kampala* sailed amid great fanfare and jubilation. Its main mast and bows bedecked in bunting. The crews, in their crisp white uniforms, neatly lined the decks, waving with their caps to the crowds of well-wishers clamored on the quay, eager to bid the *Kampala* bon voyage and safe passage. Joseph was our cabin Steward. I was quickly able to take him into my confidence. He came from Goa, and I felt a certain tie with him from the start and instantly knew that I could trust him. He did not bat an eyelid when I introduced him to Rafiki. Our passage to Mombasa was uneventful but enjoyable.

The *Kampala* docked in Mombasa on a hot and steamy Saturday morning. The wharf was crowded with shirtless coolies, their bodies gleaming in the bright, hot sun. They all had jute sacks covering their heads, and they waited patiently to offload the luggage from the ship. I admired their well-formed and muscular bodies. Each and every one of them appeared to be a prize weight lifter.

Rafiki was perched on my shoulder, taking his first sniff of Kenya's air and keenly surveying the scene. By now, he had wormed himself into the family's heart and became a welcome member of the clan. We took the night train to Nairobi. It was a fascinating journey, creeping its way through the Athi plains, teeming with wildlife. The sun setting through the acacia trees was a spectacular sight. I could not help thinking about all those poor Indian railway construction coolies who died at the rate of four per mile of track that they built and over twenty-five who were taken from their tents at night and eaten by lions who became known as the man-eaters of Tsavo. The regularity of the locomotive huffing and puffing, belching steam and clouds of smoke into the air soon sent me to sleep.

Francis welcomed us on arrival in Nairobi Railway Station amid chaos, shouting, and under the watchful eye of British soldiers in their starched battle fatigues. He was immaculately dressed, his hair sleek and brushed back, and his mustache neatly trimmed. We drove home in an ancient cab. Rafiki soon got accustomed to his new abode and normally slept under the sheets in my bed. I gathered that in our absence, Francis had grown accustomed to the party scene at the club. He stayed out later, drank more, and definitely smoked less, but no mention of him dating.

I looked with trepidation at the prospects of going back to school. The Dr. Rebeiro Goan School was a community school that provided the Goan community with a quality Catholic education. We were obliged to wear school uniforms. Boys wore a gray wool blazer, white shirt, and gray shorts with stockings. I am sure that this was a replication of some British school garb, and although distinctive, the blazers were entirely inappropriate for our warm tropical climate.

Because of the security constraints, we were bussed to school. The journey was always loud and boisterous, with the boys striving to show off to the girls. I was now nearing puberty and could not help but notice some of the pretty girls on the bus. However, I was far too shy and insecure to even dare engage any of them in a conversation.

Over this period, I could not help but notice a change in Luis's political stripes. He certainly was not a chameleon that changed its colors to blend into the prevailing surroundings. He was a person who had the courage to stand up to his moral convictions even though his opinions may have been distorted and different from my own. I admired him for this. Luis was disappointed and disillusioned by the prevailing state of affairs in Kenya, but he never discussed politics or his work at home.

It was evident that many middle-class folk had started to recognize the fact that the Mau-Mau was not really a terrorist organization but rather a movement committed to achieving self-determination and independence. Most, though, did not agree with their savage and brutal techniques. This was governed by the fact that as part of the initiation, a ritual tribal oath that had its origins in witchcraft was significant. It was administered clandestinely to all inductees to guarantee absolute obedience, loyalty, and unflinching commitment to the Mau-Mau movement.

The well-educated and widely traveled Asians were now playing an increasingly significant role in the political struggle for independence modeled on Mathma Gandhi's philosophy of passive resistance. They were committed to bringing about change through dialogue and understanding rather then through belligerence. Was Luis now associating with this splinter group?

I certainly was not the brightest student in my class. My mind often strayed, adversely affecting my results at school. Although I never failed an exam, some of my test scores were marginal at best. Latin was my worst subject. Despite my resolute endeavors, I never attain better marks then Derrick, who was in a grade lower then me at school. This infuriated me. Algebra and geometry were my best subjects. These fields of study were stimulating, there was no ambiguity involved, and the results were apparent.

The headmaster of the school was an Irish Jesuit priest called Fr. Frank Commerford. He was a disciplined perfectionist who befriended me at an early stage. He dared me to reach out beyond my self-perceived and self-imposed limitations out of my normal comfort zone. I cherished his advice because I sensed that he really wanted the very best for me. He argued that in order to make an impression, an individual must excel. I often had doubts about whether I had the capacity to be worthy of his expectations.

However, I recognized the fact that his counsel always formed the basis of my aspirations. Fr. Frank understood that I was more interested in extracurricular alfresco activities and instead of scholastic pursuits.

He also demonstrated that this was not an either-or situation. A person could do well in both with the right focus, generating a win-win situation.

Fr. Frank was aware of my fascination with the outdoors, but he never attempted to stifle this pursuit. He was always supportive but, in his own way, made me comprehend that in order to succeed, one had to compete with the best, generally on their terms. A sound education was therefore a prerequisite for success. One day, he handed me a circular from the Outward Bound Mountain School in Loitoitok on the Kenya-Tanzania border, inviting high school students to enroll in a three-week program at the school that culminated with climbing Mt. Kilimanjaro. I quickly noted that the minimum age requirement was eighteen years.

Fr. Frank said that he would try making a special of case why I should be permitted to attend if I got written parental consent. This would not be easy. My parents had warned that I had got into a habit of pushing boundaries with them. The good news was that my father would not have to pay for the course as Fr. Frank had identified a sponsor.

I set in motion a very gentle but consistent strategy to bring about a change in Luis's thinking, never demanding but quietly outlining the benefits. Luis eventually signed the consent, and it was submitted by Fr. Frank to the Board of Governors of the Outward Bound School. Unfortunately, they ruled that I should be at least sixteen years old before reapplying. This meant waiting for another year.

Paul was my best friend at school. He was raised in Parklands on what could be described as acreage. We had similar pursuits and spent most of our free time together. Some days after school, we walked over to his place and using slingshots, hunted for birds in the neighborhood. There were many fruit trees on the property with lots of sweet corn growing near a stream. When hungry, we would pluck and roast corn on an open charcoal fire or pick fruit and then lie under the shady trees and tell yarns while watching the world go by. Despite our nearness, both of us were extremely competitive, with each trying to outdo the other.

The Boy Scout Movement inspired me. I started of as a Wolf Cub at an early age, later graduating to the Boy Scouts, after that to the Senior Scouts, and subsequently becoming the troop leader. I was one of the first Queen Scouts in the school. This achievement was not without its responsibility. It required time, management skills, and leadership. Responsibilities included organizing all-troop activity and the training of younger members in all aspects of scouting, including first aid, cooking, and basic survival techniques. I coordinated fund-raising activities, planned bonfires, and made plans for singsongs and street theater. To me these activities highlighted the importance of team, which was essential for kids of diverse backgrounds to work and play together in unison.

I looked forward to camping trips, and our troop frequently went on expeditions to Rowland Camp, a beautiful tract of woodland just out of Nairobi. This park was specially set aside for the exclusive use by the Boy Scouts and Girl Guides in memory of Baden Powell, who lived in Kenya from 1938 until his death in 1941. It had excellent facilities, including hiking trails, cleared campsites, showers, toilets, and pits for camp fires. Lord Baden Powel of Gilwell, the founder of the Scout and Girl Guide Movements, first came to East Africa in 1906 and returned frequently to visit his old friend and colleague, Major E. Sherbrooke Walker, MC, who built the famous Outspan Hotel in Nyeri and the legendary Treetops Lodge where Princess Elizabeth first learned that she had become Queen of England.

On one of our camping trips and in the middle of the night, I heard loud rummaging sounds coming from our food-storage tent. My teammates were seized by panic. I immediately feared that a Mau-Mau gang from the nearby Ngong Hills had descended upon us and were foraging for food. We were the only people in the park, and our cries for help would surely fall on deaf ears. In emergency situations like this, the troop leader took charge. For better or worse, I would have to take the bull by the horns. Suppressing my anxiety and watched by the others, I put on a brave face, climbed out of my sleeping bag, grabbed a flashlight, and went outside to investigate.

My exit from the tent was intentionally boisterous. Perhaps I wanted the intruder to hear me approach and take flight.

The night was pitch-dark and still. The black rain clouds were being blown towards the south, not a star in the sky and a bad omen according to Jugay. The burglar had obviously heard me coming, and that was why everything was now hushed, I surmised. Visions of them lying in ambush, waiting, watching my every move, and plotting flashed through my psyche. The circumstances in which I was were partial and iniquitous. They could see me, but I could not see them. The longer I remained paralyzed, the more edgy I became.

Immediate engagement was now called for. Taking a deep breath, I dashed into the food tent, my eyes squinting in the dark. There was a wild scurry out of the tent, and I collided with large ant bear pounding a hasty retreat. When I gave the all clear, the rest of the team joined me. We quickly took stock, and to our dismay, there was no edible food left. With no options, we decided to abort the outing first thing in the morning. This experience brought about a profound change in me. I was now able to contend with fear and remain rational in even the most threatening of situations.

Goans are raised in strict Catholic traditions, and every evening, the whole family, with no exceptions, were obliged to congregate to say the family rosary. Mother's assertion was that a family that prayed together stayed together. To me, this was an imposition on my freedom and time. I cannot claim to be a devout Catholic, but I have faith in the belief that one should only do unto others as you would have them do unto you.

I learned to serve mass, and I was gratified that my basic Latin skills helped me to quickly learn the prayers. We lived a long way from our parish church, St. Francis Xavier's. I served at morning mass and woke up before dawn to jog all the way to church on an empty stomach. Besides the security implications, I arrived at the sacristy famished. My brain refused function without nourishment and often had to mumble the prayers I could not remember.

The British Army often conducted predawn cordon and search operations to weed out weapon caches and the Mau-Mau. They swooped down onto a neighborhood in the middle of the night to carry out their maneuvers, and often I came across their makeshift camps on my way to church. The soldiers had erected large razor-wire pens where detainees were held without charges prior to being screened and interrogated. I recognized many of the detainees to be innocent domestic servants whose only crime was that they could not speak English when questioned. They were therefore suspect and arrested.

Once I went past an army field kitchen. The smell of frying bacon, eggs, and toast made me crave for food. The army appeared to provide a good life and certainly took excellent care of its soldiers. Perhaps I would try to join the army someday. At this point, I realized that if the army was hunting Mau-Mau in our area, then there must be an element risk in my trying to reach church on foot each morning through deserted streets. The recollection of Luis's attack was still fresh in my mind. A bike would solve the problem, but I understood that getting the money to buy one would be complicated.

It was a real pleasure serving mass for Fr. Frank. As I helped him get into his robes, he spoke to me as if I was an adult, all substantive stuff, and he joked and teased but always provoked serious thought. I was invigorated with these encounters and in his presence. We were friends, and he had an immense impact on my development and future. He instilled into my psyche the notion second best was just not good enough.

Our summer vacations were fast approaching, and we all were excited about the prospects of going the coast and staying with my aunt, uncle, and three cousins. A. Maud, like her sister Charlotte, was a real character. She was full of vigor and vitality. Besides, she was lively and had a great sense of humor, an excellent cook, and fun to be around. Hazel was nominated as chaperone for the overnight train journey to Mombasa. We all looked forward to spending quality with cousins Greta, Ingrid, and Stafford, whom we had not seen for years.

Mombasa met all my expectations, and we all had a memorable vacation at the coast. I was particularly fascinated by the old part of the city that was steeped in history and untouched over the years. It was awesome scrambling through the celebrated Fort Jesus built by the Portuguese in 1593 and majestically occupying the most strategic and commanding position on a coral cliff at the mouth of Old Harbor.

This fortification played a crucial role in protecting trade routes to India and their interest in East Africa. It is probably the best example in the world of sixteenth-century Portuguese military architecture. It was easy to visualize the major role the fort played through its tumultuous history as it changed hands between the Portuguese and Omani Arabs at least nine times. The British later used the fort as a prison, but it now is a museum dedicated to the early adventurers and colonizers of this part of Africa.

In 1448, the Portuguese explorer Vasco De Gama landed in Mombasa. The objective of his mission was to spread the Christian faith and expand Portugal's trading empire. He met stiff opposition from the natives, and in order to deal with the situation, he formed a key partnership with the king of Malandi, whom he later made the sultan of Mombasa. The main activity of the port was the exchange of slaves for merchandise from ships from Europe.

Next to the fort is the magnificent old Mombasa Club. A sign outside warned that membership was reserved for Europeans only. Anyone who was white fitted into the category of being European.

This allure and splendor of the old city is hard to describe or to resist. It was a magnet that drew me to it often. It is steeped in the past, and its grandeur dominates the present, shrouded in romance and the mystical. Traditional architecture dominates the setting, with structures shimmering spotless under their fresh coats of whitewash.

The city is honeycombed with narrow winding streets flanked by "dukas" (shops) hawking spices, fragrances, Indian foodstuff, silks, and handmade garments. Also on the water was a large uncovered fish market offering the best of the day's catch at prices that were affordable to all. Mosques dotted the neighborhood scene with their white minarets reaching out to heaven and sparkling in the noon sun.

Then there is the old "dow" harbor. Dows are ancient, traditional, handcrafted wooden vessels with a central mast and triangular cloth sails. They were built to withstand the rough monsoon seas and, in the early nineteenth century, transported thousands of Indian manual workers to Mombasa. They have plied these waters for as long as man can remember, using a significant wind system that seasonally blows in opposite directions to get them to their destinations exclusively under sail. The crews were weathered sea dogs who navigated the high seas, guided only by the stars. I was enthralled by these grand old ships that regurgitated from their bowels tons of mysterious cargo that were then sold all over East Africa.

We also spent time on the water. Romero, a friend of my cousins, had a small rowboat, and he frequently took us for jaunts in Matwapa Creek. He loved the ocean, knew a lot about it, and was an excellent fisherman. I viewed him as a rough diamond because aside from the positive aspects to his character, there were a number of coarse edges too. He was also very impulsive.

Once he casually inquired if I could swim, knowing full well that I could not. I revealed that I would like to learn. Without a qualm, he immediately grabbed me and dumped me overboard. I thrashed about wildly and felt that I was drowning, fully expecting that Romero would dive into the water and rescue me. He did not but instead calmly instructed me to relax and let my body float in the saltwater. I did, and to my amazement, this worked. Then he gave me my first lesson at a distance in swimming. After the fifth session, I was no longer afraid and began to enjoy swimming in the sea. Romero, thank you.

Being it was a Friday, Francis went to the club, and it was not unusual for him to return home late. I went to bed early as I had an early start working on an extremely exciting project. True to form, Francis returned home as expected. He did not bother to change into his pajamas and just crashed into bed still wearing his street clothes. Rafiki was not in my bed that night, but I was not worried as he often slept elsewhere in the house. In the morning, Francis entered my room and announced that Rafiki had gone away. I pleaded with him to explain. The night before, Francis collapsed into bed and inadvertently squished poor Rafiki to death.

I could not hide my grief and knew that nothing could compensate for the loss of my dear friend. It made me appreciate how fragile life was and knew and understood that because of the Mau-Mau, we could be here today but gone tomorrow.

Joseph, a neighbor, was a civil servant, and his friend Raymond was an electrical engineer. They were planning a major safari to Central Africa and the Congo and had purchased an old Renault van for this purpose. It was dated and dilapidated, requiring major body and engine work. For reasons best known to the owners, they started work by painting the body black, cutting extra windows in the back, and installing a supplementary fuel and water tank. A large map of Africa was stenciled on the back of the van, showing the exact route of the expedition. Both men were mature adults with careers and far more money than I could ever dream of having.

I used to walk past the yard where they worked and stare in admiration at what they had initiated. They noticed me but showed no interest whatsoever. I had a burning desire to ask them to consider making me a member of their team. All I could offer was sweat equity and a willingness to work especially hard. Charlotte used to wear a corset to shape her waist and breast. It was a very restrictive garment limiting movement and breathing. I now felt as if I was wearing a corset. My shyness and inhibitions were major constraints to myself-determination because they restricted me in so many ways. I decided that I would not allow anything to preclude me from achieving my goals.

I was angry, and throwing caution to the wind, I approached Joseph and Raymond and broached the subject. My audacity not only startled but also amused them. They were gracious enough to put down their tools and hear me out. But I was just a kid, they argued. I was not and would soon be fifteen, I aggregated. What would my parents say? Being involved would keep me out of trouble and teach me how to work with my hands. They sort of agreed. As a start, I would be their "spanner boy." Something was better than nothing, so I dashed home, delved into a box for old clothes, and was ready to start work on the project first thing in the morning.

I had never worked with my hands before, and it soon became apparent that I was clumsier than I had realized. The work was novel and demanding. However, Joseph and Raymond were excellent teachers, and in a short period, I became familiar with combustion engines, transmissions, gearboxes, and suspensions. Progress on the repairs was slow and tedious because we lacked spares. Improvisation was the name of the game, but how would these nongenuine items perform under grueling conditions that we would face on the expedition?

The day for the long-awaited test run had finally arrived. We decided to drive up and down the Rift Valley escarpment. The rough terrain and varying gradient would be real test for men and machine. There was great excitement when we set off, with most the neighbors turning out to wish us well. We felt proud and were ready to conquer the world, dressed in our impressive new blue coveralls. Morale was high, and on board, there were refreshments and snacks. But all of us were far too excited to even think of eating. Raymond, the electrical engineer, had devised numerous gauges to measure compression, oil pressure, carburetion, engine temperature, and on and on.

The Great Rift Valley forms a rift system of about six thousand kilometers. Extending from the Dead Sea in the Middle East through the Red Sea, Ethiopia, Kenya, Tanzania, and on into Malawi. Numerous ecological disturbances produced a number of lakes, including Elementeita, Naivasha, Turkana, and Baringo. Some of these lakes are freshwater while others are saline and rich in algae and tiny crustaceans, which are the source of food for millions of flamingo that live in these waters. The features of the Rift Valley are unparallel anywhere in the world. Extinct volcanoes like Mt. Longonot and Mt. Suswa line the rim of the valley. The views are breathtaking, and the landscape looks astrophysical. We were fortunate having the chance to put our much loved automobile through its paces in such wonderful surroundings.

I was seated in the back and could only gather snippets of conversation from the cockpit. It was obvious that the roar of the engine did not equate to power output. But now the conversation in the front was getting more anxious. The vehicle's performance was just not what we had expected or hoped for. We made a pit stop at the bottom of the escarpment. After a detail scrutiny of all vital functions, the experts made a bleak prognosis. The mission had to be abandoned, and we planned to limp back to Nairobi to avoid further damage to the vehicle.

But this was not to be. A loud explosion under the hood dashed all hopes of ever being able to get the van to Nairobi. A fire reduced the vehicle to scrap. We were pleased that none of us were hurt but depressed to see six months of hard work reduced to ashes. In my mind, I tried to put a positive spin on things. I had learned a great deal about vehicles in general, working with my hands was no longer alien, and I had made two incredible friends as well. We embraced each other and hitched hiked back to the city. I did not see Joseph or Raymond again.

We had just finished a class in math when the teacher called me to one side and told me in a stern voice that Fr. Frank wanted to see me immediately. It's not normal for a student to be summoned by the headmaster except for severe disciplinary reasons. I developed a nervous twitch trying to figure out what crime I had inadvertently committed. I was not late for classes, had done all my assignments, and was not rude or insubordinate to any of my teachers. Fr. Frank's secretary was mean and old who was not capable of smiling. She asked me to wait in the corridor, as was customary. After what appeared to be an eternity, the man in charge appeared. He was very tall, slim, with silver gray hair and stabbing blue eyes. He looked imperial in his white cassock.

From the twinkle in his eye, I knew that Fr. Frank was not cross. He asked me into his office. This was the first time I had been into this spartan room that was sparsely furnished. I stood as Fr. Frank went behind his desk and handed me a letter. It was from the Board of Governors of the Outward Bound Mountain School (OBMS) saying that as a special concession, they had approved my application to attend the next course at the school that would last for three weeks. Fr. Frank's intervention on my behalf succeeded, and I was grateful.

I was energized and could not wait to share this fantastic news with the family at dinner. They acknowledged the report with cool indifference. I felt let down and alone. Subsequently, I came to understand that their reaction was based on trepidation for my safety and well-being. I had two weeks to prepare. This would be the first instance when I would be leaving the nest on my own for an extended period. I needed to prepare myself both physically and mentally. The joining instructions from OBMS were detailed but did not answer all my questions. I was venturing out of my comfort zone and therefore felt unsure of myself.

But this was something that I always wanted to do.

Full of excitement I trotted to the bus stop. Our journey to the OBMS at Loitoiktok was by bus. This was the first time I was engaged with a diverse, multiracial group of people. For the first time, I was the only Goan in the crowd, and this made me feel ill at ease. Sitting next to me was a student from the Alliance Boys High School in Nairobi. Gus was Kikuyu and much older, bigger and taller than I was.

Soon we found common ground, I became more relaxed, and we jovially swapped accounts of our daily and school lives. Our backgrounds could not have been more dissimilar. Their family came from Limuru, not far from Nairobi. Being Kikuyu, they had been subject to ruthless treatment by the security forces. Their crops were destroyed and livestock stolen. Gus had resentful memories of his childhood, and these provoked him to strive for excellence. To our surprise, we shared a common prediction. One day there would be the United States of Africa, a global superpower.

Soon we forgot our woes and joined in the communal singing designed to wile away the time during the long, bumpy, and dusty journey in Loitoitok. Nearing our destination, we could see the imposing Mt. Kilimanjaro loom in the distant background. It dominated the whole countryside, and my first impression was that it looked like a gargantuan Christmas pudding with icing on the top. Kilimanjaro is a colossal volcano reaching an elevation of 19,335.6 feet. In Masai, it's called "oldoinyo ibor," which means "white mountain." In Swahili, the name is Kilima Njaro, meaning "shining mountain." Besides being the largest volcano in Africa, it is also among the largest on earth.

The school is built on the mountain slope, in the forest area, with a fast-flowing stream of cold, clear water meandering through the grounds. The accommodation consisted of spotless but austere dormitory cabins with bunk beds. Each dormitory had a bank of communal cold showers and three pit toilets. After being served tea and sticky buns, we were split into four patrols and allocated beds where we deposited our gear. We then congregated in the mess hall, and raising our right hand, we took a pledge not to drink or smoke for the period that we were at the school and to obediently follow the school's rules and regulations. I had never made such an undertaking previously and presumed that it was probably as binding as the one taken by the Mau-Mau.

Mt. Kilimanjaro revealed itself to the first foreigner in 1848, when a German missionary, Johannes Robmann, came within sight of the mountain. He did not attempt to climb it but instead traversed its lower slopes. He was so flabbergasted with this finding that he submitted a detailed report to the Royal Geographic Society in England. The experts of this organization dismissed his report because they felt that what he described was not plausible. What? A snowcapped mountain in eastern equatorial Africa? Various attempts were made to scale this majestic mountain, but none were successful. It was, however, first conquered on October 6, 1889, by a Dr. Hans Mayer accompanied by Ludwig Pwtscheller, an experienced alpine mountaineer. The feat took the pair six weeks to accomplish.

Outward Bound Schools provide opportunities for young people during a decisive time in their lives to engage in straightforward, extraordinary experiences, in new and out-of-the-ordinary surroundings, to take part in demanding but satisfying activities to identify their strengths build their principles and values.

My sentiments were on a roller coaster during the first night at the school. Everything was poles apart from what I was familiar with. They were diverse on a material, educational, communal, and emotional levels. I recalled what Fr. Frank once said to me. "In order to win, you must be able to compete with the best on their terms." These terms were certainly not my own. They therefore must be theirs, whoever they were. I glanced out of the curtainless window and saw the majestic mountain beckoning me. My resolve was firm. I would overcome and conquer.

The routine at the school was mostly physical—early morning jog around the rope and obstacle course, followed by a cold shower and breakfast. Activities were designed to demonstrate that we all are capable of more then we know or give ourselves credit for. Racial, social, religious, cultural, and political differences were fundamentally immaterial. Through selfishness and service, it was a joy to celebrate humanity.

We learned to live as a team in the forest, where elephants roamed freely and where it became necessary to connect with and sustain each other. We were encouraged to spend time on our own, reflecting on our being, and to resolve any differences through dialogue. Compassion was the essence of leadership, and the motto of the school reminded us "to serve and strive but not to yield."

One day when climbing a tree to get on to a newly constructed high rope course, I accidentally knocked over a hornet's nest. It was like an explosion that generated a furious outburst from the hornets. Soon I was engulfed in a halo of heated hornets. Their buzzing was boisterous, their stings excruciating, and the result was hot and puffy inflammation. Nobody on the ground grasped the gravity of the situation or realized that I am extremely allergic. The ground was sixty feet below, and struggling to keep calm and retain coconsciousness, I jumped. With both feet firmly on the ground, I ran and dived into the frigid waters of the river, keeping my head submerged for as long as I could hold my breath. This saved my life. The wasps were gone but not the smarting or the swelling. I was carried to the sick bay, where I received expert medical attentions.

Soon we started packing for the final ascent up the mountain. There were two peaks, Gillman's Point and the absolute summit known as Kaizer Willhellem Spitz. Ascending the former was desirable, but the latter was optional. It would take three full days to climb and two days to descend. We had to carry all our own food, water, warm clothing, boots, sleeping bag, rope, and ice ax. Nights would be spent in caves en route, and water had to be conserved until we reached the snow line.

At dawn, our patrols set off from base camp, each led by a Masai tracker whose task was to navigate around the numerous herds of wild elephants and other forest animals. The rainforest belt was dense, with trees so tall that they formed a canopy at the top, shutting out most of the natural light. Narrow, winding tracks twisted their way through marsh, streams, and dry riverbeds. The bird and butterfly life in the forest was fantastic. They presented a spectacle of multihued colors and shades. I am not capable of illustrating the exceptional eminence of the environment I was in. It was in pristine condition, relatively unaffected by human activity, and the home to a multitude of birds and insects.

I cogitated about the Mau-Mau, who used forests like these as their hideouts. To survive, they developed the instincts of wild animals. Their garb was made from the skins of the animals that they hunted for food. They did not bathe and wore their hair in long dreadlocks. Scent, hearing, and sight were fundamental to their survival. At the beginning, their weapons were homemade, which were as much a danger to the user as they were to the target. Later, they captured or acquired more sophisticated weapons, including the pistol belonging to Francis, I surmised. Among the main military leaders of the resistance were Warihu Itote, better known as "General China," and Dedan Kamahi, both of whom achieved notoriety. Through skill, stealth, and cunning, they were able to evade the dragnets of the security forces for years.

My rucksack now felt heavy, and the straps cut into my shoulders. I now understood why the school had set a minimum age for admission, but nevertheless, I had no regrets. We climbed steadily through the day, only stopping at predetermined intervals for brief periods of rest. We had ascended above the tree line and were now in the high heather belt. I knew that this would turn into semidesert and, further up the mountain, into total desert and finally into the alpine region with permanent ice glaciers. We stopped at the first cave for the night. Dinner was a soup made of Marmite and crackers. After that, we immediately fell asleep, in exhaustion.

It was a crystal clear morning, with the forest and plains plainly visible way in the distance below us. Kilimanjaro dominated the skyline, once again offering an intimidating challenge to me. I could now distinctly see steep slopes of scree. They resembled gravel to me, which would make climbing difficult.

As we ascended, the air became rarer. Some members of our patrol were affected by the altitude, their pace slowed, and their rate of breathing increased. Fortunately, the altitude was not having an effect on me—not for now at least. This was a forsaken part of the mountain, bare, forlorn, and uninhabited. It was much colder, and I got my first glimpse of snow. By the time we reached the second cave on the second day, most of us were pooped, having no desire for food. The third day was spent climbing to the last hut for the final assault on the mountain.

Our patrol leader was a British Army officer who was an unpretentious manager. As we huddled in a tight circle, trying to keep warm, he told us anecdotes about himself. He was born into privilege and went to public school in England. He then gained admittance to one of the most famous military academies in the world, the Royal Military Sandhurst, where only the crème de la crème were selected for admission. I fell asleep before the conclusion of this yarn.

We started the final ascent at 3:00 a.m. the following morning. It was important to scale the very steep scree slopes in the dark as this avoided view of sheer gradient of the ultimate ascent. Without the spectacle, the climb was less daunting. Unaware, I assumed the lead. Most of our gear was left in the second cave, and without the weight, I was able to reach Gillman's Point just in time to see the sun rise. The skies were swathed in an orange glow, and I felt a sense of serene harmony within myself. I waited till the second climber joined me, and then decided to set off for the pinnacle. I was undaunted doing this alone because we had been well primed for the task.

I proudly recorded my details in the register at Kaiser Wolhem Spitze. It was stored in a vacuum container where climbers documented the date and time they conquered this peak. This done, I started my way down the mountain with a clear mind and an open heart. I greeted the many climbers on their way up, and they were spurred on by my good news. The descent was monotonous, but I took pleasure in gleefully sliding down the scree. Our patrol congregated at the second cave before our concluding descent to the school. This experience had transformed me from a boy into a man—not in age, but certainly in maturity. I now recognized who I really was as an individual, accepted the limits of my personal capacity, and understood that to achieve, one must dare.

Every morning before classes, the school congregated in the courtyard for the ritual of the morning assembly. The proceedings would begin with a short prayer led by the principal. This would be followed by general administrative announcements, after which we would all adjourn to our class rooms. Today, things appeared to be different. Nothing visible or tangible, but it was easy to detect an undercurrent of tension. The teachers did not mingle with the students as they normally did. Instead, they stood stiffly and anxiously to the side.

Fr. Frank then appeared. He was solemn; his voice was measured and restrained. He spent the first few minutes gazing in silence and meditation. Clearing his throat, he then started to pray. Typically, only a few students joined in the prayer. Today was somehow special.

We all connected in unity and harmony and joined in the prayers. The events that followed are indistinct. The bottom line was that the Board of Governors had lost confidence in Fr. Frank and demanded his resignation. I saw wretchedness in his eyes as he shared the news of his imminent departure with us.

I knew the chairman of the Board of Governors and often behaved in a playful and alluring way with his attractive daughter, who sat next to me in class. She sometimes spoke of her father as a man saturated with ego, who demanded nothing but absolute submission from others. Without question, he had power, fame, and wealth. However, in my humble opinion, he was an individual who was egotistic and pretentious.

My spontaneous reaction to the announcement was that this was blatant exploitation, injustice, and harassment. Integrity must be made to prevail. Without assessing the consequences, I boldly and deafeningly announced that I would boycott school until Fr. Frank was reinstated or we were given an adequate reason for his abrupt dismissal. To my incredulity, all the students started chanting in support. We clasped hands and walked out of the school gates together.

The occurrence made the evening national news, and I was named as the instigator. I did not see myself as such. I was only doing what at the time came naturally. Luis behaved awkwardly in the spotlight, and Charlotte remained very much in the background, enjoying every moment of this newfound stimulation. I was badgered by the media to make statements but had nothing to say about this deliberate form of destructive manipulation. Luis arrived home early one evening and got everyone scurrying around in preparation for a visit by members of the Board of Governors. They wanted to negotiate, I was told. I did not understand what about.

Their spokesperson was charming, although I had not previously met him. He treated me like a pampered adolescent and was indistinct in what he was trying to say. I therefore could not and did not react, which he deemed as insubordination. I was asked what I was after. This was not a personal issue but a question of what was best for us students and the school. Reinstatement was the only remedy. That evening, the chairman of the Board of Governors made a radio broadcast unashamedly stating that his words had been misconstrued. According to him, Fr. Frank was a respected and capable headmaster and that we were fortunate to have him as the person in charge of the school.

This Irishman, who wore the frock of God, had made an indelible impression on me. He had wrought my life, made me grapple with the inconsistencies of beings, forcing me to strive for nothing but the preeminent. I could no longer be satisfied with the status quo. He was optimistic that given the right mind-set, we as individuals are capable of transcending all barriers and attain our avowed goals. Life is not a bed of roses, but to succeed, we must retain control of all the ingredients that affect our daily lives and persevere. I have never looked back in disappointment.

My future depended entirely on the outcomes of the external O-level exams. I was uncertain about what I wanted to do after graduating from high school. University was a desirable option, but excellent grades were a precondition for admission to universities at home or abroad. I was confident, but this poise was based on ignorance. From now on, I would wholeheartedly dedicate all my time to studying.

Concentration was not easy at first, and I was easily distracted. I now realized how much work remained to be done if I was to come up to par. Not easy but there was no alternative. The exams were a mixed bag, and my results fell short of expectations. Though disheartened, I accepted full responsibility. My solace was in my belief that success or failure is relative to the individual's aptitude. Luis was content with the outcome of the exams and promptly arranged for me to be hired as a revenue clerk at the Ministry of Agriculture. He spoke of the tremendous merits of a career in the civil service. To keep the peace, I started working but certainly had no intention of making this a vocation.

An engineer with a long distance telecommunications company invited me to an interview at their receiving station at the foot of the Ngong Hills. The offer I received was appealing. The firm would hire me as an apprentice for a short probationary period. If suitable, I would be sponsored for a degree program in radio engineering at a university in Britain. I resigned from government and seized this opportunity.

We worked in shifts, and my responsibilities were interesting, challenging, and not desk bound. I was used to working with my hands and had been exposed to things electrical and mechanical. This helped me get acclimatized and able to work without supervision. The facility was a high frequency repeater station that received voice and data radio transmissions from all over the world. The incoming signal was then boosted for rebroadcast to its final destination. I selected and tested appropriate frequencies and then tuned in hefty transmitters and receivers to carry the interchange. All traffic was constantly monitored for quality, and I intervened if atmospheric conditions or the quality of the signal deteriorated.

Listening in to people's private conversations was enlightening. The chatter varied from intimate, to business, and to top secret government conference calls. My reaction to this eavesdropping varied from being amused, educated, stunned, and scandalized. Because of the classified nature of government calls, these transmissions were scrambled prior to broadcast. It was frightening to be associated with this top secret information, and I understood how badly informed or misled the public were.

Luis gambled on foreign horse races, and from his betting stubs, I could tell which horses he had placed his bets on. He also had a list where he ticked the horses he fancied. Because of the time difference, many of the races that he was gambling on had already been run, and I knew the winners. I would have been a hero and he a rich man had I shared this information with him.

My supervisors were pleased with my performance and increased my duties and responsibilities. I was rated highly in a performance appraisal and told that I would be sent to a university in Wales at the end of the year.

Thumbing through an old issue of the *Kenya Gazette* during one of my graveyard shifts, I saw an advertisement inviting applications for admission to the Royal Military Academy Sandhurst in England. Sadly, the last day for applications had passed. Despite this, I decided that I would call on the office of the secretary of defense when my shift ended in the morning. I sweet-talked my way into being allowed to go up to the Executive Floor. The receptionist, who greeted me with astonishment, was an old English lady. She politely regretted that there was nothing she could do to assist. From a sign on the door, I noted that the permanent secretary of defense was a gentleman called John Arap Koitie.

This was the bastion of power, and he was the person in charge. As I was about to be shown the door, Mr. Koitie stepped out of his office. He was tall, slim, his gray hair receding, and dressed in a tailor-made gray pinstripe suit. To me, he was imposing and daunting and spoke with authority and self-assured dignity. He said, "May I inquire to whom I have the honor of speaking?" or words to that effect. It was anomalous for a young Asian male to be there in the first place. I preempted the receptionist and responded. Taken aback by my audacity, he asked me into his office.

Mr. Koitie asked me to explain myself. His attention initiated a spark of hope in me. I was hesitant about how to react, but his soothing demeanor let me relax, and I responded courteously, clearly, and concisely. Mr. Koite instructed his secretary to give me a set application forms, which I immediately completed in the outer office. I was ecstatic but was cautioned that this was only the start of a long and difficult selection process. Prayers came to my lips as I completed and handed in my application. Descending in the elevator, I felt battered, drained, and vulnerable.

My place of work was on the outskirts of the city, with no public transportation serving the area. Luis kindly bought me a Vespa scooter that was made in Italy. It was metallic-silver gray in color, sleek, and economical. Not good as the mean machine owned by Francis, but good enough. At dinner one night, Luis declared that he wanted the criminal in the family to identify himself. All of us were perplexed and stared at each other with blank faces.

Reacting, he reached into his pocket and pulled out a brown government envelope that boldly affirmed "On His Majesty's Service." Luis then ceremoniously read the summons it contained. "Criminal Case Number 7680, the Crown v. Rudolf Rodrigues." It was the confirmation of a speeding ticket that I had received two weeks ago. There was hush around the table as I was handed the ticket, instructed to pay the fine, and was absolutely humiliated in front of the family. I finished my supper in silence, only staring directly at my plate. If only I could spirit myself away from this demeaning situation.

A few weeks later, we were exposed to a similar tantrum. On this occasion, Luis muttered something about having received a personal communication signed by none other than the permanent secretary of defense. Much ado about nothing, I felt, as I assumed that it was a form letter, informing me that my application to enter Sandhurst had been rejected. Not so. Luis proudly went on to say that I had been chosen and invited to attend a defense panel interview, chaired by Mr. Koitie. My heart skipped a beat on hearing the news.

Francis kindly coached me on how to conduct myself during the interview. I would have to wear trousers and a tie but owned neither. On the way home from work the following day, I stopped off at Ahmed's, a fashionable and expensive clothing store, and invested in a pair of gray slacks, white shirt, and matching tie. My ignorance and poor taste were obviously apparent to the salesperson who kindly guided my choice with persuasive recommendations.

Looking at myself in the mirror on the day of the interview, I felt positive and prepared. I was propped up because I had attended early morning mass to plead for spiritual intersession and support. Candidates assembled in a large anteroom decorated with military figurines, paintings, and other armed forces paraphernalia. The environment I found myself was as alien, as were the other aspirants. The Europeans were well dressed in dark business suits and the Africans in smart casuals. I was the only Asian and realized that the people who were short-listed for interview came from Kenya, Uganda, and Tanganyika.

There were twenty-five of us in the room, of which only five would be selected to head to the next stage of the selection processes. The interview panel was chaired by Mr. Koitie, with the General Officer Commanding, British Land Forces East Africa, the Brigade Commander, the King's African Rifles Brigade, and a civilian from the Office of the Governor General as members. Before leaving, we were asked to leave a contact address.

I used my work address rather then my home address. To my mind, the other contenders seemed to be a cut above me in every respect. Many of the Europeans had gone to boarding schools in England. Many came from well-connected settler, military, political, and business families. The remainder belonged to the emerging African elite. All had excelled scholastically and were talented sportsmen. I was relieved when this tribulation finally came to an end.

I felt rejected and inadequate but found solace in the fact that I was fortunate to have another viable alternative. In order not to throw away this opportunity, I worked exceptionally hard. In my spare time, I studied all the technical and operating manuals and could now carry out with my colleagues who had all graduated in engineering from universities abroad, credible technical discussions on radio communication theory. The English supervisor of the mail room handed me this bulky manila envelope from the Ministry of Defense. As this facility was a classified installation, management was hypersensitive about security, and I was quizzed as to the content of the package. I said that I would respond once I became familiar with the subject matter.

I could not wait to be alone to open the envelope. The letter notified me that I was one of the five candidates selected to undergo basic officer cadet training with the Fourth Battalion, the King's African Rifles in Jinja, Uganda. The inserted joining instructions were comprehensive and included information about a medical examination, terms and conditions of service, travel, housing, and pay.

Our departure date from Nairobi by train was in exactly two weeks. I read the instructions over and over again and had to keep reminding myself that this was not a daydream but reality. I decided to take the medical exam before notifying my employers. The medical tests and checkup were done at the British Military Hospital in Nairobi in a well-organized and proficient way. I was certified as being fit to enlist.

It was my eighteenth birthday over the weekend, but I did not have the disposition to celebrate. This was a defining point in my life. I would have been consoled if there was someone in the family with more experience and wisdom, with whom I could rationally discuss my options. My birthday celebration was a letdown because there was no happiness in my heart, only the burden of hesitation.

The general manager of the station where I worked was astonished when I handed in my notice. I provided no reason, and it perplexed him that anyone in their right mind would throw away such an excellent opportunity to embark on an exciting and well-paid career. I owed him an explanation, to which he commented that many were called but few were selected. This sounded ominous and was discouraging. I had however decided, and this was not to be a revolving resolution.

The train journey from Nairobi to Jinga was very different from the one from Mombasa to Nairobi. This time, we twisted and puffed our way through the lush, fertile, and cool White Highlands of Kenya, where the land was parceled into large productive and profitable settler farms. Vast tracts of land had been turned into coffee and tea estates, and the luxuriant grazing nourished herds of high yielding pedigree dairy cattle. Tight safety measures were evident at every station we passed. When the train stopped at a particular location to take on coal and water, it was instantly encircled by Tribal Home Guards and British Army.

On arrival at Jinja, we were met by a British Army drill sergeant. He was immaculately turned out in his starched khaki uniform, with his black boots glistening in the morning sun. Once we disembarked, he introduced himself as Sergeant Major Killing. He inquired if we were acquainted with each other. We had not met. The African was called Bob. Tom, Jack, and Richard were Europeans, and I was the only Asian. The fifth person had failed his medicals and would not be joining us.

Jinja was a small town and mainly owed its existence to the Owen Falls Dam. In 1947, Sir Westlake, an engineer, recommended to the colonial government in Uganda to build a hydroelectric dam on the White Nile near its source at Lake Victoria. The dam was completed in 1954 and submerged the Rippon Falls. Lake Victoria is the world's second largest freshwater lake covering an area of approximately sixty-eight thousand square kilometers. It is the main source of water for the White Nile and is notorious as the breeding ground for bilharzia.

Bilharzia is a disease common in the tropics where lakes, ponds, streams, and irrigation canals harbor bilharzia- transmitting snails.

The parasites' larvae live in snails, from which they infect humans, their ultimate host, in whom they mature, mate, and reproduce. The worms are about one centimeter long and go around the veins that carry blood from the intestine to the liver. They feed on red blood cells and dissolve nutrients such as sugar and amino acids, making the patient feeling listless and exhausted.

S. M. Killing wanted to give the impression that he was a battle-scarred veteran who, despite being semiliterate, had clawed his way up the ranks in the army. He was dumpy, and this gave him a neurosis, which he tried hard to hide and redirect. Now that he was in a position of power, he would make sure that we obeyed his orders instantly and without question. At first, I did not understand why he spoke in such a loud, barking voice, using language that was profusely infused with vulgarity.

We were made responsible for running our own officer cadets' mess, which was sparsely but tastefully furnished. Each had our own room, with communal living and dining space. There was a pleasant garden, and I enjoyed being out of the family nest, not having to worry about Luis and his anomalous behavior.

Idi Amin Dada descended on us the following morning. He was an "effendi," a rank especially created in the colonial army for Africans who were noncommissioned officers and who displayed latent leadership capabilities. He informed us that he was the most senior native in the battalion and that he would supervise our cadet training. Amin was a giant of a man, a star rugby player, popular with the British officers because of his outwardly jovial manner and his excellent physique.

Through daily contact, I got to know him well. He had a rudimentary education, was ambitious, ruthless, and in love with himself, and had a reputation of being almost all bone from the neck up. I decided to steer clear of him as much as I could even though he often confronted me to offer meaningless advice about the virtues of a good officer. On one such occasion, he told me that I would not be an officer because I did not smoke, drink, or womanize.

I felt ineffective for not having been previously initiated or indulged in these manly pursuits. So when we went to Rippon Falls Club on our next day off, I ordered a large bottle of Tusker beer and fifty Clipper nontipped cigarettes. Sitting with my colleagues, I tried to convey the impression of doing what came naturally. But the beer tasted vile, and after the first drag on the cigarette, I felt nauseated. Making a pathetic excuse, I rushed back to the mess to be sick, after which I went straight to bed. Never again would I act on the idiotic counsel of Idi Amin Dada.

Amin became president of Uganda in a coup d'etat he staged on January 25, 1971. He ruled as president from 1971 to1979. His full official title was "His Excellency President for Life, Field Marshal, Al Hajji, Doctor Idi Amin Dada, VC, DSO, MC, Lord of all Beasts of the Earth and Fishes of the Sea, Conqueror of the British Empire in Africa in General, and Uganda in Particular." He proclaimed himself as King of Scotland and proposed marriage to Princess Ann of Britain. He got the name "Dada" because every time he was caught with a woman in his tent during the Mau-Mau offensive in Kenya, he claimed that she was his "dada" (sister) in order to be let off the hook by his commanders.

He was alleged involved in the murder of Mau-Mau General Gitau Matenjagwo, whose body he paraded around the village of Muranga for days. In 1962, Amin was ordered to suppress the cattle rustling between the Karamonjong tribe of Uganda and the Pokot from Kenya. Amin directed his troops to shoot every Pokot they caught sight of and leave their bodies to rot in the sun. To disarm the Karamonjong of their homemade spears, he ordered his heavily armed soldiers to arrest all the men they spotted and line them against a table, with their penis stretched out on a table. Amin then personally cut of the organs of the screaming men.

In 1972, he gave fifty thousand Asians, who were the backbone of the economy and who had been living in the country for more than a century, ninety days to leave following a dream in which he alleged that God had appeared to him and instructed him to get rid of them.

He then issued a declaration dispensing their substantial assets to his henchmen. Amin presided over the bloodiest dictatorship in Africa, and in 1976, he achieved international notoriety when he granted safe haven to Palestinian hijackers of an Air France Airbus carrying 256 Israeli passengers on a flight to Tel Aviv to Paris. The hijacker demanded the release of 53 PLO held in Israeli detention. They were supported and reinforced by the Uganda Army, who provided them with weapons, food, water, and ammunition during their stay at Entebbe International Airport. Amin regularly visited the hostages dressed in a Scottish kilt and waving and shouting "Shalom" to them.

At midnight on July 3, 1976, Israeli commandos attacked the airport and freed all but one of the hostages. The Uganda forces were badly crippled in the action and their entire air force destroyed. This military intervention crippled Amin during his final years in power, and eventually led to his downfall. His erratic behavior is attributed to a chronic Syphilis. In 1978, Amin ordered the invasion of Tanzania with the help of Libyan troops. President Julius Nyerere of Tanzania then declared war and, with the help of Rwandan guerrillas, entered Kampala, forcing Amin to flee the country.

We all graduated from officer cadet training with flying colors and were notified that we had been enrolled at the Army School of Education at Beaconsfield in England. The authorities felt that the standard of our academic qualifications was below the British norm. The whole family accompanied me to the airport on the day of departure. I was the first person among them to fly in an airplane.

Prior to departure, Luis told me that he was proud of me. I was taken aback by this statement.

We took off in a De Havilland Comet, the first jet aircraft to enter global service in 1952. It had a cruising speed of 490 mph at an altitude of 35,000 feet, a range of 750 miles, with a payload of forty-four passengers. We made a refueling stop at Tripoli in Libya before finally landing in London. We were met and taken directly to the Army School of Education. Sentiment permeated my judgment, and I do remember what my first impressions of England were.

The Army School of Education was larger than I had expected and was located in park-like surroundings. It was so very dissimilar from the Goan School in Nairobi, which now seemed rudimentary. However, the education that I had received there was exceptional as my test scores now demonstrated. The rest of my time at Beaconsfield was spent serving tea and thinking about the next major stumbling block that I faced. The Regular Commissions Board at Leighton House, Westbury in Wiltshire, managed the selection process for entry into Sandhurst. It had to be passed before one was offered a place at the academy.

At the prior two-day briefing course at Leighton House, we were told that we would be evaluated as part of the sorting out. If suitable, we would be permitted to proceed to the Main Board as soon as one desired. I had now become anesthetized by these copious analysis and assessments and was worried about becoming blasé. Aspirants are judged by four categories ranging from immediate approval to rejection. I was informed that I could continue to the next stage.

The main board was a four-day program of diverse elements, including academic, physical, mental, and aptitude tests. The intent is to put candidates under stress while promoting their team spirit and competition. We were all given a number that replaced names and other personal details and placed in teams for the duration. Applicants were assessed against a standard and not each other. On the last night, we attended a formal dinner that many regarded as the final test in manners and social skills.

As we departed, we were told that the results would be out in four days. A bulky envelope would indicate approval. Over the duration of the main board, I developed a strong alliance with David, an Englishman. He had attended Eaton, a famous public school in Britain, and his father was a retired general who had served in the Indian Army. David kindly invited me to his home in the country to await the results.

His parents were delightful, warm, and welcoming. I was invigorated by the English country air and thankful to be able to spend a little time outside the confines of the military environment. Devoid of stress, I enjoyed Dave's music, his friends, the parties, and his mom's home cooking. The day of judgment was upon us at last. We both went down to breakfast in silence, suppressing our nervousness. On the dinning table were two brown envelopes, but one was thin. Without hesitation, Dave gave me a hug and congratulated me. He was the perfect gentleman, and I could see that despite this setback, he bore no malice. It hurt me to see him so upset, and at the core of my being, I knew that he was a better man. Once he gained self-control, Dave insisted hosting a party to celebrate.

At breakfast the following day, Dave's mom told me that I was inappropriately dressed to enter Sandhurst. She had arranged for us to visit the general's tailors later in the day. My clothing often invited frowns and stares, and I now understand why. Once killed out, my appearance altered from a Park Road adolescent to a brown English squire. This bigheartedness touched a cord within me. It made me conscious of the fact that not all people are biased. Dave's Mom looked upon me as a son for whom she wanted nothing but the best. I will never again compartmentalize people because of their ethnicity, hue, or creed.

My aspirations of being admitted into Sandhurst had been realized, but I also recognized that this was only the start of a far-reaching and multifaceted road into the future. Traditions on which this Academy was founded go back over two centuries. I appreciate that many an illustrious global figures were alumni of this establishment. Sandhurst continues to engage in the highest principles of professional distinction in training officers from Britain and many other countries. Without a doubt, the academy is a quintessence for excellence.

As we lined up to register, a black Rolls Royce pulled up. Out of it emerged a short Arab dressed in a suit, followed by an Englishman. The Arab introduced himself as Qaboos bin Said from Muscat and Oman. I wore a battle dress with an East African formation sign of two crossed machetes on the shoulders. I was slighted when Qaboos queried if I was a cook in the army catering corps. One of the questions on the admittance form baffled Qaboos. It related to the military unit he would join on graduation. He looked to the Englishman who was his private tutor and was instructed to write private army. Who was this guy who owned a private army?

I was assigned to Marne Company in New College, and Qaboos was my next-door neighbor. The first six weeks of training were a nightmare. The pace was frenzied with no letup. I just did not know if I was coming or going during this period. We were later told that that the physiology was to break down an individual and then to rebuild them into what was known as the Sandhurst mold. During this phase, we were not permitted to wear civilian clothes, were obliged to march in squads from one point to another, and could not leave the academy grounds. The training under Idi Amin Dada played a central role in helping me to continue to stay alive and surmount the rigors of this initiation period. A few colleagues were less fortunate and dropped out because they were unable to emotionally and physically tolerate the severity, strictness, and harshness of this treatment.

One of the key tests during our junior term was the Academy Company cross-country race, which covered an uneven course of ten miles. It demanded stamina, speed, and determination. Failure to complete the competition could easily lead to discharge from the army. In no way was I able to enjoy running, and distance running was something I never previously attempted. I was physically fit, but this was just the most basic prerequisite.

I soon learned that all training must be precise, and one's ability to run well came with experience and training. To improve on endurance, it was important to do regular long and slow runs, coupled with intermittent speed spells for faster running. I practiced resistance training to increase oxygen capacity and strengthening muscles. Getting into a rhythm and exercising correct control of inhalation was also central to successful running. I was persistent in my workouts and, to my utter amazement and in time, thoroughly mastered this form of workout. It gave me time on my own to contemplate, to think seriously, carefully, and relatively calmly. In simple terms, it grew to be fun, and I became an enthusiastic runner and jog to this day.

All overseas cadets at the academy had a British sponsor, a sort of surrogate parent who provided help, guidance, and support as needed. Lady Ann was my sponsor, and she lived in a castle in Mulranny, in County Mayo in Ireland. One summer, I visited and was truly enthralled by the sincerity, kindness, and geniality of the Irish. Their easygoing ways made getting on familiar terms with them straightforward. Many were poor, but they made the best use of what they had. In many ways, they are akin to the Goans. Perhaps this similarity was based on their shared Catholic faith. Lady Ann was a Protestant, and I guess that she was not native Irish.

The castle was located in the middle of immense wild splendor and the property used to ranch sheep. I enjoyed the grandeur of the castle, but being alone, I felt cut off. Ann owned a number of horses, and these were the only means of transportation. To entertain myself I often rode down to the village of Mulranny, which in Gaelic means "hill of ferns." The village was located in tranquil settings on the sea between Clew Bay and Blacksod Bay. This region is the home of the giant fuchsias and numerous varieties out of the ordinary plants.

I enjoyed visiting the Mulranny Mediterranean Heather Festival and spent many happy hours walking the long sandy beaches. The fishing is reputed to be excellent on Achill Island that I decided to check this out. Achill is a large island that is connected to the mainland by a bridge. The rustic beauty of the village was warm and alluring. I ended up spending most of my time in pubs drinking Guinness, talking politics, and arguing about the Irish Republican Army (IRA).

The locals were fascinated with my views because I was a cadet at a famous British Military Academy and because I was a native of a country fighting the British to fulfill proindependence aspirations. The original IRA was founded in 1919 and reactivated in Belfast in 1969. Its structure centered on locally recruited militant volunteers. Subsequently, it became the military wing of Sinn Fein. The IRA claimed responsibility for the bombings in Belfast, London, and Ulster in the 1950s and then reverted to a state of inactivity until the late 1960s.

On Sunday, I rode to the village church and sat next to a family with two young children. During the service, I was taken by surprise when the young girl started stroking my arm. Then with a very heavy Irish accent that I could barely understand, she muttered that I was really lucky that my mommy did not compel me to take a regular bath. I was probably the first nonwhite person that she had ever seen.

I was surprised by the dissimilarity between the two main English social classes one encountered at the academy. Those who had the privilege of attending public school considered themselves superior to the remainder of the cadets who were stigmatized because they did not speak the speak. The former would rile the latter at every opportunity. It was demeaning, upsetting to be privy to, and in many ways reminded me of the unfairness I had experienced growing up.

With time, I was able to get into my own, really enjoying our daily activities, which were varied, challenging, exciting and rewarding. We were permitted to go away on weekends, eat out, and stay late. Besides the academic and military training, we "gentlemen cadets" were encouraged to improve on our social graces. Ballroom dancing was considered important, and once every two weeks, we went to a girl's finishing school near the academy to take dancing lessons. I was attracted to this pursuit by the possibility of meeting someone nice and exciting from the opposite sex. But sadly, this never came to pass. I totally lack rhythm and found the steps and the beat of formal dances difficult to follow. In order not to appear too much of a klutz to my partners, I pretended that I had a wooden foot.

Qaboos was no dancing fan either, and in an extraordinary way, we aligned, notwithstanding the fact that our personal circumstances were very different. We became friends and did many things together, both professionally and socially. I later found out that Qaboos was the only son of Sultan Said bin Taimurand and is one of the eight generations of the Al Busaidi dynasty.

On the July 23, 1970, Sultan Qaboos bin Said succeeded his father and acceded the throne, declaring that his country would no longer be called Muscat and Oman but the Sultanate of Oman. Sultan Qu boosn bin Said is a forward looking leader, who transformed Oman into a modern country with excellent infrastructure, health care, and education facilities using massive amounts of oil wealth.

Roderick (Rod), an Englishman who was the heir to a cat-food empire, and I were buddies. We naturally shared deep feelings, attitudes, had common traits and benefited from our comradeship. Life outside the academy was now characterized by continual social goings-on. Every Friday evening, there was a mass exodus from Camberely to London.

The early evening train was packed with cadets, as were all the roads and pubs leading to the City. One and all looked forward to the weekends as the workdays were intense, stressful, unrelenting, and challenging on both body and mind. Rod was well connected in the social context and was a pacesetter at the parties and social events. An earl was part of our social orbit, and on an occasion, a known social creep came up and wanted to know when the nobleman's sister was coming out. His spur-of-the-moment response was that she was not coming out but only seeping through.

Out of sheer necessity, I learned to boogie and met many charming and exciting women as a result. But the one person with whom I became infatuated was Charlotte. She was a student at the Royal Academy of Music in London, and besides being gorgeous, she was extremely gifted. Despite Rod's words of warning, Charlotte was my constant companion. My education and knowledge of music was zilch. I knew nothing about tunes that were serious, formal, and scholarly. I did not play an instrument and could not read composition. Despite these innate differences, Charlotte and I were well matched and suited.

She soon became bored with the party scene and wanted to do things together and unaccompanied by Rod and his numerous partners. This did not correspond with my buddy's goals, and he became aggravated by the fact that we no longer hung out with the boys. Charlotte and I continued to date for awhile. She was a passionate writer, and we spent hours talking on the phone.

For our next recess, Rod suggested that we hitchhiked together in Europe. I was embarrassed to ask what hitchhiking meant. However, it soon became apparent during the planning. We took the train to Dover and then crossed the channel by ferry into France. Each of us carried a large backpack. It was easy to hitch a ride in Europe in those days. People traveling alone were glad for company, and we covered considerable distances quickly and cheaply. We had no game plan and therefore were flexible in terms of destinations.

The only constraint in traveling through France was that people expected us to speak in French. In Paris, we went to the famous Moulin Rouge show, courtesy of Rod's parents. I was staggered by the spectacle, the slickness, the special effects, the dance routines, and the costumes. All were out of this world and so remarkable that make them difficult to forget.

In Rome, we stayed with Rod's relatives. We slept during the days and partied at night. My mother once asked me if I had visited the Vatican and prayed in St. Peters Cathedral. I could not lie, but the reality was that we went nowhere near to the holy city. I had arranged to meet Charlotte at Waterloo station in London on our return. At the appointed date and time, I went to platform 12 and waited for her train. I was upset that she was not on it. I was not only looking forward to seeing her but was also almost broke.

The next train was due in another five hours, so I platform walked and people gazed. It was a blustery London evening, and after the warm sunshine of the continent, I started to get cold. Taking refuge in a nearby pub was a way out. Nurturing half a pint of Bitter, I pondered over my options. I had sufficient change for a ticket back to Camberley, but the academy did not open until the following day. I had no valuables to pawn, only smelly clothes in a worn-out rucksack. I would just have to wait, hope, and pray that Charlotte would show.

Soon, a tweedy country squire came and stood by me and started a tête-à-tête. He wanted to know what I did and bought me a drink. He too had a long wait for a train, so he proposed that we take in a movie. He was indifferent to my pecuniary predicament, and being the vicar of a large parish in the north of England, he appeared loaded. When I asked his name, he said, "Oh, just call me Dennis." I was happy for the company. In the cinema, Dennis kept dropping his hand on my knee. I understood that it was inadvertent and took no notice. Dennis accompanied me to the platform to check on Charlotte. On the escalator, he always intentionally stood below me and started caressing my bum and thigh's. Then the penny dropped. This guy was gay and trying to pick me up. The notion repulsed me, as this was my first encounter with a homosexual. Unwittingly, I had encouraged Dennis during the movie.

Alas! No sign of Charlotte, so I was destined to spend a cold windy night on a hard wooden bench on Waterloo station. I was fortunate to have a sleeping bag with me. In the middle of the night, I was brusquely awakened by a hobo, who used the other side of the bench as his makeshift bed. He was interested in some boxing results and wanted to negotiate a loan to buy alcohol.

The raison d'etre for the trip with Rod was because I wanted time to mull over who I really was. To recognize that man in the mirror. Occasionally, I felt like being ablaze and approaching meltdown. Justifiably, Charlotte felt it necessary and appropriate to anticipate more from our relationship. My life was in flux. I knew what I wanted but would only make it if I continued to be totally focused. This obsession with her had come to an end, like all good things must.

The last two terms at the Academy were hectic. Maneuvers in the field, practical instructions in command and control under simulated battle conditions, live firing exercises, historic battle field tours, civil military relations, and of course academic examinations.

Rod and I had also been working on a project proposal for the Ford Foundation. Once a year, the foundation made a grant to support an activity in adventure and leadership development. We requested support for a rock climbing, potholing, and caving expedition in the former Yugoslavia.

We were successful, and Rod and I set off in a new Ford car supplied by the foundation, complimented by ample funds to support our activities. Traveling in luxury was something we had yet to get accustomed to. The region that our journey took us through was part of the Austro-Hungarian Empire. In 1918 the Serbs, Slovenes, and the Croats joined up to form Yugoslavia.

We drove along Italy's most eastern formed by a strip of land, which curves around the west coast from Aguiteia to Trieste. The area has particular geographic, political, and cultural characteristics that distinguish it from other parts of the country. The ancient city of Trieste, steeped in history, is surrounded by rocks, cliffs, and caves. An old Roman road runs through it to Pula in Croatia.

We stayed at a charming B and B overlooking the water and hired an experienced guide who assisted us with some very difficult rock climbs. From here, we drove to Rovinj, situated on the southwest coast of the peninsula that is surrounded by twenty-two islands. The whole coast is a protected natural heritage site rich in sea flora and fauna and is sheltered by a well-cavernous coastline. The Baredine Cave is situated near the town of Parec. It is about sixty meters deep and runs for about three hundred meters. Exploring its five large chambers was exciting and fun. I learned a lot about the value and significance of conserving our precious environmental heritage.

Sadly, our expedition was coming to an end. We decided to spend the last two days in Dubrovnik. George Bernard Shaw called this city paradise. To us, it was beyond doubt the seventh heaven. It has a remarkable history of being an independent merchant republic, with flourishing trade links with Turkey and India. In fact, the republic maintained a large consul in Goa to safeguard its interests in India. The city was completed in the thirteenth century, and my words would never do justice to its magnificence and exquisiteness.

The climax of the Sandhurst social calendar was the June ball. It was a must for the "in set," and women openly expressed their desire to be invited. At dinner, the cadets boasted about their date for the event, and everyone spoke in glowing terms about what a memorable occasion the ball was. The closest I ever got to a gala was reading Cinderella as a kid. For better or worse, my existence had been altered. Having left the party circuit, I had nobody to take to the ball. Rod produced a whole list of aspirants. He had someone to fit every category and circumstance. It was the classical mail-order syndrome, for which I could muster little passion.

On graduation from Sandhurst, I received a Queen's Commission in the British Army and was posted as a subaltern to the Devonshire and Dorset Regiment based in Honiton in England. Soldiering in the British Isles was monotonous and ceremonial. One morning I was instructed to report to my company commander. Kenya was to become independent soon, and all locally born officers were encouraged to return to the country and serve in the King's African Rifles, which would eventually become the nucleus of the Kenya Army.

My family was delighted to see me back in Nairobi. Their first reaction was that I had completely changed—in behavior, temperament, outlook, the way I dressed and conversed. We sat down to a meal together, and I told about all that had happened during my absence. Luis had retired from government but was active in a number of activities, including providing some sort of technical support to the Kenya African National Union. The family now lived in an upscale Asian neighborhood called Parklands. Although delighted with the reunion, the experience was odd. Perhaps the cause was that I had no time to adjust.

I was picked up by an officer from the Fifth Battalion the King's African Rifles, and we started our long, bouncy trip in an army Land Rover to our base in Nanyuki. The town was small, tidy on the slopes of Mt Kenya., and the camp was magnificently located on a vast track of land on the edge of the forest on the slopes of Mt, Kenya. It was a modern facility with an excellent officers' mess. I was glad to back in Africa, and the transition into regimental routine was easy.

My large, comfortable room was well furnished with its own toilet and bath. Big glass sliding doors led to a hug balcony that let in the cool, pure mountain air but also offered a superb view of Mt. Kenya. Mt. Kenya, where the Kikuyu god "Ngai" resides, is the highest mountain in Kenya and the second highest in Africa. Formally it was known by the Kikuyu as Mt. Kirinyaga, and it is an extinct volcano that formed about two million years ago.

At dinner that night, I met the single officers who lived in the mess. The more senior were all English. The rest were African who had risen through the ranks. It was evident that the processes of Africanization had been greatly accelerated because of impending independence. Those Africans who were promoted from the ranks had demonstrated themselves to be excellent soldiers. However, they were uneducated and spoke and wrote little English. They struggled to make the transition from a noncommissioned to a commissioned officer. At the time, I was the only homegrown officer to have graduated from Sandhurst.

The following morning, I reported to Captain Nigel, the adjutant. He was a tall, skinny, blond Englishman who paid little attention when I smartly stood to attention and saluted him. The longer he disregarded me, the more diminished I became. I formed the opinion that his strategy was having the intended result in creating a strong and favorable impression on me.

After what seemed to be ages, he looked up and said yes. "Second Lieutenant Rodrigues reporting for duty, sir," I retorted.

He became slightly more welcoming and asked me to sit down. I would be taken to meet the battalion commanding officer, but first, he would quickly orientate me. The Regimental Standing Orders contained all the dos and don'ts. I was assigned as a platoon commander to Alpha Company. The battalion commander emerged and was demanding. He was succinct in his greeting, and in many ways, he reminded me of Luis.

I then marched off to A Company to be welcomed by the English Company commander. As his name suggested, he was a member of the Rolls Royce clan in Britain. He was wealthy, obese, pampered, and perhaps, like Charlotte, banished to the colonies in search of fame and excitement. The second in command was Captain Keith, also an Englishman, who was a member of the Household Cavalry, an aristocrat oozing wealth.

The rest of my brother officers were African of similar backgrounds to my own. They were warm in their welcome and were happy to see me, and we immediately connected. The troops under my command were skilled, disciplined, but aloof. I would have to prove my proficiency before gaining their trust and loyalty. I immediately noticed that there were no Kikuyu among them, only Somali, Wakamba, Turkanah, Samburu Kalenjins and Rendelli. All of these were branded as the warrior tribes of Kenya.

Besides the pomp and ceremony relating to the approaching Independence Day celebrations, the battalion and A Company devoted most of the time to training for counterterrorism operations. Intelligence indicated that an insurgency very different to the Mau-Mau was brewing. The ethnic Somali, who inhabited the northern frontier district of Kenya, wanted to secede to Somalia after independence. As this act was unacceptable, the factions were committed to backing up their demands by armed struggle. At the outset, I was selected to be the ensign bearer during the Independence Day celebrations. I was flattered by this honor and was thrilled at the prospects of going down in history for playing such an important role during this very special occasion.

This duty station offered a whole host of recreational activities to those with privilege of accesses. The difference now was that enty was not based on color. Captain Keith devoted all his free time hunting with the hounds. The battalion had a pack of beagles, and being the master of the hounds, Keith tried his best to get me interested in sport. Besides, if the sport was to continue in Kenya after independence, he had to get local officers to participate. Because of the cost, the exotic nature of this activity, and the strange garb that huntsmen wore, he found no takers.

I loved the unblemished scenery of the forest and quickly took up trout fishing in the numerous rivers that flowed through the Mt. Kenya Forest. But nothing could surpass the fly fishing on lake Rutundu. Located at about 10,500 feet, this small mountain tarn offered the finest rainbow trout one could ever hope to hook.

The species was introduced into Kenya in 1920 from Scotland. The average fish weighed about 2 ½ to 3 lbs., but the massive ones could go up to 8 lbs. One got a splendid view of the mountain from here. Sitting on the banks of the lake, casting my line, I often formed images of the daring accent of Mt. Kenya in 1943 by Felice Benuzzi accompanied by his two Italian compatriots, who escaped from a British prisoner of war camp with the sole aspiration of climbing the mountain. They succeeded in doing so using primitive handmade equipment and rations that they were able to forage. They published a book called *No Picnic on Mount Kenya*, which is a classic tale of out-of-the-ordinary adventure and a thrilling narration of their determination, enterprise, and daring.

The flies used for trout fishing were tied locally. Apparently, they are extremely popular with fishermen and are exported all over the world. The secret to their success is the use of the down feathers of the wild vulturine guinea fowl, which was found in abundance in this region. I was not a particularly good fisherman but enjoyed the solitude and the clean, fresh forest air. Whenever I did catch a trout, the whole world knew about it.

The battalion had a gun club, and many of the officers hunted wild animals for trophies, for meat, or on game-control duties. I was an active member and one evening was called out to cull an old bull elephant that had gone on a rampage in a village located on the perimeter of the forest reserve. Once a bull gets too old to lead, they are ousted by a younger and stronger substitute. Once separated from the herd, they often run amok and have to be put down.

My batman and body guard, Lakous, accompanied me. He was a Samburu who was not only a good and intrepid soldier but also an excellent tracker and a marksman who was completely at home in the bush. As we drove up to the village, we noticed the trampled maize fields and the knocked-down banana trees. The rogue had now gone through the village and headed up a jungle track. His fresh dung was clearly evident. The trail was now too narrow to drive on, so we left the vehicle and stalked on foot. I loved the whiff of an African village. Inhaling the aroma of wood fires, the fresh cooking, the livestock, and the wildflowers was palliative to the mind and soul. The setting was vibrant, natural, and genuine.

As we moved further into the forest and away from the village, I lost track of the animal. Lakous was now clearly in his element. He loved a hunt, and it consumed his very being. There was now anticipation in his movement; he was mentally focused and concentrated, giving attention to even the smallest of detail. It was a pleasure watching him work, and I kept well out of his way. Here was a man in perfect harmony with his environment. I could see no tracks and would have gone astray.

But to Lakaus, every blade of grass, a broken twig, and the ruffled earth told a tale. We had stopped talking and only used signs to communicate. He now recognized the exact route taken by the elephant and when it had gone past this spot. Suddenly, he made a sign indicating that he had caught a glimpse of the animal. I must admit that I could see nothing. In order to get closer, we moved stealthily down wind. The area was so impenetrable that I worried about being able to shoot accurately. We must have been about two hundred yards away from the animal when Lakous indicated that I should take a shot. He did not think that it was possible to get any nearer.

I raised my 7.62 Magnum, took careful aim through the telescopic sight, and fired. Lakous, through his binoculars, confirmed that my shot was accurate and that the bullet had penetrated through the left ear. If this was the case, the elephant should have dropped, but it did not. Instead, it came charging toward us, trumpeting in pain and anger. We dashed back to the vehicle. I slammed the vehicle into reverse, but the Land Rover did not move as the clutch failed to engage. Lakous jumped out and took aim for a second shot. But just before he fired, however, there was a loud crash as the elephant went down barely twenty feet from the vehicle.

I don't know how, but in no time at all, the whole village descended on the carcass. Among them were some Ndorobo a tribe of hunters and gatherers that lived mainly in the forest. With axes, they cut a hole into the stomach, removing the innards. This gives them access into the huge ribcage, where they resembled pygmies hacking away at the flesh. The meat was their compensation for the damage they had suffered. While Lakaus supervised the removal of the enormous tusks, I worked on removing a sapling from the pressure plate of the vehicle. The training that I had received from Joseph and Raymond stood me in good stead for this task. We got back to camp just after dark all covered in blood. The game department collected the tusks the following morning, as they were the property of the government.

The Mt. Kenya Safari Club that straddles the equator is an opulent hideaway built by the American film star William Holden in partnership with the eccentric Ray Ryan and the Swiss financier Carl Hirchmann. It became renowned as the retreat and hideout for the international jet set. The club used a military approach road, and as courtesy, all army officers were afforded honorary membership of the club. The amenities were excellent, but the high cost prevented many of us from indulging too often. This facility served as an eye-opener to the newly commissioned African officers because it was a clear example of the delineation between the haves and have-not's in Kenya.

After spending nine years in detention, Jomo Kenyatta was freed in August 1961, taking over as leader of the Kenya African National Union, a party made up mainly of Kikuyu and Luo. Preindependence elections were held in May 1963, after which Kenyatta was named as prime minister. In December 2003, Kenya became independent, and Kenyatta the first head of state. Instead of taking part in the Independence Day on December 12, 1963 celebrations, my platoon was flown into active service to Mandera, a town in the epicenter of the uprising on the shared border with Somalia and Ethiopia in northern Kenya.

The "Shifta" rebellion had begun. Landing in Mandera, I was ordered to go to immediately report to the ancient fort of El Wak on the Kenya-Somalia border. We immediately set off by road through uninhabited desert that looked as rough, gray, bleak, and barren as the moon's surface. The soil was bleached and scorched by the burning sun, and the wind howled through the stunted thorn bushes, whipping up billows of dust. A few Somali nomads with their camels ran for cover as we approached. This was out of the ordinary as the army was always welcome by these wandering pastoralist nomads. We got there at dusk, much to the delight of the police who were defending the fort at El Wak.

I was briefed by the British police officer in command of the fort at the time that he was expecting to be attacked that night. I supervised the distribution of ammunition and prepared for my first active-duty military assignment. I had seven Somali soldiers in my company, and most of them were noncommissioned officers.

Before being deployed to El Wak, there was a lot of debate in the regiment about the loyalty of the unit's Somali soldiers. There was a strong line of reasoning in opposition to their deployment. I refused to accept this logic and decided to discuss the issue frankly and freely with my men. Their response was that they were loyal and taken an oath of allegiance.

That night, I slept on the parapet of the fort with the men. At about midnight, we were fired upon from a distance. We stood to, but as the attack was of no consequence, the men went back to sleep while two Somali soldiers acted as sentries. At dawn, I noticed that all the Somali soldiers were missing. All of them had deserted with their weapons during the night. When our tour of duty ended, I returned with my platoon to Nanyuki. We were exhausted after having spent the past six months on active service.

From January 20 to 25, there were mutinies by soldiers of the King's African Rifles in Kenya, Tanzania, and Uganda. The reasons for these uprisings differ, but the most common was that the soldiers were disgruntled because of their pay, conditions, and the fact that they were still being commanded by British officers. Fearing a creeping coup syndrome, the local governments requested the British Army to put down these mutinies.

I was woken up by the orderly officer who informed me that all officers were required to evacuate the barracks because of what was taking place at the Eleventh Battalion, the King's African Rifles at Lanet. I was not aware of what was going on in Lanet but obediently got dressed and walked out of our main gate to the brigade headquarters. The quarter guards were disciplined and well turned out. We were then given details about the uprising and told that we could not return to our barracks. All the local officers disagreed with this order as we felt it compromised our ability to command our troops in the future. We felt that the men would think that we were deserting them in their hour of need.

However, if we disobeyed these orders, we would be branded as mutineers as well, so in order to preserve our authority, we would have to be more novel in our approach. The mitigate risk, the armories had to be secured. The only way in which this could be done would be for the local officers to remain in barracks and maintain surveillance. This was agreed to, and we carried out foot patrols throughout the night. This saved the situation, and we were able to sustain our status with our troops. When the trouble subsided, the unit was disbanded. After sixteen years' service, I resigned my commission and migrated to Canada.

About the Author

Rudy Rodrigues was born and raised in Kenya. He graduated from the Royal Military Academy Sandhurst and the British Army Staff College. He was commissioned and served as an officer in the Kenya Army in both command and staff appointments. Resigning after sixteen years of active service, he then immigrated to Canada with his wife and three children. He immediately formed a security guard company in Alberta that focused on providing services for shopping malls. He was appointed country director of a Canadian NGO in the Sudan, with a mandate to provide leadership, strategic planning, and delivery of UN (WFP) emergency relief supplies to more than three million starving people displaced by the famine of 1985, using a fleet of 350 cargo vehicles and a staff of over 3,000 people. The operation was later taken over by the UN, and Rodrigues served as its director. In 1989 he went to Afghanistan during the Soviet occupation with UNICEF and later with UNDP, spending over ten years in that country. He established a UNICEF office in Kyrgyzstan soon after the breakup of the Soviet Union and ended his career as UNICEF country representative in Papua, New Guinea.

CPSIA information can be obtained
at www.ICGtesting.com
Printed in the USA
FFOW04n0536110317
33254FF

9 781684 099801